MURDER UNDERGROUND

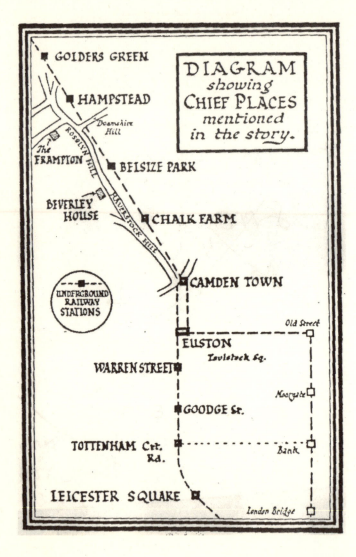

DIAGRAM showing CHIEF PLACES mentioned in the story.

GOLDERS GREEN

HAMPSTEAD

Downshire Hill

The FRAMPTON

ROSSLYN HILL

BELSIZE PARK

BEVERLEY HOUSE

HAVERSTOCK HILL

CHALK FARM

UNDERGROUND RAILWAY STATIONS

CAMDEN TOWN

Old Street

EUSTON

Tavistock Sq.

WARREN STREET

Moorgate

GOODGE St.

TOTTENHAM Crt. Rd.

Bank

LEICESTER SQUARE

London Bridge

MURDER UNDERGROUND

MAVIS DORIEL HAY

——

With an Introduction by Stephen Booth

THE BRITISH LIBRARY

This edition published in 2014 by

The British Library
96 Euston Road
London NW1 2DB

Originally published in London in 1934 by Skeffington & Son
Reprinted with thanks to the Estate of Mavis Doriel Hay
Introduction © Stephen Booth

Cataloguing in Publication Data
A catalogue record for this book is available from The British Library

ISBN 978 0 7123 5725 8

Typeset by IDSUK (DataConnection) Ltd
Printed and bound in England by TJ International

CONTENTS

LIST OF DIAGRAMS

INTRODUCTION

Among Golden Age mystery writers, Mavis Doriel Hay is one of the most unjustifiably overlooked. Although she published only three novels in the 1930s, her work encompassed many of the themes which would later become familiar to readers. They also range across the genre, from an urban setting in *Murder Underground* to death in academia, and finally to a classic country house mystery.

Very little has been written about this author until now. She was born in 1894 in Potters Bar, Middlesex, and had a middle-class upbringing, her father being a company secretary in the insurance business. Their home in Epping boasted a governess for the children, as well as a cook and a couple of housemaids. Two of Mavis's brothers joined the Malayan Civil Service and helped to run the British Empire. Yet the Hay family had more humble origins in previous generations. Mavis's grandfather was a shoemaker in Shropshire, and her great-grandfather was known as "Landsman Hay," a Scottish sailor who served below decks during the Napoleonic Wars, and whose memoirs Mavis later edited.

Perhaps it was through her grandfather that Mavis Doriel Hay became fascinated by rural crafts. In the 1920s she had published several books in the *Rural Industries of England and Wales* series, co-authored with Helen Elizabeth Fitzrandolph. This was an interest which not only lasted to the end of her life, but was to have another major consequence. In 1929, when she was 35 years old, Mavis married her co-author's brother, Archibald Menzies Fitzrandolph, the son of a wealthy Canadian banker and lumber mill owner.

With her contemporaries Agatha Christie and Dorothy L. Sayers at the height of their success, it was during this period that Mavis began to write mysteries. For her debut novel in 1934, she may have taken to heart the advice to "write what you know." She and Archibald were then living in Belsize Lane, North London, only a few hundred yards from where the murder in *Murder Underground* takes place. In later books, she went on to invent a fictional Oxford college and the imaginary county of Haulmshire.

P. D. James wrote recently in *The Spectator*: "The detective stories of the interwar years were paradoxical. They might deal with violent death, but essentially they were novels of escape. We feel no real pity for the victim, no empathy for the murderer, no sympathy for the falsely accused." She might well have been describing *Murder Underground*, in which the affluent and unpleasant Miss Euphemia Pongleton meets a grisly end on the stairs of her local Tube station, having been strangled with her own dog lead.

Writers of Golden Age mysteries found it useful to have a murder victim who was universally unpopular. It means the remaining cast do not have to spend much time grieving over the death, but can happily get on with their efforts to unmask the murderer. And in *Murder Underground*, Miss Pongleton's fellow guests at the Frampton Private Hotel certainly have plenty of theories. Hay does allow Euphemia's nephew Basil a bit of sympathy for the victim: "Whatever you may feel about your relations, you don't like to hear of them being strangled with a dog-leash. It gives me a sort of sick feeling." But this is essentially a novel of escape, and it is the puzzle which drives the story.

The treatment of the police is interesting in Hay's work. Readers of Golden Age mysteries are accustomed to a depiction of local bobbies as clodhopping yokels, and Hay nods towards this tradition with her description of a policeman on surveillance duty as "a fishy-looking fellow with police feet." But an evolution seems to have been taking place in this novel, even as Hay was writing it. In the early chapters, she relates her characters' amateur speculations rather than record their interviews with the police. Inspector Caird is an invisible presence, summoning people to answer questions, then disappearing from the Frampton with a bang of the front door. But the inspector makes a rather unexpected appearance halfway through the book, "approaching unobtrusively," as if slipping into the story against the author's intentions. And he is an intelligent, sympathetic policeman too, though of course the murderer is finally unmasked by the efforts of the amateur sleuths.

Notable among these sleuths is the rather Marple-like figure of Mr Blend, who divides murders into "tidy" and "messy." "It's the little details that count," he says, and: "It struck me I'd heard of something of the same sort before, but I couldn't quite place it somehow." Like Miss Marple, his recollection of an earlier experience leads to a vital clue, but it is a clue which might ring a bell for readers of contemporary serial killer novels.

This is a London novel, yet Hay approaches her setting as though it is a more rural location. In the manner of many mysteries of the time, *Murder Underground* demands concentration on timings and the whereabouts of suspects. But many readers will be delighted by the inclusion of maps – the layout of Belsize Park underground station, and even the Pongleton family tree.

Mavis Doriel Hay went straight on to write her second mystery, *Death on the Cherwell*, picking up on themes which were both contemporary and still have resonance today. Sadly, after her third novel was published in 1936, Mavis's career as a mystery writer came to a premature end. By 1937 the Second World War was approaching, and her family would be ripped apart, like so many others. Perhaps, by then, she no longer found murder mysteries to be an effective escape from the horrifying realities of the world.

Though she continued to write, Hay returned to her first love – rural crafts. It would have been interesting to see what else she might have produced, since her surviving novels bear comparison to some of the best work published in that period. Readers will appreciate the opportunity to discover her writing in this new British Library edition.

Stephen Booth

MURDER UNDERGROUND

CHAPTER ONE

MISS PONGLETON ON THE STAIRS

DOZENS of Hampstead people must have passed the door of the Frampton Private Hotel—as the boarding house where Miss Euphemia Pongleton lived was grandly called—on a certain Friday morning in March 1934, without noticing anything unusual. When they read their evening papers they must have cursed themselves for being so unobservant, but doubtless many of them made up for it by copious inventiveness and told their friends how they had sensed tragedy in the air or noticed an anxious look in Miss Pongleton's eyes.

Actually there was nothing to attract the attention of the casual passer-by in the usual morning exodus of the Frampton boarders. Young Mr. Grange and middle-aged Mr. Porter, both quite unremarkable, stepped briskly out at about half-past eight and took the road to Hampstead underground station. Shortly before nine Betty Watson, trim and alert, opened the door and stood there rather impatiently, gazing alternately at the sky and back into the hall of the Frampton. Punctually at nine Miss Euphemia Pongleton herself pottered fussily out, hugging an enormous handbag and looking perhaps rather shabbier and more out-of-date than usual. Betty informed her that it was a nice morning, in response to which Miss Pongleton wrinkled her nose as if she didn't like the smell of it. At the end of Church Lane she turned to the right and doddered slowly down the hill towards Belsize Park underground station.

Before Miss Pongleton was out of sight Cissie Fain came bounding out, pulling on her gloves, and she and Betty followed Miss Pongleton almost at a run, but turned to the left, up the hill, at the end of Church Lane. Five minutes later Mr. Joseph Slocomb, swinging his neatly-rolled umbrella, sallied forth sedately.

Mr. Basil Pongleton's departure from his lodgings in Tavistock Square, a little later on the same morning, was less sedate. He was obviously in a hurry; yet it was after ten o'clock when he passed almost directly beneath the Frampton, whizzed along through the tunnel in the direction of Golder's Green. The underground train which he took from Warren Street at about 9.25 would have passed that spot nearly half an hour earlier, and his subterranean wanderings on that morning were to cause him a good deal of trouble.

As he sat in the train he held before his eyes a copy of *The Times* which he had bought specially so that he might be able to make some suitable remarks to his aunt, Miss Euphemia Pongleton (quite forgetting that she disapproved of spending tuppence on a newspaper, even for the benefit of getting the standard point of view). But he was too agitated to understand anything that he read. His sight laid hold of the single sentence: *The death penalty is a subject on which every citizen ought to form a reasoned opinion, free from sentimental bias*, and went over it again and again without being able to convey the sense of it to his mind. The bowler hat flung on the seat beside him seemed to have no connection with him;

it was strangely out of keeping with his blue shirt and vaguely artistic appearance.

At the same time Mr. Crampit, a cheap dentist in Camden Town, was beginning to be a little put out by the lateness of his important patient, Miss Euphemia Pongleton, for her ten o'clock appointment. She usually came at least fifteen minutes before the time booked, in order to settle herself before the ordeal. Mr. Crampit was wondering if it would be safe to squeeze in old Mrs. Boddy, who was moaning with distress in his waiting-room.

Mr. Slocomb was, in accordance with the usual order of events, the first of the boarders to return to the Frampton that evening. He found the household in a very unusual state of agitation. In the "lounge hall"—where a couple of unused rickety wicker chairs attempted to justify the epithet "lounge"—he met the maid, Nellie, carrying a pile of plates.

"Oh, sir!" she gasped. "'V' you 'eard?"

He held up his evening paper gravely. "Yes; I have just read it in the *Standard*. A dreadful affair! That poor old lady!"

"An' my poor B-Bob!" spluttered Nellie, tears shining in her eyes. "'E's bin took by those p'lice. 'E couldn't 've done sich a thing, though the ol' lady did say she'd tell on 'im."

"Now, now; what's all this?" enquired Mr. Slocomb with paternal concern. "Do you mean to say your young man has been arrested for the murder of Miss Pongleton on the underground stairs?"

He had followed the girl into the dining-room on the right of the hall, where she set down the plates and extracted a handkerchief from the region of her knees in order to blow her nose defiantly.

"They took 'im this arternoon; 'is sister Louie come an' tell me 'bout it. Seems the ol' lady 'ad that brooch on 'er with 'is name on a paper, an' 'e bein' down in that toob station a-course it looks black for 'im; an' 'e may be weak, but brutal 'e never was, an' I *know* 'e couldn't've done any such thing, not if 'e wanted to which 'e wouldn't."

Nellie gave way to convulsive sobbing punctuated by loud sniffs.

"Now look here, my girl," said Mr. Slocomb kindly, patting her shoulder. "If your young man is innocent he'll be all right. British justice is deservedly respected all the world over."

"But the p'lice, they're something chronic; they'll worm anything out of you," blubbered Nellie.

"Don't get any wrong ideas about our excellent police force into your head," Mr. Slocomb admonished her. "They are the friends of the innocent. Of course this is very unfortunate for your young man, but surely——"

"There 'e is, my poor Bob, in a nasty cell! Oh, sir, d'you think they'll let me see 'im?"

"Well, really——" began Mr. Slocomb; but the conversation was interrupted by a strident call.

"Nellie! Nellie! What are you about? Pull yourself together, girl! We have to dine even if …"

Mrs. Bliss, the proprietress of the Frampton, flowingly clothed in black satin, paused in the doorway. "Dear me, Mr. Slocomb; you must be wondering what's come to me, shouting all over the house like this! But really, my poor nerves are so jangled I hardly know where I am! To think of dear Miss Pongleton, always so particular, poor soul, lying there on the stairs—dear, dear, dear!"

Nellie had slipped past Mrs. Bliss and scuttled back to the kitchen. Mr. Slocomb noticed that Mrs. Bliss's black satin was unrelieved by the usual loops of gold chain and pearls, and concluded that this restraint was in token of respect to the deceased.

"Yes, indeed, Mrs. Bliss, you must be distraught. Indeed a terrible affair! And this poor girl is in great distress about young Bob Thurlow, but I would advise you to keep her mind on her work, Mrs. Bliss; work is a wonderful balm for harassed nerves. A dreadful business! I only know, of course, the sparse details which I have just read in the evening Press."

"You've heard nothing more, Mr. Slocomb? Nellie's Bob is a good-for-nothing, we all know"—Mrs. Bliss's tone held sinister meaning—"but I'm sure none of us thought him capable of this!"

"We must not think him so now, Mrs. Bliss, until—and unless—we are reluctantly compelled to do so," Mr. Slocomb told her in his most pompous manner.

"And Bob was always so good to poor Miss Pongleton's Tuppy. The little creature is very restless; mark my words, he's beginning to pine! Now I wonder, Mr. Slocomb, what I ought to do with him? What would you advise? Perhaps poor Miss Pongleton's nephew, young Mr. Basil, would take him—though in lodgings, of course, I hardly know. There's many a landlady would think a dog nothing but a nuisance, and little return for it, but of course what *I* have done for the poor dear lady I did gladly——"

"Indeed, Mrs. Bliss, we have always counted you as one of Tuppy's best friends. And as you say, Bob Thurlow was good to him, too; he took him for walks, I believe?"

"He always *seemed* so fond of the poor little fellow; who could believe … Well! well! And they say dogs know! What was that saying Mr. Blend was so fond of at one time—before your day, I daresay it would be: *True humanity shows itself first in kindness to dumb animals.* Out of one of his scrap-books. Well, the truest sayings sometimes go astray! But I must see after that girl; and cook's not much better, she's so flustered she's making Nellie ten times worse. She can't keep her tongue still a moment!"

Mrs. Bliss bustled away, and Mr. Slocomb, apparently rather exasperated by her chatter, made his escape as soon as she had removed herself from the doorway.

As Mrs. Bliss returned to the kitchen she thought: "Well, I'm glad he's here; that's some comfort; always so helpful— but goodness knows what the dinner will be like!"

CHAPTER TWO

THE FRUMPS

DINNER at the Frampton that evening was eaten to the accompaniment of livelier conversation than usual, and now and again from one of the little tables an excited voice would rise to a pitch that dominated the surrounding talk until the owner of the voice, realizing her unseemly assertiveness on this solemn evening, would fall into lowered tones or awkward silence. The boarders discussed the murder callously. One's fellow-boarders are apt to appear in the foreground of one's daily view unpleasantly larger than life but rather less than human.

Cissie Fain and Betty Watson, who shared a table and worked in the same office in the City, jabbered excitedly. Cissie was fair and round-faced with a slightly petulant mouth and innocent blue-grey eyes.

"It was nothing to do with the brooch that took Pongle to town this morning," she announced, tossing her fashionably long curls.

"It didn't take her to town," objected Betty, whose literal accuracy was invaluable to her firm. She was quieter in her manners than Cissie, brown-haired and brown-eyed; perhaps not so pretty but with more decisive features.

"Well, it was taking her and it would have taken her if she hadn't been 'took' on the way, as poor Nellie would put it," continued Cissie shrilly. "It was an appointment with the dentist. Too sordid!"

"You don't suppose the dentist throttled her on the underground stairs because he couldn't bear the idea of looking down her throat again?" enquired Betty.

"Don't be so asinine! I mean there is no reason why Bob should be so desperately anxious to stop her journey."

"But how d'you know Pongle wasn't going on afterwards to see the police about that brooch?"

"I don't believe she was. I don't believe she would ever have done a thing about it, except hold it over Bob's head as a threat. She simply loved a sense of power and she loved to be in the know."

"*And* in the limelight," Betty pointed out. "She would have revelled in the position of informer—all for the public good, y'know! Setting the police on the track of a dangerous gang; appearing as witness. Oh, can't you just see her?"

"P'rhaps so. But my idea is that Bob murdered her just out of revenge, because she'd threatened him and simply infuriated him. People *do* do that sort of thing. He never thought of recovering the brooch."

"That all sounds most unlikely to me, and there's no need to make up theories to show that Bob did it. I can't believe that he had anything to do with it. It's just his bad luck that he's connected with it, as it was his bad luck to get mixed up with the burglary."

At another table Mrs. Daymer was discussing the subject with Mr. Grange. A casual visitor would have wondered how they came to share a table. Mrs. Daymer was a middle-aged lady who liked to accentuate the gaunt strangeness of her appearance by unfashionable clothes. She would explain proudly that they were of hand-woven material—"by that wonderful man Blympton Torr; does the whole thing, right from the sheep's back!" Perhaps their intimate connection with the sheep justified their peculiar unwieldiness.

Francis Grange was an unremarkable, youngish man who had not been long at the Frampton. Mrs. Daymer would have explained that she was studying him, for she was a novelist. She often told her friends, "I like to study types. When I have sucked one dry, then …" A flick of her bony hand indicated the fate of the sucked type. Meanwhile Francis Grange seemed to be submitting meekly to the sucking process. A careful observer might have concluded that Mrs. Daymer's chief reason for keeping him by her was that he formed an attentive audience, and might have guessed also that even the best audience will in time feel that the performance has gone on long enough. But Mr. Grange was still sedately enjoying the first act.

"This is peculiarly interesting to me," Mrs. Daymer was informing him. "It would be hypocritical to pretend that any one of us is overwhelmed with grief at the removal of Miss Pongleton, though of course we all deplore the horrible nature of her end. The criminal type is one which I have in the past studied intensively. I have not formed any theory about the crime yet—it is too soon—but I shall see the whole thing plainly before long."

"What I can't understand," said Mr. Grange—"and perhaps you as a student of human nature can explain it—is how we all seem to know so much about Miss Pongleton's affairs and Bob Thurlow's affairs immediately she is dead and he is suspected of her murder."

"An interesting point," conceded Mrs. Daymer, nodding at him and waving a large knuckled hand encumbered with several enormous silver rings obtrusively "hand-wrought". "It's partly due to the fact that our interest is now concentrated on these figures and automatically we rake up from our minds any scraps of information about them which may have lodged there unnoticed. And it's partly due to lack of reticence in the lower classes. That poor child Nellie has been blurting out the whole story of the brooch to anyone who would listen to her."

"I suppose that's it. That brooch affair makes the whole case against Bob Thurlow look pretty black, I must say. And his being on duty in the station, too."

"Ah!" Mrs. Daymer gloated over Mr. Grange's uncritical acceptance of the obvious. "That's just the sort of coincidence that leads the police astray in these murder cases. You must consider all the probabilities: an underground station, to begin with. Anyone might be there—an ideal scene for a murder. Then Miss Pongleton's character: she was a hard old woman, without doubt; she was reputed to be rich; she was secretive and revengeful. She may have had hundreds of enemies. She was just the kind of apparently respectable old lady who may have had a questionable past."

"But really," Mr. Grange protested; "isn't that going a bit too far—I mean about her past? You don't know anything?"

"You mustn't take me too literally, Mr. Grange. As a novelist, I am surveying the possibilities of the situation."

"And then about the place of the murder," Mr. Grange went on. "Anyone might be in an underground station certainly; but on the stairs—the stairs at Belsize Park too; why, it's the deepest of the lot, next to Hampstead. And, by the way, why was Miss Pongleton at Belsize Park? Hampstead station is much nearer."

"Although Miss Pongleton was rich she was fantastically miserly," Mrs. Daymer informed him solemnly. "That is why she always walked to Belsize Park and so saved one penny. Also she had a horror of lifts. Whether it was purely the sort of unreasoning fear which sometimes afflicts even the most sensible types, or whether there was some reason for it hidden among the secrets of her past, I cannot say—at present. But she always walked down the stairs."

"Perhaps she just disliked the sensation of leaving one's stomach behind," Mr. Grange suggested. "Well, that accounts for her being there, but it doesn't explain how the murderer came to be there. Belsize Park station stairs are not worn hollow with constant use, I should say."

"No. That points, of course, to someone who knew her habits—and it doesn't point very strongly to Bob Thurlow. Why should he know that?"

"Well, he works on the underground and lately he's been at that station. He may have noticed her coming down the stairs on other occasions."

"But equally anyone who had known her for long, or had lived in the same house with her for some time, would know her cranky ways. Moreover, such a person would be more likely to know of her appointment with the dentist this morning."

"She struck me as a secretive old lady—and I think you said that she was so—not much given to discussing her affairs with others."

"She was secretive, true; but she had her confidants," Mrs. Daymer told him. She glanced hastily round at the other tables and then leaned forward and hissed: "Mr. Slocomb may know more about her affairs than he cares to admit. Cissie Fain was in her favour, but I think only for the sake of the services she rendered in running errands, posting letters and so forth. The brooch affair shows that Miss Pongleton was not above sharing a secret with the maid, Nellie."

Even that very unsuspicious young man Mr. Grange guessed that Mrs. Daymer felt some resentment towards the late Miss Pongleton because the old lady had never confided in her. With a vague idea of offering a sop to her pride he said, "I, for one, was never admitted to her confidence."

"Probably you are lucky," said Mrs. Daymer viciously. "Before this case is over everyone who knew anything about Miss Pongleton's intended movements this morning will be suspect!" Her steely eyes glittered at him fiercely.

"I say! Not *us*—the Frumps, as Miss Fain calls us all in the Frampton."

Mrs. Daymer merely nodded severely. She was not pleased by his quotation from Cissie.

"But you have to have a motive for a murder, you know, Mrs. Daymer," Mr. Grange protested. Involuntarily he glanced round the dining-room as if looking for signs of criminal intent on the faces of the people gathered there: Cissie and Betty, young and sleek and modern, still chattering earnestly over their coffee; Mr. Joseph Slocomb, greyly respectable in melancholy solitude at the table which the late Miss Pongleton had usually shared with him; old Mr. Blend also alone, ruddy and bearded like a countryman, who was as usual a course behind the others because he was poring over a paper and marking paragraphs with a gold pencil; the Porters, a middle-aged couple who sat in their bed-sitting-room a good deal and therefore had little to do with the other boarders. Finally Mrs. Bliss, plump and important, who from her corner table seemed to preside over the company. Mr. Grange saw Nellie scuttle up to her and whisper agitatedly in her ear, meanwhile casting scared glances over her shoulder.

Mrs. Bliss rose majestically. "Ladies and gentlemen," she announced. There was a sudden cessation of clatter and chatter.

"A police inspector is here and wishes to interview each of you in turn. Just to see if you can tell him anything that will help, you know," she added, abandoning the grand manner. "I think we had better adjourn to the drawing-room as soon as we have finished dinner, and the officer can see us in the smoking-room."

"I'm through, Mrs. Bliss," volunteered Cissie. "Shall I go first?"

"Just a moment, my dear," said Mrs. Bliss. "I have to say a word to the officer myself." She sailed out of the room. The Porters followed her with their noses in the air and departed upstairs to their room, their demeanour declaring emphatically: "We're not playing this silly game."

Mrs. Daymer and Mr. Grange, followed by Mr. Slocomb, rose and crossed the hall to the drawing-room. Cissie and Betty sat for a few moments patting their hair and touching up their complexions in preparation for the interview. As Mrs. Daymer strode from the room Cissie leant forward and, emphasizing her words by beating the air with her lipstick, whispered, "Mrs. Daymer's studying the crime; you'll see; too sinister! But she may have arranged it herself as an opportunity for gathering data. I wouldn't put it past her."

CHAPTER THREE

GERRY BLUNDERS IN

In the drawing-room Tuppy, a fat elderly terrier, was snugly settled on the hearthrug, his nose resting on the fender. He showed no symptoms of pining. Mrs. Daymer entered the room first, with Mr. Grange and Mr. Slocomb at her heels, and settled herself in an armchair at one side of the fireplace, drawing over her shoulders a scarf of shot blue and green which had been slung between her elbows. Before sitting down she hesitated a moment, casting an uncertain glance at the opposite armchair, with a higher back, which had the additional advantage of being on the side of the fire furthest from the door from which draughts were apt to stray over Mrs. Daymer's back. Directly opposite the fire was a sofa, and Mr. Grange seated himself on this, at the end nearest to Mrs. Daymer. Mr. Slocomb hovered round the room, picking up papers, glancing over them and then refolding them more neatly before laying them down again.

Cissie and Betty arrived and flumped side by side on the sofa, and then old Mr. Blend toddled in with his newspaper and his gold pencil and sat down at a little table with a reading-lamp which stood against the wall beyond the still vacant armchair.

Cissie was tickling Tuppy with her toe and remarking to him: "Well, well, diddums; poor old Tuppy!" The obese dog only stirred sluggishly, tucked his hind legs and his tail in tighter, and continued to stare at the fire.

No one seemed to know how to start conversation. Each was uncertain, perhaps, as to the appropriate note to strike. Mr. Slocomb, having set in order all the papers which were lying about the room, proceeded very deliberately to the empty chair and sank into it. There was a distinct stiffening of attention among the others, but no one spoke. Mrs. Daymer shot at him a look of cold hatred for his superior tactics and inwardly cursed her own timidity.

Mrs. Bliss entered. "Now, Cissie dear, perhaps you will go in," she suggested. Cissie shot up from the sofa with alacrity.

"I shouldn't give him any of your theories if I were you," Betty warned her.

With a toss of her head and subsequent anxious patting of possibly disarranged locks, Cissie left the room.

Mrs. Bliss hovered uncertainly. "If you don't mind, I'll just bring my knitting and sit here with you. Really I feel all upset, what with identifying the poor soul's body this afternoon and the dog-leash and all——"

"I should have thought they'd have fetched Basil to identify his aunt's body," suggested Betty whilst Mrs. Bliss was fetching her knitting.

"Probably this address was in her bag—she was very meticulous," Mrs. Daymer pointed out. "Just the type to have her name and address and age and height and weight entered in a notebook."

"And I should think they know her at Belsize Park station," said Mr. Grange. "It isn't everyone who walks down the stairs."

Mrs. Bliss returned and Mr. Slocomb rose ceremoniously.

"Will you take this chair, Mrs. Bliss?"

"Oh, really, I couldn't, thanking you all the same, Mr. Slocomb." Mrs. Bliss fluttered into Cissie's vacated seat on the sofa. "Though of course there's no sense in leaving it for poor Miss Pongleton now," she added. "I don't know when I've been so upset!" Mrs. Bliss smoothed out her satin lap and began to click the shining needles.

"The identification of the body must have been a harrowing experience," Mrs. Daymer told her soothingly. "And a dogleash, did you say?"

"Why yes; he did it with her own leash—poor Tuppy's leash—tight round her throat! Brutal, I call it; and to think how often Bob has taken poor Tuppy out on that very leash!"

"Are you sure it was the same leash?" asked Mr. Slocomb. "After all, one dog-leash is very like another."

"A strap, the *Evening News* said," Betty pointed out.

"Well, a leash is a kind of strap. Anyway, I know Tuppy's leash; haven't I had to hunt for it only too often? It was broken, and poor Miss Pongleton mended it herself with brown thread that she borrowed from Mrs. Porter. Why, Bob took it home in his pocket; we thought it was his forgetfulness, and to think he may have been meditating this dastardly act!"

"But he brought it back," cried Betty. "I distinctly remember seeing him in the hall with it one evening, explaining to Pong—Miss Pongleton."

"I don't know as much about all this as the rest of you do," began Mr. Grange apologetically; "but I thought the idea was that Bob Thurlow might want to murder Miss Pongleton because of the brooch affair, and surely that only happened a day or two ago—some time after Bob went home with the leash."

"I just mean to say," explained Mrs. Bliss, "that what a man can do once he can do again. We all know Bob had access to that leash, and it was that leash that strangled the poor lady."

"I must say I can't see why Bob should want to call attention to the fact that he could get hold of the leash if he was going to murder anyone with it. And then, of course, when he did take the leash home with him he can't have had any thought of murdering Miss Pongleton, because the brooch affair hadn't occurred. It's all very muddling," Betty complained.

"It's as plain as daylight to me," said Mrs. Bliss decisively. "Only too plain. If you'd seen the poor lady laid out there in the mortuary and that old purple coat of hers—I really felt ashamed, but she always said it was no use dressing up for a dentist. I went to the station to make enquiries, you see, and then they found her, but I didn't go down the stairs to see her myself; I went to the mortuary later on and there she lay——"

"Isn't it possible," Mr. Slocomb interrupted hastily, "that if the young man did contemplate murder his thoughts might turn to the leash just because of that chance occurrence when he took it home in his pocket? Of course I feel very strongly that we should all refrain from passing premature judgment on a fellow man. We do not know yet who else may have been upon those fatal stairs this morning."

Cissie Fain swung into the room. "That's over! Your turn, Betty. Like one of those games we used to play at children's parties, isn't it?" Cissie suggested brightly as she took her friend's seat on the sofa and began to smoke a cigarette with puffs of relief.

"What I want to know," she told Mrs. Bliss, "is why, if Bob murdered Miss Pongleton because of the brooch, he didn't take it away with him—or did he? The inspector wouldn't tell me a thing, and he didn't seem awfully interested, either, in what I had to say!"

"Bob didn't get the brooch," announced Mrs. Bliss, full of importance. "And my theory is that he was disturbed too soon, or else he couldn't find it. Anyway, there it was, laid out with her other things at the police-station. They found it on her, right enough."

"Just what was the story of that brooch?" asked Mr. Grange. "Everyone is talking about it, so I suppose there is no harm in telling the true facts; some version of them is sure to be in the papers to-morrow."

"Mrs. Bliss can tell us, I expect," suggested Mr. Slocomb. He sat judicially in the deep armchair, appreciating its comfort but not relaxing to it. His small, well-kept hands tapped against each other gently above his knees. He wore his customary severe expression, with the corners of his thin mouth drawn down from the point of his upper lip. He might have been pre-siding over an official enquiry into Miss Pongleton's death.

"I expect I do know more about it than most people, see-ing that poor Nellie has been talking of it all day," Mrs. Bliss admitted with pride; "though in such a random way that sometimes it's hard to make head or tail of what the silly girl says. It seems that Bob was mixed up in this burglary at Lady Morton's house in Surrey on Tuesday night. I don't rightly know, but it appears that he got in with a lot of lads who were worse than Bob ree-lized. He hadn't been in any crime before and didn't know one when he saw it, and when they took him with them that night they didn't tell him till they got there what they were after."

"But why should they take such a noodle as Bob with them?" asked Cissie.

"It seems, according to Nellie's tale, that one of their gang failed them and they wanted someone to drive the car and keep watch. When Bob ree-lized what was up he was too scared to do anything but what they told him. They got away with

some money and things from the bedrooms, and they gave
Bob as his share an old-fashioned brooch—and it's my belief
they gave him more than that and we shall hear of it in time.
Anyway, Bob comes up here Wednesday afternoon, Nellie's
day out, and takes her out, and he gives her this brooch—no
doubt thinking it an ordinary thing that no one would notice,
though he did tell her not to go showing it about. Well, it's
a kind of brooch that was ordinary enough in its day; my
mother had one just like it, but that's neither here nor there."

The story was interrupted by the return of Betty.

"Perhaps Mr. Slocomb would like to go now?" suggested
Mrs. Bliss.

"Ladies first!" declared Mr. Slocomb gallantly.

"Mrs. Daymer?"

"What about Mr. Blend?"

"We'd better not keep the inspector waiting—such a busi-
nesslike man," declared Mrs. Bliss. "Mr. Blend, would you
mind going into the smoking-room now?"

"Eh?"

"The inspector. He wants to see us all in turn; if you
wouldn't mind going now, Mr. Blend."

"Ay, I'll go, though I could tell him more about past crimes
than this present one." He put down a pair of long-bladed scissors with which he was clipping strips from the papers, and
stumped out of the room. Betty settled herself on a humpty
in front of the sofa.

Mrs. Bliss's knitting-needles began to click and flicker again.

"Now where was I? Ah, the brooch! Well, Nellie had it
on when she took up Miss Pongleton's hot-water bottle that
evening, and of course the poor lady noticed it."

"She always was inquisitive," snorted Cissie.

"Naturally," said Mrs. Bliss with a touch of acerbity, "the poor dear lady would notice a fine old piece of jewellery worn by a girl like Nellie. She asked Nellie about it and Nellie let out that Bob had given it to her."

"And Pongle wanted to know where Bob had got it!" Cissie finished triumphantly.

"Really, Miss Fain, if you are going to tell the story—and doubtless you can do so more brightly than I—then of course I've no more to say." Mrs. Bliss knitted furiously.

"Please go on!" Betty urged her. "Cissie just couldn't resist a bit of detecting. We're all jumpy, Mrs. Bliss. Now, don't be offended!"

In response to a nudge from Betty, Cissie added her plea: "Yes, please, Mrs. Bliss; I'm sorry."

"It's not that I mind being interrupted," said Mrs. Bliss solemnly. "But whatever may be the fashion now, in my young days we were not accustomed to speak with disrespect of the dead."

"But we call everyone by nicknames nowadays, Mrs. Bliss. It's really rather complimentary," said Mr. Grange.

After a pause to indicate dignity slowly unbending, Mrs Bliss resumed her tale. "Poor Miss Pongleton came of a fine old family and she knew good jewellery when she saw it. It struck her as strange that Bob should give Nellie a brooch like that. Then she got reading the paper—you know she always took the *Standard* up to bed with her—and there she found a list of the stolen things, and sure enough there was a special description of the brooch because Lady Morton set great store by it—it was of sentimental value, as they say; she had it from her mother, I'll be bound—and she offered a reward for it. Well, next morning, when Nellie takes in her early tea, Miss Pongleton asks Nellie to show her that brooch again, and sure enough it's the one described in the paper. 'You'd better leave that here with me', she says, and so she keeps it, telling Nellie it's too valuable for her to have about. Nellie was upset, for Bob had been particular that she wasn't to show it to anyone and not to say who gave it to her. She takes the opportunity when I send her out on an errand to go and find Bob at Belsize Park, where he's on duty, and tell him what's happened. Bob comes up here in a great to-do that same evening—Thursday, it would be—and it's my belief that he got hold of the leash from the lounge hall while he was waiting—and sees Miss Pongleton. But she doesn't give him back the brooch, quite rightly. I think it was her idea to put him on probation and try to bring him to better ways. Well, well; so this is the result of her kindness and interest in a young good-for-nothing!"

"I presume no one else heard about this brooch until to-day?" enquired Mr. Slocomb from the depths of his comfortable chair.

"Not so far as *I* know," Mrs. Bliss told him. "Of course I knew nothing about the business, but I don't know who Miss Pongleton may have thought fit to consult. What I do know is that the brooch was found on the poor dear lady's body, sealed up in an envelope with that Bob Thurlow's name on it."

Mr. Blend at this moment returned from his interview with the inspector and made his way back to his little table, breathing heavily.

"Thought I knew all about it, did he?" he chuckled. "That's where he was mistaken!"

"I'm quite willing to go now," volunteered Mrs. Daymer.

"Well, if you don't mind," said Mrs. Bliss.

Mrs. Daymer arranged her scarf and departed majestically.

"What did he ask you?" Cissie enquired of her friend Betty, who was squatting at her feet.

"Just when I went out this morning and how I went to town and whether I saw Pong—Miss Pongleton start. The inspector was rather a dear and thanked me for being clear and concise." Betty, hugging her knees tipped her little head up with a momentary air of self-consciousness.

"I think he's a perfect pig," grumbled Cissie. "I wonder how Mrs. Daymer is liking him."

"I suppose he will want to know when any of us last observed the dog-leash hanging on the umbrella stand," suggested Mr. Slocomb in a tone that implied that if the inspector did not want to know this he was ignorant of his own business.

"Oh yes," agreed Cissie and Betty together. "I couldn't remember," added Betty. "It's impossible really to be sure when it wasn't there, though one might remember an occasion when one had actually seen it there."

"I don't see that it's easier to be sure one way than another," objected Cissie. "I don't think it was there last night when I went to bed."

"You had some special reason for noticing its absence?" asked Mr. Slocomb.

"Oh no, I didn't. But I didn't notice it there."

"Why should you?" asked Betty.

Hearing the door open they all looked round to see how Mrs. Daymer looked after her ordeal. But it was Nellie who stood timorously on the threshold.

"Please'm, Mr. Plasher. Says 'e wants to see everybody!"

"Good!" exclaimed Cissie with enthusiasm. Gerry Plasher was engaged to Beryl Sanders, Miss Pongleton's niece, and he might be able to add further details to their speculations, she thought.

"Show him in, Nellie," Mrs. Bliss instructed the girl.

"One moment," called Betty after her. "Excuse me, Mrs. Bliss; I think Nellie can tell us something. Nellie, do you remember when you last saw Tuppy's leash in the hall?"

"Why yes, miss; I'm sure it was there when I put Mr. Grange's umbereller away in the stand las' night. It'd bin dryin' in the kitchen an' I put it away las' thing, so's it'd be ready for 'im in the mornin'. An' I got that there leash tangled up with it when I stuck it in, so I know it was there."

"And this morning?" Betty asked.

"That's the funny thing, miss. It weren't there this mornin' when I tidied. Leastways, I was certain sure of that, but the p'lice kep' on astin' me about it an' how did I know an' all, an' mebbe it was another mornin' I didn't see it or another evenin' I did see it, an' reelly I don' know me own mind about it now."

"That's queer!" mused Betty as Nellie went out. "You'd think Nellie would be the one person who'd be sure to notice if it weren't there when she was dusting and putting things straight, especially as she was often the first to be blamed if the leash couldn't be found. 'Last thing' last night would be after Bob had been to see Miss Pongleton and gone away again."

"I shouldn't take much heed of her," Mrs. Bliss began, but was interrupted by the entrance of Mr. Gerard Plasher. Nervousness caused by anxiety as to the right method of greeting the company on this unusual occasion made him more exuberant than usual.

"Good evenin', people! This is a state of affairs—what! Awful business—so disgustingly sordid, dog-leash and all! But that young Bob didn't do it!"

There was a babble of exclamation: "How do you know?" "Have they caught someone else?" "I knew he didn't! He's really a very nice young man!" (This last from Cissie.)

"I know he didn't do it because I was talking to him just when it was done!"

"Just when …?" began Mr. Slocomb, fixing Gerry with a stare of amazement.

Betty got the question out more quickly. "How do you know when it was done?" she demanded. "The body lay there till this afternoon."

"Ah! But I went down those stairs this morning and I passed the old lady on the way. No mistaking her, with her old purple coat and all; besides, I wished her good morning." Struck by a sudden idea, he paused. "Good morning! So I did! Not much of a good morning for her!"

"But what on earth made you go down the stairs, Gerry?" enquired Cissie.

"Y'see, I had a wager with a fellow in the office that there were more than two hundred stairs. 'S a matter of fact it all arose out of my telling him how the old lady always walked down them. I had heard that from Beryl. I said I'd count them; and when I got to the station this morning there wasn't a lift ready, and I thought of the bet and, being brisk and active, what did I do but skip down those stairs. A little way from the top I passed old Miss Pongleton, and then in the passage at the bottom, on my way to the platform, I met Bob with a pail of paste—he'd been sticking up some notices on the platform, I s'pose—and I thought I'd ask him about the stairs because, 's a matter of fact, saying how-d'ye-do to Miss Pongleton put me off my count and I wasn't quite sure."

"But do you know Bob?" asked Betty.

"Oh yes; he came in with Tuppy once when I was here with Beryl having tea with Miss Pongleton; and then seeing him afterwards at Belsize Park I remembered him. I go from that station every morning, y'know."

"But you can't have kept him talking long," objected Betty.

"No, but there he was with his pot of paste and all and not a sign of a dog-leash about him, and I'll bet my bottom dollar he wasn't on his way to do a murder. And then the old lady wouldn't have taken long to get to the bottom of the stairs."

"Did you observe anyone else on or near the stairs?" Mr. Slocomb asked.

"Not a soul; not so much as a blackbeetle," Gerry declared. "Though it's a beetly place, isn't it?" he added, looking at Mr. Slocomb enquiringly.

"Really, I can hardly tell," said that gentleman severely. "I suppose you have informed the police of all this? They would be interested, I think—although perhaps it is not an incident which you will be anxious to make public."

"Y'mean it might look fishy against me? Yes, I thought of that: young man admits seeing murdered lady on the stairs; no one sees her alive afterwards. Yes, but that can't be helped."

"Oh, Gerry, had you better say anything about it?" asked Cissie.

"Don't you see, it may clear Bob?" Mr. Plasher insisted. "Of course I rang up Beryl when I read the news in the paper and she told me about Bob. She was going down to see Basil—he'd been out all day—so I thought I'd come up here and see if you knew any more. As I walked up the hill I sorted things out in my mind, and I'm going to the police-station now."

"We have a police inspector in the house at this moment," announced Mrs. Bliss with pride, as if he were some rare specimen whose capture was due to her prowess.

"Really! Where is he? What luck!"

"One moment!" Mrs. Bliss admonished him. "He is interviewing Mrs. Daymer."

"Gosh! Reminds you of the papers, doesn't it? 'The person whom the police are anxious to interview …' I guess I can tell them a lot more than Mrs. Daymer."

"I should advise you, young man—if you will trust the judgment of one who has had twice your years in this world," said Mr. Slocomb—"to relate your news circumspectly unless you want to find yourself under suspicion. For my part, I cannot see how this will help Bob Thurlow much: no one can tell how long the old lady may have paused on the stairs. She was considerably less brisk in her movements than you are, remember."

"It might help him. Anyway, there's no sense in keeping it back. Ten to one that half a dozen people noticed me make a bolt for those stairs. The man who clipped my ticket, f'rinstance; he sees me every morning and probably knows my striking face by now. And Bob might think of it himself, as a sort of alibi—I wonder he hasn't done that already. If I'm going to be under suspicion, as Mr. Slocomb kindly suggests, it'll look better for me to own up at once."

Mrs. Daymer came in and Mr. Plasher shot up out of his chair.

"Good evening, Mrs. Daymer! Here's your chair. No, it's all right; I'm off to see your inspector."

Mrs. Daymer smiled at him graciously as she resumed her traditional seat, and cast another glance of dislike at Mr. Slocomb, who sat firmly in the desirable chair that had been Miss Pongleton's. When she had resettled herself the others told her of the latest development.

"Has it occurred to any of you," she remarked grimly, "that if Bob Thurlow were innocent he would have thought of Mr. Plasher as providing an alibi; but if he were guilty he would know that it wasn't an alibi and it wouldn't occur to him to try to make one out of that chance meeting. It is helpful in these cases to study the mental attitude. That is only one point, however."

"I don't know that it helps much, but I'll go and tell Nellie what Mr. Plasher has told us," said Mrs. Bliss. "It may hearten the poor girl a little, but I'm afraid she's got a black time ahead of her. And I wouldn't be surprised to find she's smashing all my best plates, such a state of mind she's in." Mrs. Bliss gathered up her knitting and left.

"About that leash," Betty began. "I really don't see how Bob could have got hold of it. It was in the hall late last night but——"

"It is only natural," Mr. Slocomb interposed in a tone of superior scorn, "that the girl Nellie should profess to remember that the leash was there after her young man left the house last night. It is not difficult to make oneself believe what will tally with one's own earnest wish."

Betty shook her head but said nothing.

"I'm going to bed," announced Cissie. "My head's simply in a swim. Coming, Betty?"

They went off together, but not immediately to bed. They sat before the gas-fire in Cissie's room, discussing the affair.

"Fancy poor old Gerry being suspected!" mused Cissie.

"And who's suspecting him?" enquired Betty.

"Old Slow-go, for one. And probably that disagreeable inspector, by now. But, Betty, do you think he could have done it? You see, he's engaged to Beryl Sanders, who is Pongle's niece, and I suppose she'll get the money—so he might have a motive."

"Don't be so ridiculous! I don't suppose Gerry ever thought of money in connection with Beryl, and anyway it's Basil who is more likely to inherit Pongle's fortune, though I think it's a bit uncertain. Basil once told me that Pongle made a new will quite often—if she was fed up with him she'd make a new one in favour of Beryl—so no one could ever be sure who would really get it."

"I wonder if she really had much. She wore such awful old clothes, and they were awful even when new. Anyway, Betty, I hope Basil gets it, for your sake. But you know, supposing Gerry did do the deed, wouldn't it be a good plan for him to pretend to be so innocent and open?"

"How can you have such ghastly ideas?" Betty protested. "And what about the leash? How could he have got it?"

"I don't know," Cissie admitted. "Unless he crept in some-how, late at night. Let's see, last night it was there; that was Thursday—that's when Basil took you to the movies. But we don't know how anyone got the leash. Of course I don't believe Gerry did it. I was just making up theories."

"Then I think you'd better wash them out and start again," Betty advised her.

Down below in the drawing-room Mr. Blend continued to pore over his papers, taking no notice of the others. Mrs. Daymer and Mr. Grange discussed mental attitudes until Mr. Grange was summoned to the smoking-room, when Mrs. Daymer retired to bed. Mr. Slocomb read those parts of the *Evening Standard* which he always reserved for steady contemplation after dinner until, after Mr. Grange's brief interview with the inspector, his own turn came. Mrs. Bliss looked into the drawing-room and found it empty of all but Mr. Blend and Tuppy.

"Dear, dear! There's that dog!" she exclaimed with annoyance. "Where's he to sleep, I wonder."

Tuppy looked as if he would sleep peacefully anywhere. Mrs. Bliss came to the hearthrug and surveyed him.

"What a day this has been, and this poor animal deprived of two of his best friends at one blow! To think of that young Bob taking him out for walks so nicely! Why, only that last Wednesday ... That ever he could do such a thing! And the poor soul on her way to the dentist too, with trouble enough over her teeth, you'd think!"

She raised her voice to attract the attention of Mr. Blend.

"Do you remember saying, Mr. Blend, that true humanity shows itself first in kindness to dumb animals? Out of one of your scrap-books, I think it was. I thought it so good at the time and little knew ... Well, well!"

Her remark had a strange effect on Mr. Blend. He laid down the page he was cutting, regardless of the fact that his long-bladed scissors scrunched diagonally across a column of type.

"That's it, Mrs. Bliss! And to think I couldn't hit on it and you should have quoted it just at this moment! I thank you, I'm sure. Now I ought to be able to find it."

He began to gather up his cuttings, pencil, and scissors in an untidy mass. His slipshod habits were a constant trial to Mrs. Bliss, because the mauled papers and cut pieces which he left about made so much litter.

"Well, I'm sure I don't know what you're talking about, Mr. Blend. It's a wonder to me that you can ever find anything, the way you have it all in such a mess."

"Untidy old beggar, that's what I am. Never mind, Mrs. Bliss; this keeps me happy. Good night, Mrs. Bliss—good night!"

"I suppose the dog must sleep here," Mrs. Bliss was muttering. "But he'll never be easy without his own basket and his cushions. Why ever didn't I get them from the poor lady's room before the police locked it up? It's been such a day as I've never lived through before, and this poor animal sleeping all unconscious!"

Mr. Blend shuffled away and Mrs. Bliss, after gathering up some of his litter and crushing it into the wastepaper basket, followed.

Mr. Slocomb returned to an empty room, and sinking again into the deceased lady's chair with a comfortable sigh, he filled his pipe and relapsed into contemplation, whilst Tuppy lay motionless on the rug at his feet.

CHAPTER FOUR

A CONFESSION

THE next morning, which was Saturday, Mr. Slocomb was rung up in his office by Basil, the nephew of the late Miss Pongleton.

"Say, can you possibly spare me a few minutes—just want your advice; no, not business exactly; private affairs—very private. You're always great nuts on advice; my aunt had no end of faith in you. Most awf'ly grateful—round in a few minutes."

Mr. Slocomb replaced the receiver carefully, as if the mouthpiece might stretch down and bite him, and sat for a few minutes delicately tapping his fingertips against one another and trying to make his eyebrows meet across the top of his long nose. He was interrupted by a clerk. Would he see a Mr. Pink, "nibbling at that fruit and greens in Highgate"? Yes, he would.

"And, Smithson, Mr.—er—Basil Pongleton will be here to see me before long. Ask him to wait in the outer office until Mr. Pink leaves."

Smithson gave a little flick of his head and opened his eyes wider as if swallowing with an effort the name of Pongleton, made famous since yesterday by an old lady's horrible end on the stairs of Belsize Park underground station.

"Ri-sir!" he assured his employer as he departed. Basil Pongleton arrived looking flustered and hot, although it was March, and was set to cool in the outer office while Mr. Slocomb extolled the merits of the "fruit and greens" to Mr. Pink, who looked more suited to "a nice butchery", as Smithson had whispered to the giggling typist after showing him in.

Basil waited restlessly until he noticed a rubicund gentle-man pass through the outer office, when he leapt to his feet ready for the summons, which soon followed, to Mr. Slocomb's inner den.

"Well, Mr. Pongleton; this is a shocking affair; most—er—regrettable. And mysterious."

"Yes, it beats me who could have done it, and I'd give a lot to find out because the truth is I'm in an awful mess. That's why I've come to see you, Mr. Slocomb."

Basil threw his black felt hat carelessly on to a chair, ran his fingers through his already ruffled hair, and made short, apparently purposeful, darts at various parts of the room, checking himself after every few steps.

"Sit down, sit down," Mr. Slocomb admonished him irrita-bly. "Please explain in what sort of a mess you find yourself."

Basil sat down hard in a low armchair and immediately hoisted himself out of it and transferred to a small upright one.

"It's like this. It's awfully difficult to explain and I had a ghastly time with the police yesterday. Wonder they didn't arrest me right away, but they're keeping an eye on me. I noticed a fishy-looking fellow with police-feet lounging opposite my window in Tavistock Square this morning at breakfast-time, and now he's outside here."

"A detective! Watching my offices! This is not exactly—er—beneficial to my business. Really, Mr. Pongleton, don't you think you might have been more careful?"

"Thought you mightn't want to see me if I explained that I was bringing a follower! But I wasn't sure about him when I telephoned. I rather wanted to make a test and see if he did fol-low me here. But I expect I'm safe for the moment. Haven't they got that young fellow Bob Thurlow under arrest? Though I can't believe he did it. But I suppose they're hardly likely to arrest two quite unconnected people for the same crime at the same time."

Mr. Slocomb's mouth was drawn into the lines of an inverted V, and his eyebrows tended to repeat the same figure. "Am I to understand, Mr. Pongleton, that there are grounds for—er—your arrest in connection with this crime—this horrible crime? Really, I had not expected this!"

"Nor had I," Basil declared. "But do you know anything about Bob Thurlow?"

"I have not heard whether any charge has yet been brought against him, but when it is brought I surmise it may merely be that of complicity in the burglary at Lady Morton's house. The police will thereby be enabled to detain him without committing themselves, for the time being."

"By Jove, I hadn't thought of that! You mean they may not think he really did it and they're probably keeping him safe, just in case, and nosing around for another murderer?"

"Of course I am not in the confidence of the police, but that occurs to me as a possible development. They may collect further evidence against Thurlow himself."

"Well, I dunno that that makes it much better for me. It's like this—really it's awf'ly difficult to explain; the hell of a mix-up. And mind you, this is between you and me. I told the police what I thought good for them—at least that's what I meant to tell them but I may have got a bit muddled."

Mr. Slocomb leant forward across his desk, tapping the top of it with one bony finger.

"You have something to conceal from the police?" he enquired portentously. "I do not know that it is quite suitable for me to hear this—and especially here." He considered. "But perhaps if I can advise you … Well, let me hear."

Basil tiptoed to the door and opened it suddenly, revealing only Smithson and the typist who, at this abrupt intrusion, became immobilized in the midst of a joke, as if a cinema film had been suddenly stopped. Basil shut the door before their faces had time to recompose themselves.

"All right," he announced. "Old Ducks'-feet is probably still in the street outside."

Mr. Slocomb had half risen, in horror at this irregular behaviour.

"Really, I should be obliged, Mr. Pongleton, if you would refrain from conduct which may tend even further to bring my offices into disrepute."

"Sorry," Basil apologized, sinking into the armchair. "I'm all of a doo-da. But your offices, you know—too respectable; nothing can harm their reputation. Why, just your own arrival every morning on the stroke of ten would be enough to allay suspicion, even if they found a corpse on the doormat. But now I'll get on with it!"

Basil drew a deep breath and crossed one leg over the other.

"Yesterday morning I set out to go and see Aunt Phemia. I'd had a letter from her—one of her snorters—saying she'd disinherited me."

Mr. Slocomb clucked sympathetically. Basil took no notice of the interruption.

"Seems that last time I had tea with her—Wednesday I think it was—she overheard me make some improper remark to Betty Watson in the hall as I left."

"Some improper remark?" enquired Mr. Slocomb with interest.

"That's her word. What happened was that I met Betty just home from her office and told her I'd been doing the dutiful, or some muck of that sort. I'm sure I'd shut the drawing-room door behind me, and if people open doors for the purpose of listening they must expect to hear the unexpected. Aunt Phemia probably did. She was already in a bit of a wax with me over something else. Anyway, when I got that letter yesterday morning I thought it might be diplomatic to rush up to Hampstead and explain it all away."

"But why in the morning?" asked Mr. Slocomb severely.

"Well, I got the *billet doux* with my morning tea—now I come to think of it, it's funny I didn't get it on Thursday, for Aunt Phemia didn't usually waste much time when she had something unpleasant to say. However, there it was on Friday, and I was going out that afternoon and was booked up for several days so I thought I'd better pop up and see her at once. If I got there bright and early it might have a good effect—she was always rubbing in my indolent habits. Well——"

"One moment," Mr. Slocomb interrupted with pointing finger—"was Miss Pongleton's letter dated Wednesday or Thursday?"

"Quite the police manner," grumbled Basil. "I don't know. I tore it up and I didn't notice particularly. Does it matter?"

"No, no. Continue."

"In the underground I remembered that she had said something on Wednesday about making an appointment with the dentist for Friday, and she'd probably start at break of day. A pity, thought I, now that I've risen with the dawn and got all togged up, if I miss her. I remembered that she always came to Belsize Park to save the coppers, and that she always walked down the stairs, and some insane idea got into my head that she'd be toddling down those stairs at that very moment. So I got out at Belsize Park, and after a look round the down platform and in the passages I got more and more convinced that Aunt Phemia was on her way down those stairs. So what did I do but start to walk up them!"

"Up the stairs!" gasped Mr. Slocomb in horror.

"You see," said Basil. "Nasty, isn't it? But I'd better finish. Well, I started up and began to curse myself for an idiot, realizing there must be miles of them—and then suddenly I came upon what looked like an untidy bundle of old clothes flung down on those stairs. I almost trod on it before I saw it, for I was panting up with my head down. There was something horribly familiar about that old purple coat, and in a moment I saw that Aunt Phemia was inside it. There she lay on her face, head downwards, as if she had stumbled and gone headlong. That's what I thought at first, but I began to lift her up and noticed the ghastly look of her face, and then I saw there was something tight round her neck. She was dead as a doornail; there was no doubt of that. It was horrible. Even if she was a bit of a trial to her family, why should she have to die like that? Whatever kind of a beast could have done it? A sort of blind rage came over me; the police must get on his trail at once. I began running up the stairs like a lunatic, but I was out of breath in a minute and I thought I'd get to the bottom quicker than to the top, so I started down again. I began to think what I'd say to the police—and then suddenly I wondered where *I* came in. D'you know, I sat down on those stairs and tried to think things out. I was properly shaken. I saw how it might look to anyone else—or how I thought it might look. What was I doing on the stairs? they'd ask. You know, Mr. Slocomb, I don't know how to make you believe this. I know it sounds pretty rum, but if only you could realize how I felt. I know I acted like a fool, but I simply couldn't think clearly."

"At what time did all this happen?" Mr. Slocomb asked coldly.

"Time? Good Lord! I don't know. Pretty early in the morning. About ten o'clock I should say, or a bit earlier." Basil looked around him in a harassed way.

"Can you prove the time, do you think?"

"Prove it? No, I can't prove anything. That's the trouble. Well, there I sat on the stairs, and the only thing I could think of was that if people knew I'd been on the stairs with Aunt Phemia they'd think I'd murdered her. Her money, you see, and being fed up with her."

"But you say she had disinherited you? That will remains to show that you would not benefit by her death," Mr. Slocomb pointed out.

"It probably doesn't exist. She may never have made it, or she may have torn it up. Anyhow, I got it into my head that the one thing to do was to get away before anyone saw me, and go up in the lift and call at the Frampton and ask for her as if nothing had happened. I went on down the stairs, and at the bottom I speered around and waited a bit, and then suddenly I felt I couldn't do that. I'd had a nasty knock, you know, and I didn't feel it would be safe to go to the Frampton and ask for Aunt Phemia, knowing all the time she was upside down on the stairs. I'd never pull it off, and besides, then people would know I was about in the station at that time. So I did a bolt for the platform and dived into a train for Edgware."

"Edgware?" enquired Mr. Slocomb, as if to say, "Does anyone go to Edgware?"

"Yes; that train happened along and the other platform was a blank. When I was in the train it occurred to me that it was rather a good idea. I'd go to see old Peter—lives at Golder's Green, Russian and quite mad; paints. It had come into my mind earlier that I might look him up after seeing Aunt Phemia; I really did want to see him about a picture of Beryl that he's to do, and the morning's the only time you can be sure of getting him."

"Did you mention to anyone your intention of going to see this man?"

"Don't s'pose so. Who was there to mention it to? Oh, I might have said to old Waddletoes—my landlady, y'know— that I would probably lunch at Golder's Green. I don't know. I sat in that damned train and tried to pull myself together, and I was feeling a bit better by the time I got to Golder's Green but still pretty wonky. I walked about on the Heath a bit before I went to Peter's house; then I thought to myself that that wasn't the best procedure—someone might see me straying about like a lost lamb and remember it later; so I went to Peter's."

"Will he be able to say at what time you called?"

"Shouldn't think so. He has even less idea of the tempus than me. His wife's pretty sane, but I think she was out—oh yes; she came in later."

"And how did you spend the rest of that day, Mr. Pongleton?"

"I had lunch with Peter and his wife and began to feel safe and soothed and inclined to stay till all hours; but I had to come away at last—before tea. I walked to Golder's Green station and then I felt I couldn't bear that underground again, and I knew I'd feel an insane impulse when we passed Belsize Park station to get out and see if the corpse was still on the stairs, so I got on a bus instead. I didn't feel like going home; thought the police might be waiting to see me, to identify the body or something, so I had supper in a low place in Soho and sat there smoking for a bit, till I shook myself up and went home."

"Did you find—er—anyone waiting to—er—interview you?"

"The police had been there and said they'd call again. Beryl was there—my cousin. I didn't tell her the whole story—no one knows that but you. I just told her I'd been to Golder's Green to see Peter and then dined with a friend. By that time I'd got a paper and read about the affair, so I thought that would account for my being a bit upset. Then the 'tec arrived and I told him as much as I thought was good for him."

"What exactly have you told the police, Mr. Pongleton?"

"Well, it was lucky I saw Beryl first, for when I told her I'd dined with a friend it came into my mind that that wouldn't wash with the police, for they might try to identify the friend."

"Actually you dined alone?"

"I did. Nothing criminal in that? I told the police what I had told Beryl, except that I filled in the evening at a cinema till dinner-time and that I had some food in Soho because it was after my usual dinner-hour and Waddletoes wouldn't be expecting me. Rather neat, that; I did go to the New Vic. on *Thursday* and knew all about the film and where I sat. They didn't ask me that, but they may do yet."

"And have you imparted any other—er—version of your activities during Friday to any other person, Mr. Pongleton?"

"Oh no. Except to Waddletoes of course. Didn't tell her much. Just that I had been to see a friend at Golder's Green and stayed to lunch and then was kept—useful word that, 'kept'—and couldn't get back in time for dinner. She's used to that sort of thing, and anyway she was in a great state of mind, having read the news in the evening paper by then, and so she didn't take much notice of what I said."

"You have not spoken of the—er—your—the way you occupied your time on Friday to any other person?"

"No. No, I don't think so. Let's see: Peter and his wife; bus, Soho, back to my rooms; Waddletoes, Beryl, police; bed. No, that's all. Oh, Gerry Plasher rang me up this morning before I was up; seems he was at Belsize Park station that morning and actually ran down the stairs and passed my aunt on the way— she wasn't dead then. 'Straordinary thing! Those stairs seem to have been positively congested with traffic that morning, and I suppose no one goes down them from one year's end to the other in the ordinary way. I told him I went up to Golder's Green in the underground on Friday morning and must have been just about passing Belsize Park when the murder was committed. Then I just said I didn't get home till after dinner. Said nothing to him about supper in Soho, with or without friend."

"Well, Mr. Pongleton, we must try to get the facts quite clear and review them and then decide on the best course. But I have a considerable amount of business to attend to before lunch, and doubtless your—er—friend outside will be getting restless. It may be wise for you not to stay here longer, but perhaps your good Mrs. Waddle——?"

"Waddletoes? Waddilove her name is——"

"Ah, yes; perhaps Mrs. Waddilove could duplicate your midday repast and I could join you there for some confidential discussion. Not a restaurant, I think, and the Frampton does not offer facilities for a *tête-à-tête*."

"Rather! That's to say delighted to ask you to lunch, Mr. Slocomb. I suppose I'd better go back to my rooms and twiddle my thumbs till you come?"

"Perhaps some occupation ...?" Mr. Slocomb suggested.

"Might toss off a witty trifle for *Punch*, or perhaps a murder mystery; that's not much in my line—never could get the story straightened out."

"Well, good-bye, Mr. Pongleton, for the present. Will one-fifteen suit you? I will walk up to Tavistock Square; I am very fond of a constitutional."

When Basil had left the office Mr. Slocomb walked over to the window and, looking down through the interstices of SLOCOMB'S BUSINESS AGENCY in white china, he saw a lounger in big brown boots and a bowler hat jump into activity and set off purposefully a few yards behind Basil's agile figure, dodging the pedestrians in Charing Cross Road.

Mr. Slocomb tapped the window-sill irritably.

"Young fool!" he muttered to himself. "Pretty thin, that story."

Mr. Slocomb returned to the consideration of fruit and greens, confec. and tobacco, and other blameless affairs.

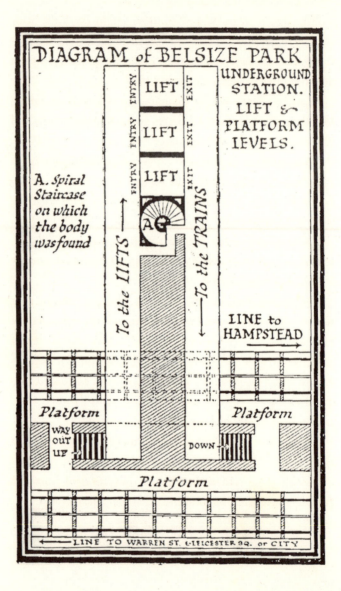

DIAGRAM of BELSIZE PARK UNDERGROUND STATION. LIFT & PLATFORM LEVELS.

LIFT

LIFT

LIFT

ENTRY ENTRY ENTRY

EXIT EXIT EXIT

A. *Spiral Staircase on which the body was found*

A

To the LIFTS

To the TRAINS

LINE to HAMPSTEAD

Platform

Platform

WAY OUT UP

DOWN

Platform

← LINE TO WARREN ST. & LEICESTER SQ. or CITY

CHAPTER FIVE

MR. SLOCOMB ADVISES

BASIL PONGLETON was executing fancy steps to the accompaniment of blaring wireless "lunch-time music" when Mr. Slocomb arrived for lunch. The latter paused on the threshold of the room, a look of pain and horror on his face.

"Sorry!" said Basil, switching off the wireless. "Must pass the time somehow, and if this is what the B.B.C. hands out to us, who am I to refuse it?"

Mr. Slocomb shut the door behind him. "I think it would be wise," he suggested, "to keep our discussion of—er—salient points until after lunch. Mrs. Waddilove coming in and out … Of course, some reference to your aunt's unfortunate death would be only natural."

Mrs. Waddilove came in with a dish of cutlets. "Now I hope you'll make a good meal, Mr. Pongleton," she admonished him. "Excuse me, sir"—to Mr. Slocomb—"but Mr. Pongleton is that upset; why, what he ate for breakfast wouldn't give a fly indigestion, if you'll excuse my mentioning it; and he gen'ally so hearty!"

They ate their lunch with a good deal of haste and little conversation. During the course of the meal Basil told Mr. Slocomb firmly: "I've asked you for your advice and I want it, but I warn you there's one thing it's no earthly use advising me to do, and that's to report it all to the police. I simply can't do that. So you've got to help me keep it dark."

The entrance of Mrs. Waddilove saved Mr. Slocomb from the distasteful necessity of admitting his willingness to become an accomplice.

When Mrs. Waddilove had cleared away with a silence and deftness which was surprising in view of her bulk, they settled themselves on either side of the bright fire and Mr. Slocomb produced a small black notebook.

"I say," exclaimed Basil in alarm; "you're not going to write down *the truth*? Seems risky, I mean. And feels a bit too much like the police."

"Rest assured that I shall not be guilty of any indiscretion. But I think we may see the relevance and importance of each fact more clearly if we jot down the items and piece them together. Of course the notes must be destroyed afterwards. Now, to begin with, Mr. Pongleton, you told me this morning that you commented to Mr. Plasher on the telephone that you must have been passing Belsize Park station just when the murder was committed. May I ask by what means are you, in what for the sake of convenience we will call your public story, supposed to know when the murder was committed?"

"Good Lord! Have I made another howler? Now, look here, Mr. Slocomb, we all know that my aunt must have been murdered soon after Gerry saw her alive on the stairs at—when was it?—nine-twenty or something like that. No one supposes she sat down and waited for the murderer to arrive."

"Ye-es. I only wish to warn you, Mr. Pongleton, of making any statements based on knowledge acquired by you on your unfortunate expedition up those stairs. That expedition did not officially take place. Please do not assume that I intend to connive at any attempt to deceive the police authorities. But I am bound to say that by your rashness and prevarication you have put yourself into a difficult situation. When once a man has been found to be untruthful, I believe the police are often reluctant to believe his subsequent statements."

"You needn't rub it in, Mr. Slocomb. I'm only too well aware what a mess I'm in! That's why I've asked your advice. But what else could I have told the police? By the way, Waddletoes has told me that the police asked her when I left here on Friday morning, and she told them it was twenty past nine. I expect that's about right. She brings my early tea at eight; and as soon as I read Aunt Phemia's letter I yelled to her to hurry up with breakfast, and I leapt out of bed and hustled around no end. I had breakfast at about a quarter to nine, she says."

"If Mrs. Waddle—Waddilove is definite and unshaken in her statement as to the time you left this house, that may be a factor in your favour. Miss Pongleton left the Frampton at nine o'clock on Friday morning. Her appointment with the dentist—Mr. Crampit of Camden Town—was for ten o'clock. At her request I had myself telephoned to him and arranged the—er—interview. The time of her departure from the Frampton can be testified to by several inmates of the boarding-house, myself included."

Mr. Slocomb noted these times meticulously in his little notebook.

"Now let us proceed with our reconstruction of events," he continued. "There are certain points on which we may be guided by assumption. I read in the paper this morning that an official at Belsize Park noticed Miss Pongleton proceed towards the stairs on Friday at, he thinks, about nine-fifteen. He is probably correct. … The next person who saw her was Mr. Plasher—if we accept what he says——"

"Oh, but surely—I mean, *Gerry* …!"

"We are considering the facts, impersonally," Mr. Slocomb pointed out dryly. "Mr. Plasher states that he ran past Miss Pongleton on the stairs a few minutes after nine-fifteen; that is his usual time of arrival at Belsize Park on his way to business. He is not quite sure of the exact time, but presumably he would be at the bottom of the stairs before nine-twenty, and there he paused a few moments to speak to Bob Thurlow whom he met in the passage."

"Going towards the stairs with a bucket, I gathered from Gerry. But he says there's nothing in it—nothing suspicious about Thurlow's appearance, I mean."

"You yourself saw nothing of Mr. Plasher, I presume?"

"Oh no; but then he'd be in the other passage," Basil pointed out.

"Yes, yes. But it is necessary to have every point clear. Officially no one else saw Miss Pongleton, dead or alive, until the afternoon, but she can hardly have been on the stairs—er—alive, for more than ten minutes after Mr. Plasher saw her. Perhaps you have heard the sequence of events that led to the tragic discovery?"

"I've had some rather scrappy accounts from Gerry and Beryl, but I'm not very clear about it."

"As I understand from Mrs. Bliss, that good lady became anxious when Miss Pongleton did not return to lunch, as she had precisely stated that she would do so at the usual hour. Mrs. Bliss telephoned to Mr. Crampit and learnt that Miss Pongleton had not kept her appointment. Mrs. Bliss then rang you up—that is to say, she obtained this number—and Mrs. Waddilove informed her that you were out and that your aunt had not been here. Mrs. Bliss hastened to Belsize Park

station and made enquiries there. No one remembered seeing Miss Pongleton—the man who afterwards stated that he
had noticed her had doubtless gone off duty—and Mrs. Bliss
telephoned to the police station. The police, learning of your
aunt's habit of going down the stairs at the station, investigated
the staircase with the results known to you."

"How did Bob Thurlow come in? Oh, I remember, his name
was on some paper my aunt had on her."

Mr. Slocomb related the affair of the burgled brooch, as he
had heard it from Mrs. Bliss.

"That all seems a bit queer, doesn't it?" suggested Basil.
"I mean, why should Aunt Phemia write his name on the
envelope or whatever it was, and why should she carry it about
with her?"

"I see nothing queer about it," snapped Mr. Slocomb. "You
must surely be aware that it was your aunt's habit to secrete
things in somewhat peculiar places, and until she had decided
on a hiding-place to her liking she would carry papers and so
forth about with her in her somewhat capacious handbag. She
was very meticulous, and it would be natural for her to wrap up
the brooch and write Bob Thurlow's name on the package."

"But look here, it wasn't in her bag but in her pocket!" Basil
declared. "I read that in the paper."

"Really, is it of any significance?" Mr. Slocomb snorted.

"Well, you said 'bag'," sulked Basil; "and I'm trying, under
your guidance, to be accurate. But what was she doing with the
brooch anyway? Either she ought to have left it with the girl or,
if she must interfere, the police should have had it."

"Certainly her procedure was somewhat irregular. Your
aunt took a great interest in young Thurlow, and possibly she

was holding the brooch until she could exact some promise from him that he would return it to its owner or to the police. It is likely that she carried it with her to prevent the girl Nellie from recovering it whilst she was away from the house."

"That doesn't sound like my aunt, except the last bit. She was a hard old woman, and I don't believe she had a spark of interest in the young man except for the services she got out of him for nothing. Why, she used to have to *pay* a girl to take that poodle for walks!"

"Poodle?" enquired Mr. Slocomb.

"Oh, I know it wasn't—isn't—a poodle; but never mind. I suppose young Thurlow's done for anyway, poor fool; even if he clears himself of the murder business he'll lose his job on the underground. And I suppose the fact that he was mixed up with a burglary will make the police ready to believe he is capable of murder too."

"Assuredly Thurlow seems at the moment to be the person with both opportunity and motive."

"The opportunity was doubtful, Gerry thinks."

"Mr. Plasher states that he passed Miss Pongleton, who moved slowly, near the top of the stairs. After he himself left the stairs he stopped for a moment to speak to Thurlow and then went on his way. It is reasonable to suppose that Thurlow, if he then went straight up the stairs, would meet Miss Pongleton before she reached the bottom—and I understand that the body was found no great distance up."

"Well, it doesn't seem likely to me and I can't say the motive seems at all clear," Basil persisted.

"The motive, presumably, was to recover the brooch. He would learn from the girl Nellie that it was in Miss Pongleton's possession. Possibly he heard you coming up the stairs just as he was searching for it. But it is not our business to detect the criminal. Time is getting on, and before I go I think we had better get your own movements clearly stated—for our private information." Mr. Slocomb consulted his notes. "You left here at nine-twenty and proceeded to…?"

"Warren Street station—ten minutes' walk."

"And bought a ticket to…?"

"Hampstead. It wasn't till later that I got that idiotic idea about Belsize Park."

"The ticket to Belsize Park would be a cheaper one?"

"Oh yes; it's another penny to Hampstead."

"And still another penny to Golder's Green?"

"Yes—I forgot that on Friday, till I got out at Golder's Green. It struck me as I held out the ticket to the collector, and I got into a panic, but I saw he was examining the ticket and I had to say something, so I explained quickly that I'd changed my mind after getting the ticket, and then I paid the extra penny."

"Hm! It might have been less noticeable if you had handed him the penny with the ticket, without saying anything."

"By Jove, Mr. Slocomb! You'd make a snappy criminal; you think of everything!" Basil exclaimed in admiration. "But it wasn't anything out of the way to have to pay on a ticket."

"And you arrived at Golder's Green at what time?"

"I've told you I don't know any times," declared Basil.

"To revert, for one moment, to Belsize Park. I do not suppose it is of the least use to ask you at what time you left the station after—er—viewing the body?"

"No, it isn't. What a hellish invention time is!"

"But can you say whether you encountered there—or caught sight of—anyone who knows you, who might recognize you?"

"Not a soul. I told you how I skulked on the stairs till the coast was clear; then I skipped along to the platform and hopped into a train. There may have been one or two people getting in or out but I don't suppose they noticed me particularly. Certainly I didn't notice them; I was much too taken up with noticing myself."

"A risk; undoubtedly a risk; especially as your behaviour in—er—skulking—er—skipping and—er—hopping may have been conspicuous. Hm! To proceed: you do not know the time of your arrival at your friend's house in Golder's Green, but have you any idea how long you walked on the Heath?"

"I'll engage a timekeeper before I get mixed up in another crime! No, I don't know; I just mooned about a bit. Perhaps a quarter of an hour; perhaps half an hour. I got my shoes very muddy," he added helpfully.

"And the distance from Golder's Green station to your friend's house is…?"

"Good ten minutes' at a fast trot. He lives in North Way."

The telephone bell rang; not with any significant note as it does in the best regulated murder mysteries, but with its usual ear-splitting insistent din. Basil rushed at the apparatus.

"H'lo! Yes—Basil. O-o-h!"

He covered the mouthpiece and turned to Mr. Slocomb.

"Police have been asking Peter's wife when I got there yesterday and how long I stayed."

Mr. Slocomb was considering the notes he had jotted down and he seemed to take no notice of Basil, but he muttered abstractedly, "About ten; yes, ten—or very soon after."

"I don't know, Delia," Basil was saying to the telephone. "You know I never know the time; but I got up rather early that morning. What time do you think it was? Oh, of course you were out when I arrived. What does Peter think? No, of course he wouldn't know. Well, does it matter? I should think I got to you soon after ten. Yes, *ten*—gives you a bit of a shock, does it, me being so bright and early? Well, I told you I was feeling very brisk. What? Rotten? Oh yes, I did feel a bit off colour later on, all through getting up so early, I expect. Yes, I'm all right now, thanks. How's Peter? You didn't go out till after ten? Well, I believe Peter said I'd only just missed you—no, of course I didn't miss you entirely, luckily. Anyway, it's not important, is it?—the time, I mean. The police are donkeys. Usual routine: they have to find out where everyone was. And, I say, Delia, you've got my hat. No, I haven't a cat. H for hell … yes, a bowler. Oh, but you must have it. I left it behind me yesterday. I don't suppose you would notice it among all the odd tiles and garments you keep in your hall, and I wouldn't be surprised if one of your disreputable friends had nabbed it. I'm sure I left it there; I know I came home without it. I'll collect it when next I come. Don't worry. Right! Good-bye!"

"Did that rather well, didn't I?" remarked Basil, returning to his chair.

"What's this about a bowler hat?" enquired Mr. Slocomb.

"I started out yesterday in a bowler—beastly thing! Oh, beg your pardon; it's all right on someone elderly and respectable, of course, but I never can feel at home in it. Only put it on because Aunt Phemia thought it looked gentlemanly— poor old Aunt Phemia! And I came home without it. Hope to goodness I didn't leave it on the stairs! No, I can't have done. It may be in the train or it may be at Peter's. Anyway, Waddletoes noticed that it was gone when I came in last night."

Mr. Slocomb gazed at Basil with the utmost disapproval.

"You can tell me, Mr. Pongleton, that you—er—mislaid a bowler hat with such incredible carelessness that you do not know where it is?"

"You've got the idea," Basil assured him. "Anyway, I shan't need it any more."

Mr. Slocomb sighed heavily. "Just what did Mrs.—er—Peter say to the police?" he asked.

"Oh, she says that she said she went out at about a quarter-past ten and that I turned up soon after. But she's one of these red-haired women, quite unreliable, y'know," said Basil gloomily.

"Now, according to this story you have told the police, you got up on Friday morning earlier than usual, called to Mrs. Waddilove to prepare your breakfast quickly, and left the house with unwonted promptitude, in order to visit Mr.—er...?"

"Kutuzov. Well, of course I didn't rub in all that about being prompt and early. I just said I went after breakfast."

"And you do not know whether Mrs. Waddilove may have expatiated to the police on your hurry and the early hour of your breakfast?"

"Oh, but surely ... well, she is rather a talker, and she's very proud of me when I'm out of bed before nine."

"Just so. Now, to consider this matter of the letter from your aunt which you received in bed on Friday morning. We know actually that was the cause of your early rising. Is there any likelihood that anyone else may know or suppose that you received such a letter and that it had any effect on your conduct?"

"Aunt Phemia's letter. . . . Let's see. Waddletoes brought it up with my tea. I expect I let out a bit of a groan on seeing it–Aunt Phemia's writing generally meant trouble. Waddletoes probably knows that writing by now, too, if she takes as much interest in my correspondence as she does in my appetite."

"Did you actually mention the letter to Mrs. Waddilove?"

"And, if so, at what time, eh? I don't know. Suppose someone brings you a letter and you look at it, and say, 'Oh, hell!' would you call that mentioning it?"

"It would be unusual for me to make *any* comment on my correspondence to a third person, especially an employee," Mr. Slocomb stated primly.

"I bet it would. Well, when I'd read the letter I yelled to Waddletoes to get a move on with breakfast, but whether I said I was going to see my aunt or had heard from my aunt, I simply don't know."

"Hm! Bad. Anyone else?"

"There was Beryl. Let's see . . . did I tell her I'd heard from Aunt Phemia that morning? No, I'm pretty sure I didn't. I didn't want her to know I had anything to do with the old lady that day. I remember now: I told her I woke up feeling very spry and thought about her picture that Peter was to do, and so I leapt out of bed and rushed up to Golder's Green to see him and nail him down. It's to be my wedding present to Gerry and Beryl—at least, it was to be. Don't suppose it will be if I'm hanged for murdering Aunt Phemia. Throw a bit of a gloom on the wedding festivities, won't it?"

"In my judgment, Mr. Pongleton, your wiser course would be to banish from your mind any possibility that you may be implicated, and at least to imagine yourself innocent."

"That's a nasty one, Mr. Slocomb. As I was saying, Beryl was rather pleased with the idea that I had set out early to see about her picture. She swallowed it as if it were an oyster—whole."

"And the police—you told them also that you went to see Mr.—er—Kut-off—er—Kut-us-off—about your cousin's picture?"

"I don't know that I told them what I went to see Peter about. I probably just said that I went to see him. But that's what I did go to see him about. I told you I had thought of going to see him about it before I—well, before I met the body."

"And presumably he or his wife will have told the police that that was what you did go to see him about?"

"I d'n 'know about that. You see, when I got there I was too dithery to talk business. I don't know what I did talk about. Though, 's a matter of fact, we did discuss the picture before I left. I b'lieve Delia mentioned it first; but, as I've told you, there's no knowing what Delia has told the police. She'll tell anyone what she feels like telling."

"This is all most unfortunate, Mr. Pongleton, most unfortunate. If you actually had been—er—guilty of—er—crime you could hardly have behaved more wildly than you seem to have done."

"If I had been a criminal I might have behaved much more cautiously. And, anyway, isn't it a good business principle not to rush at your business the first moment you meet your man?"

"I should hardly have thought that this business was of such a delicate nature as to require that kind of indirect approach."

"You don't know old Peter. Any business with him is of a delicate nature. But, look here, you seem awfully suspicious.

You don't really think I *did* it? Aunt Phemia may have been tiresome, poor old girl, but I swear——"

Mr. Slocomb raised his hand. "Enough, Mr. Pongleton. It is always my habit to believe in the word and the good intentions of my fellow men until I am compelled to believe otherwise. But there is one other point. You did not trust your cousin enough to tell her the whole story, and there is at least one discrepancy between what you told her and what you related to the police. You informed your cousin that you had supper in Soho with a friend—I presume you gave her to understand that you met a friend by appointment? The other version was that you went to a cinema and then took a simple meal alone because it was too late to return to your rooms for dinner. These two stories have, as it were, been launched, and before long both may reach the ears of one person. How do you propose to deal with this?"

"Just a minute. It wasn't because I didn't trust Beryl that I didn't tell her the whole thing. It was just because it was so beastly—finding Aunt Phemia upside down like that with Tuppy's leash round her neck; and also because I had been a bit of an ass, and it might worry her. As for dealing with it, I don't see what I can do, and, after all, does it matter? It's only a question of how I spent a few hours of the evening, long after Aunt Phemia had been discovered."

Mr. Slocomb wagged his head to express exasperation and despair.

"Is it impossible for you to understand, Mr. Pongleton, how important it is that all your behaviour should at least seem to be above reproach? Persons who have nothing to conceal do not usually give contradictory accounts of their movements."

"I tell you I've no experience of crime," Basil insisted; "and I don't understand the first thing about it."

"Flippancy will not assist you," said Mr. Slocomb severely. "And yet another point: that restaurant in Soho. Are you well-known there? The police may make enquiries, and may find that you spent more time there than is consistent with your story."

"I don't suppose they noticed me specially. I look much like all the others, and lots of people sit there for donkey's years."

"In any case I do not see what steps we can take with regard to that. Perhaps you had better not frequent the place for the next few days."

"All right. I don't frequent it, anyway."

"Now we really must consider, Mr. Pongleton, what action you ought to take about this story you have told your cousin. Can you trust her sufficiently to tell her that there was some trifling inaccuracy in what you said to her on Friday night—owing, doubtless, to the fact that you were—er—upset at the news of your aunt's death?"

"Trust Beryl! Of course I can trust her. But I don't want to worry her, y'know. She's upset enough already about the whole beastly affair, and then Gerry being mixed up in it makes it worse. To think that Gerry and I should both be inspired to go gadding about on those godforsaken stairs on the same day! Looks as if Aunt Phemia had a sort of malign influence, y'know, drawing us both to the fatal spot. Lord! How she must be chuckling! I s'pose I might tell Beryl——"

"I think, Mr. Pongleton, that it would be better for me not to know what you tell your cousin. I need hardly say how repugnant to me is all this—er—prevarication. But I beg you to bear in mind the possibility that she may be questioned closely by the police, and a young woman is liable to be confused by close interrogation, so it would be as well to avoid any unnecessary complications."

"Oh, Beryl's as cool as a cucumber. She won't get flustered. She has a quiet sort of way of saying things so that you'd have to believe her even if you knew she was telling a whopper. She was wonderful with Aunt Phemia! And the whole of Scotland Yard backed by all the Archbishops couldn't make her tell them anything she didn't want to say."

"I leave it to you, Mr. Pongleton, to exercise suitable discretion. Now there is one more point. Do you happen to have any information about Miss Pongleton's will? I understand that you and your cousin were her joint heirs, and that you were to have the larger portion of your aunt's estate."

"Aunt Phemia was always making wills, and one of the things she said in that letter was that she had made a new one and left most of it to Beryl. So you see, I shouldn't have had any motive for murdering her on Friday morning, should I?"

"Ah!" This seemed to strike Mr. Slocomb as a good point. "And that letter is destroyed?"

"It is—confound it!"

"Your aunt did not state in that letter what she had done with the new will?"

"Heavens, no! But she probably tucked it safely away under the mattress."

Mr. Slocomb put the tips of his fingers neatly together and considered them. "If an opportunity should occur, Mr. Pongleton, you would be wise to mention that letter to the police and to say—quite truthfully—that it implied that you were disinherited. You will realize that would eliminate what would seem a possible motive on your part for—er—committing the crime."

"Yes, I see. Of course, I don't know that she really made a new will, and if the police hear about the letter and don't find the will, mightn't they think I'd destroyed it? She was always talking about making new wills, but I don't suppose she made half of them, though she certainly did keep a supply of those printed forms—she showed them to me once. When she was more or less normal—I mean, when she wasn't specially annoyed with me, it was to be as you say, most of the fortune to me. But I wouldn't be a bit surprised to find she had no fortune at all. She was awfully close."

"But she is known to have inherited a large sum at some time? And she lived in very modest fashion. The Frampton is, of course, highly respectable and reasonably comfortable, but not what one might call extravagant."

"Extravagant! Good Lord, no! It's certainly true that my aunt came into some thirty thousand from her brother, my Uncle Geoffrey. She can't even have spent all the income from that; she saved every penny she could—couldn't help it; a sort of disease. Goodness knows she wasn't so anxious to leave me well provided for. But she may have given it away to a dogs' home or a society for teaching the working man not to waste his wages on gramophones."

"Hm! Doubtless we shall have more definite information on those points before long." Mr. Slocomb consulted his notes once more. "The matter of the ticket to Hampstead—if you should be questioned about that perhaps it might not be unnatural that you should have asked for a ticket to Hampstead out of habit? You go frequently to Hampstead, and habit is strong."

"Good idea!" Basil agreed. "I might easily do that."

"Well, Mr. Pongleton, I will see you again before the inquest, which is on Monday, I think? In a case of this kind it is usually brief and formal. Now I must think over all the somewhat—er—disturbing information you have given me."

"But, look here, aren't you going to tell me what to do?" cried Basil in distress.

After a discreet knock at the door, Mrs. Waddilove entered.

"Miss Sanders and Mr. Plasher to see you, sir. I told them you were engaged with a gentleman, and they're waiting to know whether you'd like to see them."

"I am about to leave," declared Mr. Slocomb stiffly.

"Mr. Slocomb's a friend of the family, Mrs. Waddy; not a policeman," Basil assured her.

Mrs. Waddilove eyed the dour but dapper little man doubtfully.

"Oh, Mr. Pongleton, sir, you will have your joke! Well, I never did think you'd be having the police to luncheon. I'll show Miss Sanders and Mr. Plasher up, shall I, sir?"

"That's the idea."

Mr. Slocomb took his leave. "Bear in mind, Mr. Pongleton, that the account of your movements on Friday that you have given to the police is the true account—for the present. And perhaps a—er—slight reluctance to discuss the affairs of that very—er—painful day would be only natural. In any case, Mr. Pongleton, no interviews with the Press, I should advise. Good day!"

"Wait a mo'. When can I see you again? You may think out something. I have to be with my people all to-morrow...."

"Hm! Not wise for me to come here too often or for you to frequent my office. Monday morning; another early breakfast might be a good move for you. Can you, Mr. Pongleton, arrange to start early enough to meet me and accompany me on a short constitutional? I will leave the Frampton at five minutes past nine; or perhaps five minutes earlier—yes, say nine o'clock. I will look for you at the corner of Church Lane and Rosslyn Hill."

"But, I say, that's awful—nine o'clock!" Basil grumbled at Mr. Slocomb as the latter slid out of the room. "Oh, well, I s'pose I must manage it!"

On leaving the house Mr. Slocomb looked round for the gentleman in brown boots and bowler hat. He was not there, but another lounger lolled against the railings of the square. "Second shift, presumably," Mr. Slocomb murmured to himself. He moved with an easy gliding step which carried him rapidly along. "What a young fool!" he muttered. "The marvel is that he had the good sense to seek my advice!"

CHAPTER SIX

THE PRESS DOES ITS DUTY

WHILST Basil Pongleton was decanting his Friday escapade into the unsympathetic ears of Mr. Joseph Slocomb, the reporters for the *Daily Chat* and the *Evening Snatch* and the *Sunday Smatter*, and their numerous colleagues and rivals, were sniffing eagerly on the trail of Miss Pongleton's murderer. None of them had been able to glean many details on Friday, although one of them had extracted some very damp reminiscences from Nellie before Mrs. Bliss had intervened. The journalist surmised that Mrs. Bliss herself would not be averse to disclosing her own views of the situation at some other time, when Inspector Caird, who was then claiming her attention, should leave her free.

The Saturday morning papers had therefore not been able to elaborate to any great extent the bare facts of Miss Euphemia Pongleton's setting forth on Friday morning to visit her dentist, and the discovery of her body in the afternoon. They endeavoured to allay their readers' curiosity with descriptions of the spiral staircase which descends beside the lift shafts at Belsize Park station. They counted the steps and they examined the narrow gutter against the wall for clues which might have been overlooked by the police, but as it was choked with cigarette cartons, paper, and scraps of tobacco—the litter of months or even years—it was impossible to pick out anything that might be significant. They noted that the stairs were covered with some hard composition on which steps sounded but faintly, and that the clang of the lift gates and the footsteps of passengers hurrying to and from their trains floated up clearly from below.

The stairs led down to a short passage connecting the two main passages along which travellers passed from the lifts to the platforms or from the platforms to the lifts. The observant reporters pointed out that experienced underground travellers often use this passage at the foot of the stairs as a short cut, so that it would excite no surprise if anyone were seen entering it or emerging from it, even though the stairs themselves were rarely used; and also that a man standing on one of the lowest stairs would have a view of the down passage and would probably never be noticed by those who hurried past with their backs to him.

All this merely tended to show that anyone could have approached the staircase from the bottom, and left it by the same route, without being noticed. Unless Gerry Plasher were the murderer—and no one seemed to think that he was—it was almost certain that the criminal had gone up the stairs to the point where Miss Pongleton's body was found, and, after strangling her, had come down again. Anyone approaching the top of the stairs would probably have been noticed by one of the station officials, who were sure that Miss Pongleton herself and Gerry Plasher were the only people who had taken that route to the platforms on Friday morning.

The relevant facts about Gerry Plasher were soon known to the enquiring representatives of the Press. He was engaged to Miss Pongleton's niece, but it was generally supposed that Basil Pongleton and not Beryl Sanders would be her heir. He was an ordinary young man, junior partner in a firm of stockbrokers, and had no cause to bear the old lady any malice. It was unlikely that he knew of Miss Pongleton's appointment with the dentist, or had any reason to suppose that he would pass her on the stairs. He had made no secret of the fact that he used them on Friday morning and saw her there. There was nothing to indicate that he had any opportunity to get hold of the dog-leash from the Frampton.

It was known that the police had examined the rail of the staircase for fingerprints, and had found these in embarrassing profusion. Gerry had left his mark there; Bob Thurlow had left his, but that was easily accounted for by his duties in the station which caused him to use the staircase from time to time—though not on Friday, so far as anyone knew. Other underground workers testified to that, and his fingerprints had been found above the body as well as below it, which implied that he had put them there on his lawful occasions.

What was more mysterious was a footprint which, the reporters learnt from the underground officials, had been found on the stairs, below the body, pointing upwards. It was difficult to get any exact information about this and the police did not want it talked about, so evidently it was important, and presumably it did not belong to anyone who was known to have been on the stairs that morning. But how any foot had contrived it to make a lasting print on the hard composition with which the stairs were covered the reporters could not discover. They referred to it in guarded but rather inaccurate terms as "an important clue" which was "in the hands of the police".

With this mysterious footprint in mind, the reporters were nosing about eagerly for something which would point to another murderer. But they did not neglect Bob Thurlow, who had been charged with complicity in the burglary at Lady Morton's house, for it was possible that the graver charge was only being held in reserve until the chain of evidence should be complete. Bob's fellow-workers were convinced of his innocence. He was a burglar—or at least the accomplice of burglars—they now knew, but he was a "damn silly one". He was a good-natured chap—look how he used to go dragging that fat dog about on the end of a strap to please the old lady! He hadn't behaved like a murderer on the day of the crime.

How did murderers behave? the reporters enquired sarcastically. Wasn't their main object to behave like innocent men? But Bob was too simple for that. Had he been a murderer he would have behaved "queer", and there had been nothing queer about him that morning. He had been seen by them at various times, going about his ordinary duties quietly and normally. Of course he had had something on his mind for some days; they had noticed that, and now knew that it was the affair of the brooch.

"And there you are," the ticket collector had said to one of the Press men. "If he murdered the old lady to get the brooch back, why didn't he get it?"

That, of course, was the problem, but one of the bright young men pointed out that everyone was barking up the wrong tree. It was absurd to suppose that Bob had any idea that Miss Pongleton would be carrying the brooch about with her. It was much more likely that he met her on the stairs by chance, and, naturally, spoke to her about the brooch, again begging her to restore it to him and not to give him away to the police. The journalist's imagination was fired. He had a vision of the telling article he would write at some future date when Bob Thurlow had been convicted of the murder.

"Who knows what happened on that grim staircase on the fatal Friday morning? We can picture the young man's entreaties; the old lady's stern refusal; her rigid adherence to her conception of her duty as a citizen—an adherence which was to bring about her tragic death. We can picture the young man's desperation"—mustn't seem to justify him, though, thought the journalist—"his rising anger, anger which flamed into blind rage. Instinctively his hand goes to his pocket, the pocket in which is the leather leash thoughtlessly placed there on the last occasion when he returned the little dog to its unsuspecting mistress"—or perhaps snatched up from the hall on Thursday night when he talked to the old lady there; snatched up when no one was looking, perhaps already with some obscure idea of revenge—must look up that point.... "He whips out the leash, takes a step upward and flings it round the old lady's neck. She is old and feeble; her faint cries of despair are quickly stifled; the deed is done!"

"Blimey! How you talk!" said the ticket collector. "But that ain't Bob Thurlow. He's a quiet sort of chap; not the one to fly into a rage. And look here—the last thing he wanted was for anything to happen that would bring that brooch affair to light! The old lady hadn't told the police nor anyone else as far as we know, and he hoped she wouldn't ever tell them. Her death wouldn't do him no good."

"He didn't know that her death would bring the whole affair to light. He realized that it would prevent her telling the police, and he couldn't guess that she'd have the brooch wrapped up in an envelope with his name on it. His natural idea would be that it would be found among her property and would excite no remark. It was the sort of thing any old lady might have, by all accounts."

"You're all wrong," the ticket collector declared. "I tell you Bob Thurlow's not that sort of chap."

Mrs. Bliss, however, thought otherwise, as a severely tailored young woman from the *Evening Snatch* was discovering. They were sitting in the little room behind the dining-room at the Frampton, which Mrs. Bliss called her sanctum, and which was furnished with Victorian appurtenances that had been banished from the public rooms to make way for the more easeful chairs and sofas that decadent modern taste demanded. It was also cluttered with an incongruous assortment of objects which had been abandoned by past boarders and were now reverently preserved by Mrs. Bliss. They provided useful starting points for reminiscences.

"That was Colonel Horsley," she would say, pointing to a small ebony elephant. "Such wonderful experiences he had had, and such an interesting man!" Mrs. Bliss had already been wondering which of the late Miss Pongleton's treasures would pass into her possession to be given a place of honour on the mahogany corner table. Would it be the ostrich egg on the teakwood stand, or the pair of china dogs gazing over their shoulders with languishing eyes, to which she would point in the future when she wanted to say: "*That* was poor Miss Euphemia Pongleton, who was strangled on the stairs at Belsize Park."

"It's a sight that will haunt me to my dying day," she was telling the tailored young woman, apparently with the intention that it should haunt as many others as possible. "The poor soul laid out there in her old purple coat! Why, only this morning, as I was putting on my last year's hat—which I keep for wet weather, you know—I thought to myself, now if my time should have come to-day—and with all these motor-cars dashing about the streets you can never tell—should I like to think of myself laid out in that old hat? It makes you careful, doesn't it?"

The tailored young woman tucked a straying lock of hair away beneath her rakish cap. "Yes," she said; "yes. I suppose Miss Pongleton had no premonition of her death?"

"We none of us know and we none of us ever shall know," declared Mrs. Bliss impressively, "what the poor lady thought when she met Bob Thurlow on those stairs with the light of death in his eye. When that young man, that she had trusted and befriended, set upon her there with murderous intent, it must have been such a shock to her that it would have been enough to kill her, let alone the leash belonging to her own little dog."

"We don't *know* yet that it was Bob Thurlow who murdered her," the young woman pointed out cautiously.

"And who else could it be?" Mrs. Bliss enquired. "It's all as clear as daylight. He only didn't get the brooch because he was disturbed, and for some reason he couldn't get back to search the body. If the poor lady hadn't been so careful and particular we might never have known that he had cause to wish her dead, but there was the brooch in an envelope, and written on it: 'Brooch believed to be stolen property, obtained from Nellie Foster, who had it from Bob Thurlow, March 15th.' If that isn't enough to hang a man I'd like to know what is?"

"I suppose no one had any suspicion that Bob Thurlow was concerned in the burglary until all this happened?"

"We had no idea of any such thing, or, of course, I'd never have had him in the house again, and poor Miss Pongleton would never have trusted him with her little dog that she set such store by, had she known. But when the body was found, and the brooch, and the police asked Bob about it, it seems he made a clean breast of all the affair of the burglary, hoping, no doubt, that he'd get off with that, and maybe thinking he could save his own skin by giving away his friends.

"It's dreadful to think how we've all trusted that young man, and he's been in and out of this house almost like one of ourselves, and one of the first things I did when I'd got over the shock was to count the silver, but I'm glad to say there's nothing missing except a little teaspoon, and I can't be sure that didn't go down the drain, for the last maid I had was something chronic, the way she'd empty everything away without so much as noticing!"

The tailored young woman was sympathetic. Mrs. Bliss had given her "quite a lot of useful stuff", and it only remained to extricate herself not too abruptly from the sanctum.

Whilst these investigations were in train on Saturday, other reporters sought out Basil, the nephew and probable heir of the victim of the crime. But he had given Mrs. Waddilove firm instructions that he would not talk to any of them; she was to say that he was too much upset, and anyway he couldn't tell them anything about it.

This refusal to interview the Press, considered in conjunction with the gentleman in brown boots and bowler hat who leant against the railings opposite Basil's front door and carefully observed everyone who went in or came out, aroused the lively interest of the *Sunday Smatter*, personified in a sleek

young man who was buoyed up by the conviction that nothing escaped him.

"I'm sorry Mr. Pongleton won't see me," he confided in Mrs.
Waddilove. "For his own sake as much as mine, you understand, for naturally the public will be interested in him, and
they are always ready to sympathize with anyone who frankly
tells them what they want to know. I'm sure you will agree
with me, Mrs. Waddilove, that no one can afford to ignore
the great newspaper public, and especially, if I may say so, the
Sunday public. But, of course, I can feel for Mr. Pongleton; a
shocking affair, and naturally very distressing to him!"

The strains of "lunch-time music" floated down the stairs.

"Mr. Pongleton enjoys the wireless?" the *Sunday Smatter*
suggested.

"He's very musical," agreed Mrs. Waddilove. "But it doesn't
seem quite right to me at such a time as this——"

"Perhaps he finds that it soothes the nerves! I expect he has
suffered from the shock?"

"That he has. Real strange he was when he came in on Friday night, with a paper in his hand and no hat; and he says to
me, 'Mrs. Waddilove,' he says, 'have you seen the news?' 'I've
heard it,' says I; 'and there's a police officer will be here to see
you in half an hour or so and your cousin's waiting up in your
room, and whatever have you done with your hat?' He gave
me a queer look at that, and says, 'I've lost it somewhere,' and
upstairs he goes. Well, I ask you, it's a bit funny, isn't it, to
go losing a good bowler hat—and he hadn't worn it so many
times either—and no more fuss about it than that?"

"Don't you think, Mrs. Waddilove, that the sudden news
of his aunt's death in such tragic circumstances might make

the loss of a bowler hat, even a new one, seem comparatively unimportant?"

"It wasn't such a new one in point of time, if you take my meaning. Mr. Pongleton's one of these writers—he's not a city gentleman—and what he usually wears is a more artistic sort of hat; black and widish. He only put the bowler on when there was some special reason for it; it's my belief he didn't really feel at home in it."

"And that special reason was…?" enquired the *Sunday Smatter*.

"Ah! That'd be telling, and I never was one to give away secrets," declared Mrs. Waddilove, peering at him speculatively from her little twinkling eyes. "But I do say that it looks like fate that Mr. Pongleton should lose that bowler hat just when he won't have any more call to use it!"

"Miss Euphemia Pongleton didn't favour that Chelsea appearance, I'll be bound," suggested the *Sunday Smatter*.

"I said not a word about Miss Pongleton," Mrs. Waddilove pointed out; "but since you say it yourself—well, she was very genteel; there's some might call her a sight too particular."

"I wonder why Mr. Pongleton chose to wear that hat on Friday?" the *Sunday Smatter* remarked to the doorstep.

"I'm not one to pry into my gentlemen's affairs," Mrs. Waddilove assured him; "but I must say it was a real surprise to me when he told me he hadn't been to see his aunt on Friday morning. That's to say, he told me in a manner of speaking, because he said he'd been to Golder's Green to see a man about a picture, which I don't doubt, but I must say I did think when he got that letter that he was up and away to Hampstead to see his aunt because of it."

"Ah, yes; the letter!" said the *Sunday Smatter* knowingly, never having heard of the letter. "Perhaps the last letter the unfortunate lady ever wrote!"

"Of course, it's not for me to say that the letter came from his aunt," Mrs. Waddilove pointed out. "I'm not one to go snooping around looking for bits of torn-up letters as some might do, though they wouldn't have found much of that one, for into the fire it went! Mr. Pongleton is what you might call hasty, and whatever was in that letter it didn't please him!"

"Perhaps he changed his mind on the way to Hampstead and went to Golder's Green instead," suggested the *Sunday Smatter*. "To see a man about a—picture, you said?"

"That's what I said and that's what he said. Some furrin painter who's to do a picture of Mr. Pongleton's cousin, Miss Sanders; and she's pretty enough, though a bit pale for my taste; but she'll look all right in a picture, I'll be bound. Miss Watson, now, she's more lively, and Mr. Pongleton thinks a lot of her."

"Watson?" The *Sunday Smatter* brooded for a moment over the name. "Lives up at the Frampton, doesn't she? No relation, I take it?"

"Not yet," Mrs. Waddilove informed him coyly.

"I suppose Mr. Pongleton has chosen a good artist to paint his cousin's picture?"

"I don't think a great deal of his painting myself," said Mrs. Waddilove, with the air of a connoisseur. "A bit wishy-washy, if you know what I mean. But he's thought a lot of; Mr. Pongleton showed me one of his pictures on the cover of a magazine. Great bearded fellow he is, with an outlandish name—Koo—Koo…." Mrs. Waddilove cooed plaintively, but could get no further.

The *Sunday Smatter* persuaded her to search for the magazine cover, and when it was disinterred he was able to deci-
pher "Kutuzov" scrawled across one corner. With the help of
a directory he ought to be able to run the fellow to earth. As
he was preparing to depart, Mrs. Waddilove had a momentary
feeling of alarm.

"Mind you, I know nothing at all about this business," she
assured the sleek young man. "I wouldn't like to say anything
that'd bring trouble to Mr. Pongleton, even if he isn't so reg'lar
as he might be with his rent; for he's in a way about his aunt's
death, goodness knows, and although she was a bit of a tartar,
it's a dreadful thing to happen to anyone. But I always did
think those undergrounds were nasty, dangerous places. And
I hope you won't go putting anything about that letter in your
paper, for people's private letters are their own affair, I always
say, and so I always said to Waddilove. Of course, when Mr.
Pongleton chooses to say anything about the letter himself,
that's a different matter—and say it he will in his own good
time, if it's of any importance to anyone."

"Quite so," the *Sunday Smatter* agreed. "Don't worry, Mrs.
Waddilove; you have been absolutely discreet, and you can be
assured that I shall respect your confidence."

The *Sunday Smatter* strode away thoughtfully. This was
all very interesting. He had sought an interview with Basil in
the hope of eliciting what the journalists call "a story" about
his aunt, and although he had drawn a blank as far as the
intended "human document" for to-morrow's issue was concerned, he had chanced on something far more interesting.
He did not see how he could make any immediate use of the
idea that Basil Pongleton might be responsible for his aunt's

death, or at least implicated. But it would be worth while to try to see this artist fellow at Golder's Green, for if this clue should really be the right one—and the watcher outside the house in Tavistock Square indicated that it might be—Basil might be arrested at any moment, and any knowledge of his movements and behaviour would then be of value.

It was Kutuzov's wife, Delia, who interviewed the *Sunday Smatter*. Directly she learnt that he represented the Press she smiled at him expansively; bade him "Come right in!" and led him into the studio. She was a big handsome woman with a flamboyant manner. Peter was out, and that was just as well, for he never would grasp the importance of being nice to the Press. Delia was fully alive to the fact that any opportunity of impressing a journalist with the idea that Peter Kutuzov was "one of the coming men"—and, moreover, had a charming wife—was to be seized and exploited to the full.

"I'm afraid I can't tell you a great deal about Miss Pongleton," she told the *Sunday Smatter*. "Unfortunately, my husband never painted her, but her niece is to sit to him, as you know, and I can show you several drawings of Basil Pongleton, her nephew. Basil is a great friend of ours, and I believe he is Miss Pongleton's heir."

"The old lady was well off, I understand?"

"She was supposed to have a fortune, but I don't really know, except for the fact that she helped her nephew a good deal. She was apt to make a mystery about her affairs, and she was rather chary of parting with her money, so that you would never have thought she was well off from the way in which she lived."

Delia was rummaging in a portfolio from which she produced a sketch of an amiable young man with a wide mouth and rather long, ruffled hair. "That's Basil Pongleton. Perhaps the drawing will be of some public interest now? My husband might be persuaded to allow it to be reproduced. Portraits are his best work. He had a show at Coryton's Galleries last month. We hoped that Miss Pongleton might commission a portrait of Basil; she suggested it herself, but couldn't bring herself to part with the money when it came to the point. Though, as I have said, she had fits of something almost like generosity when she was pleased with any of Basil's work—perhaps you know his writing?—and would hand him a fiver neatly sealed up in an envelope. He's not well off, and he'll miss her a good deal—but, of course, I suppose he'll come into her money, so it will be all right in the end."

"I'm afraid I'm not familiar with Mr. Pongleton's work. Short stories?"

"Yes; and newspaper stuff, and poems; all free lance work. But I don't think he's really found his own line yet. That's so important for an artist, isn't it? My husband has been drawing portraits since he was five, and he would have made a greater name for himself by now if he hadn't always been so terribly shy of publicity. I understand his feelings utterly; I shrink from it myself, but one can't afford to hide one's light under a bushel, can one?"

"You're right there," the *Sunday Smatter* agreed. "I'm sure you must help your husband a lot. When Mr. Pongleton comes into his aunt's money I expect he will be ordering some more of Mr. Kutuzov's work—perhaps a portrait of Miss Watson?"

"Betty Watson at the Frampton? He might do; it's an idea. Of course, there's Beryl Sanders' picture to be done first. He was talking to my husband about that on the very day Miss Pongleton was murdered—yesterday, in fact. It was a curious thing: Basil came up to see us in the morning, by the underground, but he was so upset that he couldn't discuss anything connectedly, and his shoes were covered with mud. I feel that he must have had some premonition of his aunt's death. It's most curious."

"Perhaps he had heard that she was missing and was anxious?"

"No, I don't think so. It was too early for anyone to have realized that she was missing. He got here at about half-past ten, I believe. I was out at the time, but I came home about eleven, and he stayed until the afternoon."

"What do you suppose upset him?"

"Really, I don't know. But he was utterly distrait. He may have some kind of second sight and not be aware of it."

As the *Sunday Smatter* walked back to Golder's Green station he wondered about Basil's muddy shoes. He, too, had heard of the footmark on Belsize Park stairs, but how could Basil pick up mud on his shoes between Tavistock Square and Belsize Park? Friday morning had been fine, but Thursday had been memorable for a heavy shower which broke the winter drought. There would certainly be muddy spots on the Heath. He dismissed that problem for the moment, and meditated on Delia Kutuzov's account of Basil's state of mind on Friday morning. He visualized a splendid headline: NEPHEW HAS PREMONITION OF AUNT'S DEATH. Would the editor stand for it? He thought it would be safe provided the "story" were carefully worded:

"On calling at the house in Tavistock Square where Mr. Basil Pongleton (photo inset), the nephew of the deceased, and heir to her considerable fortune, occupies bachelor apartments, our representative was informed that Mr. Pongleton had not yet recovered from the shock occasioned by his aunt's death in such tragic circumstances, and that he was too distressed to receive visitors. He finds his only consolation in music, being a devotee of the more serious items in the radio programmes. Our representative learnt from an intimate friend of Mr. Pongleton that he appears to have had a strange premonition of his aunt's fate, though at the time he could not account for the feeling of depression that overcame him at the moment when she met her tragic end...."

THE PONGLETON FAMILY TREE

Grandfather Pongleton
d. 1907

m. (i) Lydia.   (ii) Emily.

Geoffrey Pongleton died, un-married, 1921. Left £30,000 to his sister, Euphemia	Euphemia Pongleton, unmarried, murdered 1934	James Pongleton m. Susan Morris	Adela, m. J. Sanders who died 1925
		Basil	Beryl

CHAPTER SEVEN

BASIL ELABORATES

"WE'RE just in time, I gather," exclaimed Gerry, panting from his hurried climb of two flights of stairs.

"What d'you mean? For tea? Yes, I suppose you are."

"Oh no; I wasn't thinking of anything so gross as my material needs. Merely anxiety for your welfare, Basil, my boy. We met old Slowgo on the stairs, with his face as long as a boa constrictor, and old Waddletoes told us he's been lunching with you. You must be about ready for spiritual consolation!"

"Did you ask him to lunch, Basil?" Beryl enquired, as Gerry relieved her of her coat. "And if so, why ever?"

"He was a great friend of Aunt Phemia's, y'know. She put no end of trust in him and always consulted him. Though, come to think of it, he doesn't seem to know much about her affairs. But, anyway, he's a wise old bird, and generally knows all about everything, and I thought he might have some theory about this rotten business."

"And has he?" Beryl asked in a weary voice.

"W-e-l-l, I dunno that he has—yet. Seems to think that Thurlow had the chance to get hold of that leash of Tuppy's and the chance to meet Aunt Phemia on the stairs, and good cause for being mad with the old lady, too; but I simply can't believe that he'd—he'd strangle her."

"It's difficult to believe that of anyone," said Beryl, sinking into a chair by the fire. "And Bob Thurlow seems a bit of a noodle but not really vicious or desperate—isn't that what you think about him, Gerry?" Gerard Plasher nodded agreement. His general tendency was to agree with Beryl unless he felt strongly opposed to her view. "I can't believe that he'd attack an old lady in that horrible way," Beryl went on, "just because he was furious with her for keeping the brooch. And the idea that he murdered her in order to recover the brooch is fantastic, for he didn't take it."

"Perhaps he couldn't find it," Basil suggested.

"That's not possible," Gerry declared. "He would have had plenty of time to search for it. It's more likely that he never thought of the possibility that she had it with her. But, as Beryl says, I don't really think he did it at all."

"He might have heard someone on the stairs and been scared and done a bolt," said Basil, without much conviction, but apparently unable to abandon conjecture as to what happened on the stairs.

"But there wasn't anyone on the stairs, except the murderer and me!" Gerry pointed out. "If there had been—I mean anyone not mixed up with the crime—Miss Pongleton's body would have been found by them, much earlier than it actually was found."

"I wouldn't be too sure of that," Basil told him. "If you, galloping down those stairs, had met Aunt Phemia dead, instead of alive, what would you have done?"

"Why, rushed down and given the alarm, of course." Gerry was quite sure. "There'd be nothing else one could do."

"I don't know. It wouldn't do any good, and I should think your one idea might be to get out of it and not be mixed up in the business."

"No one could be so silly," declared Beryl impatiently. "It might easily be found out afterwards that you had been there, and then, of course, everyone would think it frightfully fishy that you had kept it dark. Oh!"—she shook herself disgustedly—"it's all so beastly! Why must we keep on talking about it? And no one seems to think about poor Aunt Phemia herself—only what did the murderer do, and what would you do, and so on without end. And it's no *use*!"

"I've often thought anyone might act like that," Basil persisted, disregarding his cousin's protests. "Do you remember the Crumbles murder, and the Crowborough murder?"

"But they *did* it, in both cases," cried Gerry. "Do shut up, Basil."

"The jury said they did," Basil continued obstinately; "but it always struck me that they had pretty plausible cases, especially the young man who said he came into his bungalow and found the girl hanging from a beam. It seemed to me that he really might have been so scared and so shaken that he'd think the only safe thing to do was to hide the body and pretend he knew nothing about it."

"That was different," Gerry explained. "That young man was to blame in any case, even supposing he hadn't actually murdered the girl; and there she was in his own bungalow. The case of anyone going down the stairs and finding your aunt's body would be quite different. I say, you're not suggesting, are you, that *I* found the old lady dead? I tell you I said good morning to her!"

"No, I wasn't suggesting anything," Basil assured him. "I was only trying to work out whether it was possible that Thurlow did murder Aunt Phemia in the hope of recovering the brooch and was then scared away before he'd got hold of it, and hadn't found the opportunity to go back again for it before they discovered her body."

"I wish you'd stop these silly speculations," Beryl implored. "I'm sure it wasn't Bob Thurlow. I suppose it couldn't have been an accident?"

"Accident?" Basil exclaimed incredulously.

"I mean that she fell headlong downstairs and the leash somehow got hooked on to the railings and throttled her?"

"Of course, it did look a bit like that at first glance," said Basil, to the astonishment of the others.

"*Look* like that? How do you mean?" Beryl asked him.

"Oh, when I read how she was found—lying upside down on the stairs; of course, the first thing I thought was that she'd stumbled and gone headlong."

"It never struck me like that," said Gerry, still puzzled by Basil's remark. "Of course, the first thing I saw in the paper was the headline: MURDER IN UNDERGROUND STATION, or something of that sort, so I got the idea of murder into my head straight away."

"I think the paper I saw had a different heading—something about a mystery; anything's a mystery to the Press; and then, naturally, reading of old Aunt Phemia head downwards on a staircase, the idea of her falling down came into my mind."

"Well, could it have happened like that?" Beryl asked.

"Not possible," said Basil. "The police would have noticed at once if the leash was hitched round the railings or anything of that sort."

"I'm afraid the accident idea really isn't tenable, Beryl dear," said Gerry gently.

"No," Beryl admitted. "But I do wish something would come to light. I hate the idea of anyone being found guilty of such a horrible thing, but it's dreadfully unsatisfactory at present, and so worrying for everyone; and I equally hate the idea of people who aren't guilty being suspected."

"Yes, that must be perfectly beastly," Basil agreed. Strolling to the window he looked out into the square and quickly retreated.

"How about tea?" he suggested. "I'll see if Waddletoes can get us crumpets or something." He left the others to themselves.

Gerry crossed to the window and looked out, as Basil had done.

"D'you remember the chap who was lolling against the railings as we came in, Beryl? He's still there; funny-looking fellow in a purple suit."

Beryl showed no interest in the lounger. She sat looking into the fire, occasionally giving it a half-hearted jab with the poker. Gerry watched her for a few minutes, realizing that what made him feel so wretched was not the untimely death of a distinctly forbidding old lady, but the droop of Beryl's mouth, and the unusually listless attitude of her slim figure bent forward in the chair. Her face, under the little black hat with her fair hair smoothed away from her forehead and tucked back behind her ears, looked very pale. All her delicate colouring seemed faded to pallor, whether by her anxiety and distress or merely in contrast with the black which she wore, he could not determine.

She hit a large lump of coal with a resounding whack.

"Can't we *do* something, Gerry?"

Gerry crossed the room towards her and whipped off her soft felt hat. "That's better. I don't like the look of you with your head encased in that object!"

"I know." Beryl smiled at him faintly. "But it's the only black one I've got, and Mother thought it looked disrespectful to Aunt Phemia to wear colours. I hate mourning, myself. I always have a feeling that it's either ostentatious or hypocritical. But as Mother felt like that about it I had to wear black. And goodness knows I feel gloomy enough at present."

"'Tis not alone thy inky cloak'... You look pretty wretched, I must say. I wish we could do something, but I don't see what. I've done what I can for young Thurlow by getting my solicitors to take him in hand. They tell me that although he's awfully upset he's quite clear and unshaken in his story, and accounts for all his doings on Friday in a way that seems perfectly satisfactory, though, of course, it's difficult to check it all. If only we could find out anything about your aunt which would suggest that anyone else had a motive for murdering her ... "

"I should think a lot of people may have disliked her. It seems horrid to say it now, but everyone knows she was mean and liked to have power over people. But I can't see what motive anyone can have had for *murdering* her, except to get her money, and, as far as we know, no one had any claim on that except Basil and me. That reminds me, I haven't told Basil about the wills."

"The police may find some clue. I hear they've been making a thorough search of her room."

"They have to do that. You know what a habit she had of hiding things in odd places?"

"Crumpets for tea!" announced Basil, flinging open the door and coming in with a paper bag, plate, knife, and butter. "I said we'd toast them ourselves. Waddletoes says she's been 'that put out' with callers. Oh, what a mess you've made of the fire, Beryl!"

"I'll soon find a red place," said Gerry, going down on his knees on the hearthrug.

"Basil, I forgot to tell you about Aunt Phemia's will," Beryl said.

"Oh; how did you hear?" Basil tried to seem indifferent.

"Mother has seen her solicitor, Mr. Stoggins. I suppose he'll write to you. The police have been searching Aunt Phemia's room, you know. I think they had an idea they might find something more to throw light on her connection with Bob Thurlow. They came across a will, made fairly recently, under the paper at the bottom of a drawer. They consulted Mr. Stoggins and found that he had another one, made some years before. They are practically the same, I gather, and of course they don't help to clear up the mystery. She has left most of her money to you, except for five thousand, I think it is, to a dogs' home, and some hundreds to provide for Tuppy, and her pearls and some jewellery to me."

Basil gave her a startled look, but he breathed a sigh of relief. "So they haven't found the other one?"

"What other one?"

"Oh, some time ago she told me that she had made another, leaving the spoil to you because I annoyed her."

"Do you mean last summer? Poor Aunt Phemia! She was rather pleased with me because I sent her three picture post-cards while I was on holiday, and you had been neglectful. But she tore that will up; you told me so yourself."

"Yes, of course; I'd forgotten. I thought she might have made another one since. She often told Betty Watson that

I wasn't going to get her money. She thought Betty was after it—and me."

"Oh, the one they found was made last spring, I think. I don't think she made quite so many as she talked about, but they may find another yet."

Gerry had succeeded in uncovering some glowing coals, and Beryl knelt on the hearthrug beside him and began to toast the crumpets, whilst he melted the butter. Mrs. Waddilove, bringing the tea, put a stop to conversation about Miss Pongleton's will. Basil strode restlessly about the room, occasionally casting a sidelong glance out of the window.

"I must say I'm relieved," he said at last, when Mrs. Waddilove had gone, "that they've found the right will. I know you didn't really want the money, Beryl, and goodness knows I need it."

"Of course I didn't want it," Beryl agreed. "It ought to go to you, and it would have gone to you anyway. But I expect you'll find you're just as impecunious after you've got it as you always have been—unless you get Betty to look after it."

"I'll be able to give you a decent wedding present, anyway. By Jove, when I was haggling over it with old Peter, I was, as it were, coming into a fortune all the time, had I but known it."

"How about the picture?" Gerry enquired. "When is Beryl to sit?"

They discussed the portrait—what Beryl was to wear, and what pose Gerry liked best.

"Do, for heaven's sake, cheer up before the sittings begin," Gerry admonished her. "Of course, you feel wretched, but you mustn't mope—that'll do no one any good."

"I'm sure Peter's quite capable of painting a smile, if a smile is asked for, even if it isn't there," Beryl assured him a little sadly. She was pouring out tea.

"But it might be someone else's smile, and that wouldn't be at all the same thing," Gerry objected. "D'you remember, we had meant to see the film of *The Constant Nymph* at the New Vic. this evening? But I don't suppose you want to go now, though I'm not sure that it wouldn't be a good thing to flout the conventions and go—just to switch your mind off this beastly affair and give you a rest from worry."

Beryl shook her head at him, but seized on the opportunity for normal conversation.

"You saw it on Thursday, didn't you, Basil?"

"Yes—no, on Friday."

"But you said you were taking Betty on Thursday?"

"We went somewhere else after all. I went alone to the New Vic. on Friday."

"Whatever for—*Friday*?"

"Yes; after I came back from seeing Peter. I was feeling rather blue and thought I'd like to see it. Of course, I didn't get the evening paper and read about Aunt Phemia until I came out of the cinema."

Beryl was looking at him intently—so intently that she continued to pour tea into a cup already full, until Gerry noticed what she was doing.

"Look out, Beryl—you're flooding the tray!"

"Oh, what an idiot I am! I'm so sorry. Gerry, take the tea-pot while I clear up this mess."

Everyone's attention was directed to the tea-tray, and by the time order was restored the cinema had been forgotten.

But Basil realized that he still had not put matters right.

"I say, Beryl," he began in a pause, looking self-conscious. "You remember what I told you about what happened on Friday—I mean the various things I did? Do you remember what I said about supper? I was all hot and bothered when I saw you that evening just after I'd read about the murder and heard that the police had been to see me, and I'm not sure what I did tell you."

"You said that you had supper in Soho with a friend. I don't think you gave any more details. Why?"

"I say, Beryl—you'd better not mention that friend to anyone. I don't suppose you have talked about it. Fact is, I didn't tell the police anything about a friend. 'S not important—not in connection with Aunt Phemia's death—but, 's a matter of fact, the friend isn't awfully reputable, and I didn't want the police nosing around on that track, so I just told them I had supper alone in Soho because it was too late after the cinema to come back here for it—which is true."

"But, Basil, isn't that frightfully rash, to cook your story to the police? It might make them think you had something to conceal? And why?"

"Well, I have. But I haven't cooked my story. I wasn't under oath to tell the whole truth—only the chief facts; and, anyway, what is the whole truth? And does anyone ever tell it? I left out lots of other details—f'rinstance, how many times I blew my nose."

"Don't be so idiotic!" Beryl admonished him. "Really, Basil, wouldn't it be better to confess to a—an—indiscretion than to let the police think you may be hiding something truly fishy? Don't you think so, Gerry?"

"I certainly do," agreed Gerry. "They'll be on their hind legs at once if they think you've got something up your sleeve."

"But it's nothing to do with them."

"That's just it," Gerry insisted. "When they know it they won't bother any more about it; but so long as they don't know it, if they get on the track of something unknown, they'll smell a guilty secret."

"Surely, Basil, it's nothing that matters telling?" said Beryl. "I don't want to know what it is, and I won't say a word about it to anyone. I'll forget it at once, and I know Gerry will, too."

"Of course," muttered Gerry, rather unconvincingly.

"But I do think it would be much less worrying for you, and prevent awkward complications, if you told the police about it now, before they happen to find out from someone else. You could easily explain why you didn't tell them before, but the longer you wait the worse it gets."

"I wish you'd let me manage my own beastly affairs," grumbled Basil. "I tell you they don't know me in the restaurant, and they won't remember whether I was with anyone or not, and no one else saw me—us."

"I don't know all the details and I don't want to, so perhaps it's difficult to judge," Beryl admitted. "But I should have thought there were enough complications in this case already. Don't be so annoyed with me, Basil. I think Gerry and I had better be going. I shall see you later on when you bring your people along. You'll stay to supper, won't you?"

"I'll go and warm the engine," said Gerry, and ran down the stairs.

"Which way are you going?" asked Basil.

"I thought we'd go for a drive. It's a lovely fine night."

"D'you think Gerry would give me a lift to Hampstead—if that's on your way? To the Frampton?"

"Why, yes. But you'll be awfully cold and uncomfortable in the dickey. The underground would be much snugger—or a bus," she added hastily.

"I don't feel specially keen on the underground; and I hate the bus route past all the Camden Town fish shops."

"All right; come along. Don't forget about the train at King's Cross."

"No; I've got time. You go down and tell Gerry. I won't be a minute."

"May I just go and look in your mirror?" Beryl asked, with her hat in her hand. She went behind the curtain at one end of the room—for Basil's apartments, grandly called "rooms", consisted only of one long room on the second floor with a partition and curtain shutting off his dressing-room at one end. His bed, metamorphosed as a couch, adorned the sitting-room.

When Beryl emerged from the curtain Basil was standing with his back to the room, looking out of the window. Beryl hesitated in the middle of the room, but as Basil gave no sign of noticing her, she went quietly out. As soon as she had gone, Basil went beyond the curtain and, tipping the small hanging mirror forward from the wall, disengaged a pearl necklace which hung behind it, looped over the suspending wires.

Meanwhile Beryl was standing on the pavement whilst Gerry caused his Alvis two-seater to execute elaborate backing and turning manœuvres, which were really designed to throw his headlights towards the centre of the square, so that he could discover whether anyone were still lounging there in the dusk. Yes, he distinctly caught sight of the purple suit, proceeding with a steady stride along the railings, as if on its way somewhere.

"Whatever are you doing?" Beryl enquired, when he drew up by the kerb. "You could have gone round the square instead of turning."

"Stupid of me! I wasn't thinking. Imagined I was outside your house at Hampstead. Where do we go now?"

"Basil wants a lift up to the Frampton, and I'd like a drive. Fresh air would do me good, and I can always think better in a car."

"Right-o! What about the Barnet Road? But don't think too much."

He climbed out and adjusted the dickey seat, smiling to himself. Basil emerged and clambered in, and in a moment the car shot off towards Euston. They nipped dexterously through the traffic of Seymour Street and Camden Town and roared up Haverstock Hill and dropped Basil at the corner of Church Lane.

"Good move, that of Basil's," chuckled Gerry. His words were drowned by the roar of the car as it crested the hill to Spaniards Road. When they were running more quietly down North End Road Beryl began to talk.

"This is nice." She tucked her hand under Gerry's arm, and he gave it a sympathetic squeeze with his elbow.

"You know, I feel that if we could go driving on and on all night, this horrible mystery would clear itself up. Perhaps it's just that driving gives you the sensation of getting away from things. I felt myself getting more and more muddled, and more and more depressed, in Basil's room. Gerry, what do you think is the matter with Basil? Of course, he always was given to unloading his private affairs on to other people and then stopping short, with a sudden access of caution, at some vital point. He has often related some secret history—nothing really important, you know—to two different people, keeping back from each one a different part of the story. It was rather embarrassing sometimes, because one of his confidants, perceiving that the other knew the story, would then refer to the part of it that the other one did not know. There's a curious strain of secretiveness in the family, I think. Aunt Phemia had it strongly. I don't suppose anyone knew all about all her affairs. She confided a lot to old Slowgo, I know, but I'm sure she kept back a good deal; and Uncle James used to complain that she made it difficult for him to attend to her business matters because she wouldn't tell him everything. But I don't think I've got any of the secretiveness in my make-up."

"I'm sure you haven't, darling," said Gerry with conviction.

"Basil kept making such queer remarks," Beryl went on. "As if he really had something to hide; but I can't see what there would be that he couldn't tell us. And he does seem to have got the police on his mind rather. That struck me when first I saw him after the murder—on Friday evening. I suppose the police must look around for anyone with a possible motive, and would naturally ask who would come into Aunt Phemia's money; but Basil has a perfectly good alibi for Friday morning, if they really should be suspicious of him, which seems preposterous. Mrs. Waddletoes told me, when I rang her up on Friday afternoon to ask where Basil was, that he went out at twenty past nine; and we know from the time when you saw poor Aunt Phemia on the stairs that she must have been—have been—killed a few minutes after that. Besides, how could the police suppose that he really had a motive, for he never knew what the state of Aunt Phemia's will might be; in fact, he seemed to think that she had cut him out of it again lately.... Oh, it's perfectly horrid the way we calmly discuss such ghastly ideas, but I'm trying to clear my mind."

"I understand, darling. You aren't really talking of the possibility of Basil having a motive, but only of a police theory unrelated to human fact."

"Yes, that's it," said Beryl eagerly.

"Your aunt was quite attached to Basil, wasn't she, in her own curious way?" Gerry asked.

"Undoubtedly. And also I think she had an odd belief in his genius. It was a form of family pride with her: she felt sure that a Pongleton could do anything he set his hand to better than anyone else."

"It has just struck me, Beryl, that the police won't know of your aunt's habit of altering her will. Basil was generally acknowledged to be her heir, wasn't he?"

"Yes—it was always understood that Uncle Geoffrey intended the money to go to him; and I'd privately made up my mind that if, through Aunt Phemia's erratic fits of dislike, it should come to me, he should have it somehow."

"I suppose Basil knew that?"

"In a general way, yes; I have mentioned it and I think my mother has. It was agreed upon between her and me. But still, he would hardly count on it. Poor old Basil, he's always hard up, you know, and, without being grasping, he couldn't help being anxious about Aunt Phemia's money."

"I'm afraid he's not making much by his writing as yet?"

"No. I wish he could make a tremendous success of it. He has a small allowance from his people, but they're not too well off. If Aunt Phemia's will is all right he'll be quite opulent now, and I'm sure the first thing he'll do is to ask Betty Watson to marry him. Perhaps he's doing it now."

"I wondered about that."

"I hope he will. Betty's a nice girl and has a lot of sense. Aunt Phemia disliked her, for some reason, and used to tell her that Basil wouldn't get her money. That was another point of difficulty lately: Aunt Phemia was sure to make a fuss if Basil took Betty out or seemed to be too friendly with her. It was too bad of her, for Betty was the only girl who was at all possible who had ever seemed seriously fond of Basil; and he really is very fond of her."

Beryl paused, and Gerry drove on in silence, realizing that there was more to come.

"I don't want to tell tales about Basil," she began again, "but you must be guessing about the mysterious 'friend' with whom he had supper on Friday, and I'm pretty sure it was a girl he picked up somewhere—probably in the cinema—and then took to supper. He told me once before about doing the same thing; I think he was just lonely and wanted someone to talk nonsense to, and, you see, he was afraid to ask Betty to go out with him too often for fear of a fuss from Aunt Phemia. The only thing I can't understand is why he should be so anxious to keep it dark."

"Probably he is anxious that it shan't get to Betty's ears."

"Yes; he would be, of course. But he knows he can trust me, and he might have enough commonsense to know that the police wouldn't give two thoughts to the affair if he told them all about it. If it should come to be general knowledge, I should think he could trust even Betty to overlook it. After all, it's nothing very desperate—we know he got back to his rooms about a quarter to nine."

"I wonder what Basil talked about to old Slowgo for so long," said Gerry after a pause during which they negotiated Chipping Barnet. "If the old chap is really as sagacious as Basil makes out, and if Basil has told him about the complications he's been creating for himself, Slowgo must have advised Basil to tell the police the whole story."

"I'm not so convinced of Mr. Slocomb's wisdom myself," said Beryl dubiously. "Aunt Phemia thought a lot of him, but although she was always very wary I'm not sure that she was a good judge of character. Look how she misunderstood Betty! He probably flattered her, and, after all, any old lady likes that! You know, I wondered at one time whether old Slowgo could be after her money. I think Uncle James put the idea into my head. It sounds a mean thing to say, and probably it's quite unfair, but I couldn't see why else he should take so much trouble to please her. After all, she was very difficult."

"Do you mean he thought she might marry him? I suppose it's possible. One hears of such things. He's not a gentleman, but old ladies do sometimes run off the rails."

"It sounds fantastic. No, I daresay he's all right. Isn't it perfectly rotten the way we all keep discussing people and criticizing them and suspecting them of this and that?—and no one gives a thought to Aunt Phemia except to her failings and to her death because it happens to be the centre point of a mystery."

"I say, Beryl…" Gerry tactfully changed the subject. "How about supper somewhere? Isn't there a good pub at Hatfield?"

"Sorry, dear; impossible. Basil's people arrive this evening and I must be there. Mother may be fussed if I'm late. Perhaps we'd better turn."

"All right. But could we just look in on Peter Kutuzov on the way home?" Gerry suggested. "Basil seems to have arranged with him about your picture, and we might fix the first sitting definitely. It's awf'ly decent of Basil to give us such a topping present. If we take the new road through the Garden Suburb we shall very nearly pass his house."

"Yes, we might do that, if we don't stay long."

In the little house in North Way Beryl found only Peter's wife Delia at home.

"Peter's dining out," she explained. "Actually with Puffin, the art critic; a useful man. I hope it really is settled about your picture, but Basil seemed awfully vague when he was here on Friday. I didn't think he was at all himself—even more woolly than usual."

"His aunt's death was a terrible shock to him," Beryl explained shortly. She disliked Delia and Delia's criticisms and was only thinking of getting away.

"But we didn't know about it then—no one knew, except Miss Pongleton's murderer," Delia pointed out coldly. "When we read about it next morning Peter remarked that it almost seemed as if Basil had second sight. He had been so distrait when he was with us—just as if he had received a bad shock already, as you suggest. Of course that sort of thing doesn't seem out of the way to Peter, being Russian."

"It seems very out of the way to me," Beryl replied. "I didn't mean to suggest that Basil knew; of course he couldn't have known. I was just muddled. I think Basil has been worried about various things lately. The editor of that provincial paper for which he was doing a series of articles on London scenes said he didn't want any more of them because Basil was so unpunctual with them. That upset him, because he had counted on it as a regular thing. Aunt Phemia was annoyed about it too, for she thought the articles very fine."

"Yes," said Delia meditatively. "You know, I don't think his aunt's influence did Basil any good, so far as his writing was concerned. The sort of thing she admired was the pot-boiling stuff. Oh, I know one has to do it—like Peter's magazine covers—but I think Basil was beginning to over-estimate its value, because not only did he get paid for it in the usual way, but he often got a fiver from his aunt as well. I told him on Friday that his style was getting aunt-ridden. Peter said he could even detect the Euphemistic touch in the poem which Basil got into the *Mercury*."

"If Peter said that to Basil it would account for him being distraught! He thinks a tremendous lot of the *Mercury* poem," Beryl told her.

"The police seem rather interested in Basil's movements," Delia remarked. "They've been to ask me what time he arrived here on Friday. I happened to be out, and of course when Peter is at work time means nothing to him whatever. But I'm sure I didn't go out till after ten. And Basil seems to have lost his hat and says it's here, but it's certainly not. He really is behaving very oddly."

"Lost his hat? Well, I'm really not surprised," Beryl declared. "Basil can lose anything. He once lost an enormous manuscript in a bus."

"I don't think the police have enquired about the hat *yet*; but if they do I really can't say it's here."

"Why should you if it isn't?" asked Beryl sharply. "But I really must go: Gerry's waiting for me in the car. No, he won't come in because we really must be home in time for dinner. Please tell Peter that I'll come on Monday week if I don't hear from him. Goodbye."

"The woman's a cat," she told Gerry as they drove back to Beverley House.

CHAPTER EIGHT

BASIL APPEALS TO BETTY

AT the Frampton Nellie opened the door to Basil.

"Is Miss Watson in?"

"Oh yes, Mr. Pongleton. Why, it seems weeks since you was last 'ere; Wednesday, wasn't it? An' such doin's since! Oh, sir, it's orful, and oo'd 'ave thought it? An' my poor Bob—you know 'bout 'im, sir? But 'is sister Louie says it's not so bad reelly; it's the burglary they've got 'im for, not the other, though that's bad enough, with 'is job gorn an' all. But won't you come into the drorin'-room, sir?"

"Look here, Nellie; I want to see Miss Watson but I don't want to see Mr. Slocomb—or any of the others. Do you know where she is?"

Nellie was not unused to a desire on Basil's part to see Betty privately. "Mr. Slocomb, sir, 'e's sittin' in the drorin'-room with the evenin' papers; I've jus' taken 'em in to 'im. An' Miss Watson's in there, too."

"Well, Nellie, just go into the drawing-room and say to Miss Watson...let's see; the old man's pretty sharp...Yes, say: 'Miss Sanders to see you and she won't come in.' Do you understand, Nellie?"

Nellie understood, and with an air of great importance she vanished into the drawing-room, whilst Basil pulled the front door nearly shut and waited outside it. When he heard steps in the hall he opened the door cautiously and held up a warning finger at Betty. Nellie hovered in the background, round-eyed.

"What's up?" whispered Betty.

"Quick! Get a hat and coat and come out—up Church Lane and you'll catch me up. Don't tell anyone I'm here. And just warn Nellie not to say I called. She can say Beryl came with some message for you."

He slipped away in the darkness and Betty bounded upstairs, after a hasty word of warning to Nellie who still lingered in the hall.

A few minutes later Basil, moving with lagging steps along Church Lane, heard quicker ones overtaking him to the accompaniment of small scuffling sounds, snorts and a kind of sneezing.

"Whatever have you brought that beastly pug for?" he protested as Betty came into the lamplight, dragging the indolent Tuppy who was raising desperate objections to her rapid progress.

"It gave me an excuse for coming out, and the poor brute must need exercise. Now we can stroll and he'll be all right. What he likes is the gentle amble of Bob and Nellie arm-in-arm. But what's the matter?"

"Look here, Betty—I'm in a hole and you're the only person who can help me. I'll have to explain things to you a bit. Is there anywhere we can talk?"

"You know how impossible the Frump-hole is——"

"Not there. I don't want Sl—the others—to see me there. You know how they all chatter; they'd talk some criminal intent into your lightest word. But there's no time to get far. What a curse it is, living in public like this. Oh damn!"

Tuppy, making a dart across the pavement towards a friend on the other side of the road, entangled himself with Basil's legs. "I wish you hadn't brought the poodle."

"I think we'd better just go on to the Heath," Betty suggested. "It'll be pretty empty now and we can find a seat."

"We'd better. I can't talk with this beastly animal scuffling round my legs."

"Tuppy!" Betty admonished him severely. "Tuppy, to heel!"

This did not seem to convey much to the stout terrier, but a stranglehold on the cord tied to his collar brought him to Betty's side, where he trotted along fairly quietly.

"What will happen to Tuppy, do you think?" Betty asked, seeing that Basil was not going to explain his difficulties to her until they were settled in some quiet spot.

"Aunt Phemia has left him some hundreds in her will."

"Not really? Oh, Tuppy, will you invest it in bones? But it can't be left to Tuppy himself!"

"I haven't seen the will, but Beryl told me that Tuppy is provided for. I suppose someone who undertakes to look after him will have it."

"Probably Mrs. Bliss will undertake the job in that case. And we shall all have to take him out in turn. We shall hear a lot from Mrs. Bliss about 'the least we can do for one who is no longer among us.'"

"I suppose Mrs. Bliss and all the Frumps are gloating over this business of my aunt's death? Do you realize, Betty, that I haven't seen you since I had tea with Aunt Phemia on Wednesday?"

"No, I don't, because you saw me on Thursday, though you may not have noticed it"—Betty sounded hurt; she had a special reason for remembering that evening, and it ought to have been a special occasion for Basil too. "You took me to see *The Constant Nymph* on Thursday evening."

"Dammit, so I did. Never mind, that's part of what I want to talk to you about, but not here."

They were dodging their way up Heath Street, towards the Spaniards Road, amongst a crowd of people oozing from the underground station.

"We're all agog in the Frump-hole," Betty told him in gasps, as she steered Tuppy among this forest of legs. "Mrs. Daymer is studying mental attitudes and forming theories; old Slowgo is being judicious and advising everyone not to talk too much. You know, he's a cunning old bird; he listens to everyone and offers advice, but never says a thing about what he really thinks. Mr. Grange is attending dutifully to Mrs. Daymer and being intelligently enquiring. The Porters are more detached from the rest of us than ever, and go about with the air of saying, 'If you had asked our advice, this would never have happened.' Cissie is simply wallowing; she seems to think the whole business is a charity matinée staged by Providence in her boarding-house for her special edification. Mr. Blend seems even less interested than usual in our affairs; he's hot on the track of something he wants to find in his books of old newspaper cuttings, which are in such a mess that he can never turn up anything in less than a week. Poor Nellie is tearful and expansive."

"What do they seem to think about the business?"

"Nothing very definite. But I've been thinking about you quite often; it must be beastly for you."

Basil grunted.

"You know the police came up on Friday night and inter-viewed us all? Then this morning they had a thorough hunt through Pongle's room—I think they looked around a bit on Friday too—and then locked it all up."

"Damn!" exclaimed Basil. They had reached the pond now and stood by its edge, wondering on which part of the Heath to seek seclusion.

"Is that Tuppy again?" asked Betty, and she jerked at the unfortunate animal's collar.

Basil did not answer her.

"Towards Ken Wood," she suggested. "There are lots of seats down under the trees."

They slithered down the steep slope from the road and wandered about in the darkness until they found a fallen tree, some little way from the path along which close-coupled pairs occasionally passed. Here they settled themselves, Betty pulling the fur collar of her coat more closely around her neck. She tied Tuppy's cord to a branch and the dog sat uneasily on the cold ground, whining occasionally.

"Now, tell me as quickly as possible," Betty instructed Basil. "I ought to be back at the Frump-hole in time for dinner, if I'm not to arouse a lot of curiosity. What about the film, to begin with?"

"Have you told anyone that we saw that particular film?"

"I expect so," declared Betty cheerfully. "Why not?"

"Who?" demanded Basil.

"I certainly told Cissie a lot about it. I'm not sure about anyone else, but I may have mentioned it to someone in the office. Whatever does it matter?"

"You haven't told Beryl?"

"Beryl? No; I haven't seen her since."

"Well, if you do see her, keep off the subject if you can. Though I suppose that if Cissie knows, it will be all over the place before long."

"If it hadn't been for all the to-do about the murder, which has been the main subject of conversation since yesterday evening, I should probably have told lots of other people. But suppose Beryl happens to ask me if I've seen that film—which isn't likely just now—what am I to say? Look here, Basil, you simply must tell me more. Why is this so vital? I don't mind telling a few lies for you, or keeping a secret for you, but I can't do it intelligently if you don't tell me more about it. And I suppose you realize that it would be hopeless to tell Cissie not to pass the information on. Ten to one she won't say anything about it, because her mind is now full of other things, but you can't be sure, and to suggest to her that there's some mystery about it would just put her in a state of bubbling excitement."

"I'm going to tell you more if you'll just give me a chance." Basil edged closer to Betty along the log and stretched out one arm behind her. "It's all to do with Friday evening. The police came to see me—naturally, I suppose, to ask when I'd last seen Aunt Phemia and so on—and they asked me where I'd been all day; they seem to have asked everyone that. Well, that morning I had been up to Golder's Green to see Peter Kutuzov, who's to do a portrait of Beryl. When I came back in the afternoon I had some business to attend to that I don't want to tell anyone about—at present. After that it was too late to go home to dinner and so I got a meal before going back to my rooms, and I bought a paper and read about Aunt Phemia's murder. That was a nasty knock. Whatever you may feel about your relations, you don't like to hear of them being strangled with a dog-leash; it gave me a sort of sick feeling. I got home feeling pretty done in, and there I found Beryl waiting to see me, and a detective came along soon after."

"Poor old Basil!" Betty murmured sympathetically.

"I told the police where I'd been all day, and to fill in the gap—the private business—after I got back from Golder's Green, I added a visit to the New Vic. to see *The Constant Nymph*. I thought of that because I had just been there and could give more details if they wanted them. I had to tell Beryl the same in case she should happen to hear what I had told the police. But apparently I'd said something to her, days ago, about my plan to go with you to the New Vic. on Thursday, and she seemed surprised that I should go again the next day. So I gave her the impression that we didn't go to see that film after all on Thursday. Now do you see?"

Betty gasped. "What a muddle! Basil, how exactly like you! Why must you always make such complications? And it all seems so needless. Wouldn't it be simpler to tell Beryl that you had some private affairs that took up your time that evening?"

"You're so good at thinking these things out, but it's too late. You see—'s a matter of fact, I've told her two different things already, and I don't want to tell her a third story. The truth is, I don't want to bother her more than I can help. It would have been plane sailing if only Beryl hadn't remembered that I went to that film with you on Thursday."

"Now I come to think of it, I did tell Cissie not to blurt it out all over the Frump-hole that I had been with you, because I didn't want Pongle to know. Cissie understood about that and she probably has kept it to herself. But I do think you've made rather an unnecessary mess of the story, Basil. A pity you're such a hopeless ass! But the police can't care in the least about what you were doing on Friday evening—why not tell them the truth?"

"I told you, I don't want to tell anyone—just at the moment. I promise you, Betty, I'll tell you the whole story some day. But, as you say, the police won't bother about what I was doing on Friday evening, and the story I told them sounds quite plausible so they'll just accept it—they have accepted it, of course."

"Well, I'm glad that's all," said Betty. "When you came to the door of the Frump-hole and were so mysterious I thought there was something really awful!"

"Oh, there's worse to come!" Basil announced. "But there's not much time. You've got to get back to dinner and I have to get down to King's Cross to meet my people—they're arriving from Yorkshire at eight-five; had a telegram this morning. Betty, I want you to do something for me that is desperately important and rather difficult, I'm afraid."

He pulled an envelope out of his pocket. "This is something of Aunt Phemia's; it's valuable and it must be put back among her things. 'S a matter of fact it's a pearl necklace, a family heirloom, worth quite a lot. No, I didn't steal it; she gave it to me herself—not gave it for keeps but handed it to me, but it ought to have been back among her things and I must get it back somehow. Betty"—Basil's arm was round her and his hand gripped her arm—"do help me over this! You must! I can trust you, I know. I'll explain it all to you later. But it would be damned difficult to explain if the pearls were missing when they go through her things. You've got to believe me that it's nothing really discreditable, and trust me to explain it all to you when there's time. You know, don't you, that if it were anything really bad I wouldn't be getting you mixed up in it? Say you'll do this for me."

Betty had put out her hand when Basil first held out the envelope to her, and then had withdrawn it as if she were afraid to touch what seemed so dangerous and fraught with mystery. She drew a deep breath and turned her head away from his, which was bent forward, his eyes eagerly scanning her face in the gloom. There was silence for a few minutes.

"You know I'll do anything I can for you, Basil—though I can't think why I should—but I simply don't see how this can be done. Is all this scheming absolutely necessary? Why must you be such a noodle?"

"There's no other way that I can see. Betty——"

"I'll take them, Basil, and I'll do my best," said Betty decisively. "As I told you, the police have already searched her room; I think they were looking for a will, and Mrs. Bliss says they found it beneath her underclothes. Pongle's, I mean."

"Yes, but you know how she hid her things all over the place. There must be lots of crannies they haven't searched yet," put in Basil, speaking quickly and anxiously.

"But how do I know which crannies they have searched?"

"If Mrs. Bliss was there you can pump her."

"Perhaps, but that's not the worst. They've locked up her room again and taken the key. I don't see that there's a hope of getting in."

"You must watch for a chance. If that's utterly impossible, could you hide them somewhere else in the house where she might have stowed them away? Did she only hide things in her own room? Remember, I'm supposed to have handed them back to her when I went to see her some time—last Wednesday, when I had tea with her, I suppose. Couldn't she have put them... Oh, I don't know. You're much better than I am, Betty, at thinking things out; you'll get an idea! And another thing, let me know somehow, secretly, when you have disposed of them and how. As soon as you can. They may be missed and someone may ask me about them."

"I can ring you up, I suppose?"

"Yes—but be careful—Waddletoes can listen in downstairs to the calls she puts through to my room. Writing would be safer, but to-morrow's Sunday and I want to know soon. You'll find how best to let me know, but remember I shall have to be up and away from my rooms early to-morrow; I'm lunching with the Sanders—my people are staying there; and I suppose I'll have to be with them most of the day. That's why I was so desperately anxious to get hold of you now. I hadn't a chance all day till this evening."

Betty put the envelope in her handbag. "That's safest," she said. "I always carry it about with me. I must fly or I shall be late. We can walk as far as the station together. Come on, Tuppy. Why ever am I so nice to you, Basil?"

Basil offered no suggestion. They made their way back to the Spaniards Road and hurried along it. A bus, and a grey Alvis two-seater creeping along behind it, overtook them.

"There go Beryl and Gerry—did you see?" cried Betty. "They might give us a lift. Look, the bus is holding them up!"

"No; better not. They brought me up to Hampstead this evening and I don't want to bother them again. We've got time."

Basil felt that he would have to meet Beryl again, and his parents as well, only too soon. He was not ready to do any more explaining at the moment.

"I wish you could have explained things more to me," said Betty as they went on down the hill. "But of course there isn't time now. When shall I see you again?"

"To-morrow's hopeless, so far as I can see, but I'll ring up if there's a chance."

As Betty hurried along to the Frampton, with Tuppy dragging wretchedly in her wake, she was musing: "Now where did Pongle hide things? In the drawing-room, perhaps? I wonder. Would she entrust anything to old Slowgo? But then he'd have to know; that wouldn't do. Oh, come on, Tuppy. I suppose you couldn't swallow them?"

The miserable terrier had probably never had a less enjoyable outing.

CHAPTER NINE

BASIL THINKS OF GLOVES

BASIL leapt off a tram and ran into King's Cross station at the moment when the train which he was meeting was steaming up beside the platform. He realized that if he could have overcome his repugnance to the underground he would have arrived in better time. "But Mother'll be fussing about her luggage," he thought, "and her bag and her scarf and her rug and the rest of it. They'll hardly get to the gate before I do."

He was right. When he arrived rather breathless at the gate where tickets were collected, he saw his mother and father approaching it from the other side. James Pongleton was a tall spare man with white hair and an iron-grey beard clipped to a neat point. Austere in expression, he closely resembled his dead sister and was utterly unlike his son Basil. It was evidently from his mother that Basil inherited his good looks as well as his impulsiveness and his vague mental processes. Susan Pongleton's once bright colouring was faded and her figure was definitely plump, but on seeing her one thought at once, "What a pretty girl she must have been!" She always dressed as fluffily as fashion would permit, favouring lace and soft materials.

At the gate Mrs. Pongleton had to hand a large shopping bag crammed with magazines and papers to her husband, already burdened with two rugs and two umbrellas, so that she might search in her purse for her ticket. Having found this at last in her pocket, where she had put it so that it would be handy, and having passed through the gate, she rushed at Basil and embraced him effusively, to his embarrassment. He tried to curtail the greeting by mumbling, "Must hurry to get a taxi, y'know—we're in everyone's way—come on."

He took an assortment of impedimenta from his parents and led the way out of the station.

"What a terrible thing this is, Basil," his mother murmured as she scuttled along beside him. "Really dreadful! There's never been anything of the kind in the family before; it's so—so—demeaning!"

"I don't suppose it's the sort of thing that becomes a family habit," said Basil unfeelingly. But his mother did not notice, being occupied with keeping an eye on the porter whom she suspected of evil intentions towards her suitcase.

"All well at Steyton?" Basil asked his father.

"Couldn't have been called away at a worse time," Mr. Pongleton replied gruffly. "This our taxi? That contraption of yours will climb a hill, I suppose?" he enquired of the driver.

Mr. Pongleton's ideas about motor-cars had been formed some thirty years earlier, and the elderly limousine driven by a promoted coachman, in which he was accustomed to proceed sedately along the less hilly roads around his home, had done little to develop them. The flabbergasted taxi-man decided that the old gent didn't know any better, and looked to Basil for instructions.

"Beverley House, Haverstock Hill," Basil directed him, when the suitcases had been stowed away, after several rearrangements, to his mother's satisfaction.

"There now, James!" exclaimed Mrs. Pongleton, sinking back in her seat. "Did I pack your pyjamas? I've been so flustered and we had to come away in such a hurry——"

"Don't worry, Mother," Basil urged. "I can get a pair of mine for Father if you have forgotten them. How are the dogs?" he enquired, hoping to stave off conversation about his aunt's murder.

"Floss has the sweetest puppies," his mother told him. "And that reminds me of poor Phemia's dog. Who is looking after him?"

"Tuppy's quite happy at the Frampton. People take him for walks," Basil explained.

"What's the truth of this unfortunate affair?" Basil's father asked him abruptly.

"Wish I knew. It's the most awful tangle," said Basil.

But Mr. and Mrs. Pongleton had not been confused by the various clues and counter-clues and inconsistencies which were bothering everyone else. Both assumed that Bob Thurlow was the murderer, and Mr. Pongleton, who had gleaned the story of the burglary and the brooch from the papers, was inclined to the "told you so" attitude.

"Many and many a time I have warned poor Phemia not to poke her finger into other people's pies, but she would do it, and now see what it has come to! She should have let well alone."

"But, James," protested Mrs. Pongleton, who had not been over-fond of her sister-in-law but felt that her husband's remarks were a little unseemly, "Phemia saw that the brooch was stolen property and had to do *something*. It's all very terrible and I can only hope it will soon be over. It seems clear enough to me, but if there's not enough evidence why haven't the police found any fingerprints? I understand that there are always fingerprints."

"Perhaps too many on a public staircase," Basil suggested.

He peered out of the window of the taxi, which was carrying them up Haverstock Hill. In doing so he put his hand on the window-ledge and then glanced at the smudges made by his own fingers, and others before them, on the polished wood.

Basil managed to get away soon after dinner. He walked down the hill, still feeling a repugnance towards the underground. Although he had been restless all through dinner, with anxiety to get back to his own rooms, now he was reluctant to return to the vigilance of "Duck's-feet"—or his purple-suited colleague. Alternately he dawdled and hurried, but in Chalk Farm Road he seemed to decide that haste was more important than the postponement of his return, and he sprinted to catch a 24 bus which came round the corner.

In Tavistock Square he saw no one, but without waiting to investigate its darkness very carefully he let himself quietly into the house, and after a hasty look round, satisfied that no one was about, he made for the telephone which stood on a table at the far end of the narrow hall.

"That the Frampton? That you, Nellie? Can I speak to Miss Watson? Quick! Right."

He had thought it would be safer to use the telephone here rather than the extension in his own room, for if he did the latter he could not tell whether Mrs. Waddilove might be listening in. But as he sat on the table, holding the 'phone to his ear, a door opposite to him opened and disclosed Mrs. Waddilove waist-deep, as it were, in the basement. She banged an enamelled tin jug, a book, and a basket of silver down on the floor, hoisted herself up the last few stairs, shut the door and locked it. Still burdened with a hot-water bottle, she stooped down slowly, with grunts, and picked up the other baggage. Basil inwardly cursed himself for that "Quick!" and hoped it would take a long time to fetch Betty, yet he imagined that through the telephone he could hear a series of thuds which marked her precipitous descent of the stairs. Why hadn't he gone to a public telephone-box? Just his insane reluctance to part with cash—even tuppence—when he might get something on credit.

Mrs. Waddilove waddled to the foot of the stairs and began a dragging and groaning ascent. Another door opened and Miss Stark, the downstairs lodger, emerged.

"Oh, Mrs. Waddilove, about lunch to-morrow—I just wanted to remind you—about my friend…"

Miss Stark was well launched into a description of her friend's idiosyncrasies of diet and of the precise way in which the coffee should be made, when Betty's voice sounded through the telephone in Basil's ear.

"I say, Betty—no, of course not; I didn't think you'd have had a chance yet. 'S a matter of fact I'm glad you haven't. I've got an idea…" He took a cautious glance towards the stairs. They would be there for hours yet. "I say—er—what about gloves? Yes, *gloves*. No, no! I thought a pair of gloves for *you*——Yes, got the idea? Bright girl! Best of luck!"

He put down the telephone. "Hope she really has got the idea," he thought as he began to climb the stairs, squeezing past Mrs. Waddilove, who turned to say "good night" to him as he passed and to shake a playful finger at him, having dumped down her load again and thus freed her hand.

"Ah, Mr. Pongleton, a birthday present, I'll be bound. I always say there's nothing so nice as a good pair of gloves for a young lady."

"Yes, they come in useful, don't they?" Basil agreed fatuously as he climbed to his room.

CHAPTER TEN

TUPPY PERFORMS HIS TRICK

"I'm sure I don't know what to do with that poor little animal to-night," Mrs. Bliss complained to Betty, meeting her on her way through the hall on Saturday evening from the cubby-hole where the telephone was installed. "Would you believe it, he seemed so quiet and peaceful on the rug in the drawing-room yesterday evening, and yet he got up and roamed and prowled in the night—poor little fellow—looking for his mistress, I'll be bound!—and he simply gnawed some papers to shreds. Quite tart about it Mr. Blend was this morning; seems they were just the ones he wanted to cut up. Dear, dear! Just one trial added to another!"

"Tell you what, Mrs. Bliss: I'll have him in my room if you like. I believe he'd settle down there. I took him for a walk this evening, you know; galloped him all over the Heath, so I hope he's tired out."

"I do believe he might settle better in someone's room. The truth is, he's not used to sleeping alone. Nervous he may be; they say dogs have nerves just the same as humans. Well, Miss Watson, if you wouldn't mind, it'd be kind of you and a weight off my shoulders. I'll tell Nellie to take his basket and cushions up to your room. Luckily I thought of them when the police came to-day and I got them out of the poor dear lady's bedroom. Not too keen on letting them go, the police weren't; seems as if they were still searching for something. You know what a one Miss Pongleton was for hiding her belongings all over the place. Why, they found that will underneath the paper at the bottom of the third drawer in the mahogany chest of drawers—under her combinations, too! She was always one to have plenty of warm underclothes; wool next the skin—well, there's nothing like it."

"They have locked her room again, I suppose?" Betty enquired.

"Locked it and taken the key, and they put seals on the bureau and drawers too. They'll be here again on Monday I understand, and Mr. Pongleton and Mrs. Sanders are to come too and look through her things."

"I suppose they had a good hunt—looking for things that might be hidden?" Betty suggested.

"That they did, Miss Watson. Behind the pictures, under the carpet—I told them about that, having found things there myself once, when the poor lady was away and it was taken up to be cleaned. And I shall never forget how Miss Pongleton turned on me for having taken it up without asking her. Seemed to think I was prying into her affairs! Well, I said to her, a carpet's a carpet and not a safe deposit, and I should have thought that with a bureau and all there'd be no need to put things there in all the dust! That was before I knew her ways."

"It must have been very awkward for you," said Betty in a soothing tone.

"Awkward's the word for it. And there's another thing, Miss Watson. There's the poor lady's room under lock and key and no more use to me than if it was occupied—let alone the difficulty of finding another tenant after all this upset! But I don't know what's to happen about the rent. It's all a great worry to me, on top of the blow of the poor lady's death like that; but it's hard if I'm to be the loser."

"I shouldn't worry about that, Mrs. Bliss. Mr. Pongleton or Mrs. Sanders is sure to settle it satisfactorily. I was wondering, did Miss Pongleton hide things outside her room—in the drawing-room, for instance?"

"Not that I know of—but who can tell? The police haven't looked elsewhere yet, but they may be all over the house before they've done. Dear, dear. Who'd've thought I should live to see such doings!"

Some hours later Betty sat in a wicker chair before the gas-fire in her bedroom, wrapped in a decorative blue silk dressing-gown. She had a brush in her hand with which she occasionally gave one or two vigorous strokes at her sleek brown hair. It was in the awkward stage known as "growing", but although it only hung to her shoulders, she was able, with her usual neat efficiency, to secure it in a demure little twist at the nape of her neck. She was puzzled but not disheartened. Her brown eyes stared into space and her pretty mouth was even more firmly set than usual. She put down the brush and lighted a cigarette.

There was a little rummaging noise behind her and Tuppy stepped deliberately from his basket, carrying in his mouth the small cushion which Miss Pongleton had sewn with her own hands in order that Tuppy's asthmatic head might rest more comfortably. He deposited it at Betty's feet and then sat down fatly in the glow of the fire.

Betty stared down at him without enthusiasm. He had performed his one trick, which his late mistress had so often exhibited with pride to the bored inmates of the boarding-house. But her uninterested gaze at the little blue cushion was turning into a wide-eyed stare.

"Tuppy!" she exclaimed, but with no trace of reproof—rather in the tone of one who shares a great discovery.

She snatched up a pair of nail-scissors and ripped open a few inches of one side of the cushion. It was filled with kapok, luckily. Miss Pongleton would have been quite capable of providing down for Tuppy—or perhaps not, in view of its price; anyhow, down would have been dangerous, fluffing all over the room.

Tuppy watched the procedure uneasily, pawing at Betty's bare leg. Betty dumped the cushion and its cover under the eiderdown on her bed for safety, though she knew Cissie had gone to bed and no one else was likely to disturb her, whilst she extracted from her handbag the envelope which Basil had given her on the Heath.

"Now for the gloves!" she said to herself. "Poor old Basil! I suppose Miss Stark was hovering around, waiting to get at the telephone."

With her gloved hands she opened the envelope and drew out the pearl necklace. She could not resist pausing to look at the creamy gloss of the pearls, even holding them against her neck and admiring the effect in the mirror. Then she retrieved the cushion, carefully hollowed out a nest in the middle of the kapok, and stuffed the pearls inside. For a moment she was horrified at the impossibility of matching the cotton with which the seam had been sewn, but reflected that, after all, Miss Pongleton must be supposed to have unpicked the cushion in order to stow the pearls away and might not have had any of the original cotton left. She studied Miss Pongleton's stitches and re-sewed the cushion with their exact counterparts. Then she stuffed Tuppy back into his basket, placed the cushion tenderly under his head, switched off the light, turned out the gas-fire, and slipped into bed, murmuring to Tuppy: "Guard the heirloom well, my lad!"

In the morning Betty's first thought was how to let Basil know. Obviously she could not telephone from the Frampton. Anyone might pass through the hall whilst she did so, and probably he would want to know exactly where she had hidden the pearls. Betty decided that she must go out immediately after breakfast to a telephone-box, and somehow she must elude Cissie, who was sure to offer to accompany her. It was lucky that Cissie had been upstairs when she slipped out yesterday evening after Basil, but she could hardly hope for the same luck again.

Cissie was down punctually. Bad luck! She sometimes overslept on Sunday.

"Glorious day!" she exclaimed to Betty. "Let's have a walk on the Heath."

Betty was unenthusiastic. "I've got letters to write. You might get someone else to go with you."

"That's likely, in this place!" declared Cissie with scorn. "You can't frowst in the house all day, and the letters can be written this afternoon. You know there's no post till the evening on Sunday."

Betty's thoughts wandered wildly among telegrams—how and whence did you dispatch them on Sunday? But anyone might open and read a telegram if its rightful receiver were out. No, telegrams were definitely dangerous. Would it be possible, if she went out with Cissie, to be struck with a sudden desire to telephone, from the underground station perhaps? But Cissie was so inquisitive; she would lounge against the door of the box and might overhear something. Betty had another scheme.

"All right, I'll come. But I want to write a letter first, to Basil, and then go down the hill and leave it at the Sanders' house. He's lunching there."

"Why not ring him up?"

"He'll be out—he was to go up to the Sanders' first thing. His people are there."

"D'you mean to say Basil will be up and out at this hour?" demanded Cissie incredulously.

"Yes; he's to breakfast with the Sanders," explained Betty wildly. "Naturally his father and mother want to see as much of him as they can while they're here."

"Ring him up at the Sanders'," suggested Cissie exasperatingly.

"For goodness' sake let me manage my own affairs! It won't take me a moment to write a note."

"Oh, all right," conceded Cissie. "But for anyone with a reputation for being sensible you do have the silliest ideas. Have some more bacon?"

After breakfast Betty retired to her room and composed a note to Basil which, she hoped, would not give the secret away even if it should fall into other hands. But it ought to be quite safe.

> *Dear Basil* [she wrote], *I was not able to telephone to you this morning, so send this note instead. If you want to ring me up I shall be at home this evening. I can be free for lunch on Tuesday, if that's suitable.*

("Just to make an excuse for writing," she said to herself; "in case anyone should read it or should ask him what it's about. Parents are so enquiring. This may sound forward, but it's not suspicious.")

> *We're still rather distraught here and Tuppy wanders about like a lost lamb. I had him to sleep in my room last night, as he was restless alone in the drawing-room, and with the little blue pillow which Miss Pongleton sewed for him herself* (luckily *Mrs. Bliss had rescued his basket and pillows out of Miss P.'s room*) *under his head, he slept peacefully. I had to stitch up a rent in the little pillow before he would settle down. He is very devoted to it and guards it as if the family jewels were inside it!*
>
> *Yours,*
>
> *Betty.*

"Now, will Basil think I've gone clean off my nut or will he have the wits to understand? Certainly if anyone else reads it they'll think I'm a blithering idiot. It ought to be all right, though."

She sealed it carefully and put on her hat and coat.

"I'm ready, Cissie!" she called, as she leapt down the stairs.

Whilst Betty and Cissie were out, Mr. Plasher arrived at the Frampton with Beryl, in the Alvis. Beryl asked to see Mrs. Bliss, who flowed into the hall, black and shiny in her Sunday clothes, before Nellie could show the visitor into the drawing-room.

"Good morning, Mrs. Bliss; I'm so glad I've caught you before you went to church," said Beryl, smiling especially graciously because she felt that her mission was a little difficult.

"Will you come into my sanctum?" Mrs. Bliss invited her importantly, and swayed through the hall towards the little room at the back.

"It's about Tuppy," Beryl explained, when she was seated on a hard, slippery sofa in the sanctum.

"The poor little fellow!" exclaimed Mrs. Bliss unctuously. "Miss Watson has been very kind—had him up in her room to sleep last night. I'd have taken him myself but I always was such a light sleeper, the least thing disturbs me and then I'm good for nothing in the morning. Tuppy's breathing isn't what it should be, Miss Sanders. But there! He was a faithful friend to poor Miss Pongleton for many years, and who'd have thought that she'd have gone before him! I always say it's the unexpected that happens."

"Yes, Mrs. Bliss," Beryl nodded sympathetically. "Mr. and Mrs. Pongleton are staying with us, as I expect you know, and we have all been talking over the question of Tuppy—what it would be best to do with him. My Uncle James has decided to take him back with them to Yorkshire. My mother can't very well do with him, so that seems the best plan. Don't you think so, Mrs. Bliss?"

"I'm sure I don't know, Miss Sanders; and of course it's not for me to say. I'll miss the poor little fellow, and I'm sure I've done what I could for him, but it's not easy for me to give him proper attention. What I always say is, my clients must come first. Everything that can be done for their comfort shall be done. Of course, poor Tuppy is one of them, in a manner of speaking——"

"I know, Mrs. Bliss, that you've been very kind to Tuppy. We are all very grateful to you in every way. But Mr. Plasher is waiting outside in his car. So will that be all right if we take Tuppy and his basket of course—at once?"

"It's lucky that the poor little fellow is here, for Miss Watson and Miss Fain have gone for a walk and Miss Watson was all for taking him, but Miss Fain said they couldn't be bothered and they might come back on the bus and that always makes him sick, so he is here right enough. I'll tell Nellie to fetch his basket; it's in Miss Watson's room, for she said it had better stay there for the present."

When Nellie came staggering downstairs with the basket, Beryl and Gerry were in the hall.

"I suppose the police have searched it?" suggested Gerry with a grin. "I hear they had a great exploration in Miss Pongleton's room—what!"

"Indeed they did," Mrs. Bliss agreed. "They prodded and poked those cushions before they'd let them go! And you'll be sure to take care of the little blue cushion, Mr. Plasher, for poor Miss Pongleton made it herself and Tuppy's never easy without it."

"I'll guard it," Gerry assured her. "You must have had a lot of worry, Mrs. Bliss?"

"That I have, with the police up and down all day. Carpets and pictures and everything, they searched. You've heard about her will, of course? Finding it under——"

"Oh yes," interposed Beryl hastily. "My mother has seen my aunt's solicitors."

"And her money goes to Mr. Basil, I understand?" ventured Mrs. Bliss.

"Oh yes," said Beryl again, unwilling to discuss these details in the hall, but not knowing how to silence Mrs. Bliss.

"They do say," continued the persistent lady, "that she used to make a new will from time to time and that she'd disinherit Mr. Basil when she felt so inclined."

"I don't suppose she really did," Beryl began, but they were all startled by Nellie, who had been quietly waiting with the basket and now blurted out: "Why, that will was only made las' Wednesday night, an' to think that Bob an' me put our names to it!"

Having given this startling information, Nellie banged the basket on the floor and hastily searched for her handkerchief.

"Surely you're mistaken, Nellie? I think it was made some time ago," said Beryl, startled out of discretion.

"A-course we didn't read it. It was folded up an' just the place lef' for our names to go, an' when we came in, Bob an' me, with Tuppy, Miss Pongleton said: 'Now I want you both to sign a dokkyment for me', an' Bob, 'e said arterwards, 'That's 'er will, you bet, on one o' them forms that you buy'. 'E'd seen 'em before an' 'e knew."

Nellie sniffed assertively.

"I think he must have made a mistake; that was probably some other document," said Beryl firmly. "Don't worry, Nellie," she added kindly. "Mr. Plasher's solicitors are looking after Bob, you know."

"Yes, your Bob will be all right," Gerry assured the snuffling girl. He picked up the basket and cushions and bolted out to the car.

"Now, where's Tuppy?" enquired Beryl briskly.

Mrs. Bliss moved towards the drawing-room reluctantly. Here was a hint of further mystery, but she could not see how to draw Beryl into discussion of it.

Tuppy was snatched from a peaceful doze in front of the fire and Beryl carried him out. Mrs. Bliss turned to find Nellie lingering in the hall.

"When was it exactly that you and Bob signed that paper for Miss Pongleton?" she enquired.

"Wednesday evening," said Nellie. "We took the dog for a turn on the 'Eath, Bob an' me, an' we brought 'im back an' I went into the drorin'-room with 'im. Miss Pongleton was there alone—Mr. Basil 'ad bin to tea, you remember, ma'am—an' she 'ad the paper before 'er; she was sittin' at the little table Mr. Blend uses. An' she said: 'Oh, Nellie, is Bob with you?' An' I said: ''E's waitin' outside for me, miss', so she said——"

"Yes, yes," interrupted Mrs. Bliss, who was impatient of garrulity in others. "And what happened?"

"As I was tellin' you, she arst us to put our names to that paper, an' so we did."

"Did she say it was her will?"

"No, she didn't *say* so, but she seemed in a fair way, an' I thought to meself, 'Mr. Basil's got across the ol' lady agin.' "

"You'd better be getting about your work, Nellie," Mrs. Bliss instructed the girl. She herself made haste upstairs. She would be late for church.

"There might be another will," she thought. "Did the police look through all the drawers?" Mrs. Bliss went through them in her mind whilst she put on her hat. "Handkerchiefs, stockings, 'larngeree', woollen underclothes—what will happen to all those?" she wondered. "And where else? Downstairs, Miss Watson suggested."

At church Mrs. Bliss's mind constantly wandered from the sermon to thoughts of underclothes and of how her own store needed replenishing, and of unlikely hiding places for wills.

CHAPTER ELEVEN

MRS. DAYMER DECIDES TO INVESTIGATE

OLD Mr. Blend was very busy on that Sunday morning after the murder. He sat at his little table in the drawing room with half a dozen large and dilapidated scrap-books piled up before him.

He was constantly devising new systems of classification for his cuttings, and as he never completed one before abandoning it in favour of another, the precious strips of paper were grouped in a disorderly medley of systems. Many of them were yellow with age and most of them referred to crimes. Kindly and tolerant in his relationship with his fellow men, Mr. Blend would gloat over the details of crimes with a chill, inhuman joy. The truth was that he did not regard them as part of life but merely as a form of art, just as many humane people wallow deliciously in the gruesome "murder mysteries" of fiction. Mr. Blend never read "shockers" or any other novels; he did not even read Mrs. Daymer's hectic "psychological" stories, which her other fellow boarders were too cowardly to ignore.

Mr. Blend would describe the crimes recorded in his scrap-book as "a nice neat little murder" or "a messy affair"—the messiness which he deplored being always in the nature of clumsiness or bad planning, not necessarily a great spread of gore. Miss Pongleton's strangulation on the stairs of the underground railway he regarded as "a very tidy business", and he had already shocked Mrs. Bliss profoundly by referring to it in this offhand way. It was curious that a man so untidy in his personal habits as Mr. Blend should have such an admiration for tidiness in crime. As he said himself, "I'd do no good at murder—I'm far too great a muddler. Like as not I'd be whipping out the blood-stained dagger to cut the cake at tea."

Although he had lived at the Frampton for some ten years—ever since he sold the "tobacconist and news agency" business in which, with the help of his careful wife, he seemed to have amassed a comfortable little fortune—yet Mrs. Bliss could not remember ever seeing him in new clothes. His dark grey tweed suits had trousers baggy at the knees and coats bulgy at the elbows. His late wife—"my old Sarah", as the Frampton knew her—must have spent all her leisure in knitting ties for Mr. Blend, for he seemed to have an inexhaustible store of them, somewhat frayed and loopy, and their ends dangled untidily outside his coat below his fuzzy, rounded beard. He was not the sort of boarder who adorns the drawing-room and gives the establishment what Mrs. Bliss called a "high-class tone", but she put up with him for the sake of her old friendship with his wife and because he always paid promptly, when he was reminded, and helped to keep the maids satisfied by tipping them generously.

"It's the little details that count and that round off a good crime nicely," he would say. "Choice of place and choice of instrument, those are important, and no untidy fingerprints left to mess up the place." The Pongleton affair had been excellently managed, he considered, and there his interest ended. He was not concerned about the tracking of the murderer, and he exasperated the other boarders at the Frampton by his indifference to their theories and his lack of curiosity as to what the police might be doing.

His scrap-books contained, in addition to the cuttings relative to crimes, many records of the sententious remarks of magistrates and coroners. He would repeat these truisms and conventional moralizings to the boarders with fatuous glee. Mrs. Bliss was the only one who appreciated them. Betty sometimes suspected that Mr. Blend had a sarcastic grin up his sleeve when he quoted, with every sign of approval, some such remark as that "when young women cut short their hair and their skirts, it seems, unfortunately, that they cut short their morals too."

Mrs. Daymer was accustomed to tell him, in reply to these quotations, that "the psychology is all wrong", and would dismiss him and his scrap-books with a dry sniff up her thin nose and a jerk of her head. It was surprising, therefore, that he should confide in her about his discovery on that Sunday morning. It may have been because he and she were the only occupants of the drawing-room. She was sitting by the fire, opposite to Miss Pongleton's more comfortable armchair which had been so basely annexed by Mr. Slocomb. The convention that that chair belonged by a sort of divine right to one particular person was firmly established in the Frampton, so that even Mrs. Daymer hesitated to sit there, though Mr. Slocomb had gone out for a walk. She was drafting plans for her next novel on a writing-pad.

Mr. Blend suddenly brought his fist down with a resounding thump on the open page of a scrap-book.

"There you are!" he exclaimed in triumph. "That's when I was classifying them under victims—unsound method, very unsound. So I've found it, and it's a pretty neat bit of work too!"

He ran his fingers into his grizzled red hair as he read the cutting again. He often talked to himself over his books, and Mrs. Daymer took no notice of him except to make a little clittering noise by rattling her long string of hand-painted wooden beads impatiently. But Mr. Blend had to talk to someone about this. He surveyed Mrs. Daymer for a few moments and then called out to her:

"Hi! Mrs. Daymer, this ought to interest you. You don't set much store by my old scrap-books, I know, but here we see the past repeating itself—repeating itself with added elegance, we might say!"

Mrs. Daymer looked at him with some annoyance. "What is it, Mr. Blend?" she enquired coldly, as if he were a tiresome child.

"Merely a little piece of the past that has acquired a topical interest." Mr. Blend's own provincial style of speech sometimes borrowed pompousness from his records of the utterances of the Bench.

"Topical—do you mean something connected with Miss Pongleton's murder?" asked Mrs. Daymer with quickened interest.

"In a manner of saying, it may be connected," Mr. Blend told her cautiously.

"Well, what is it? I can't get up." Mrs. Daymer indicated her homespun peacock-blue lap, papered with lists of characters and notes on their psychology.

Mr. Blend picked up the loose-limbed scrap-book gingerly and bore it across to her. He sat on the edge of the sofa and balanced the book on one knee, extending the important page towards her and pointing with a stubby tobacco-stained finger at a yellowish cutting printed in smeared type.

"Here you are; one of the earliest cuttings I ever took, that must be. From the *Coventry Globe* you see, some thirty years ago. That would be when I was in business there."

Mrs. Daymer read the account. "I don't quite see…?"

"It's the little details that count," Mr. Blend pointed out. "Put that poor dog out of your mind, or picture it as a human being. It's the method that's interesting. A dog-leash, you note—the animal's own leash—whipped round its neck and pulled tight from behind. Quick and neat! Not a sound! The dog must have been without a collar, or it may have been removed by this young fellow before he got to work."

Mrs. Daymer shuddered. "Revolting! And it's certainly curious; they say that is how it was done in the case of Miss Pongleton, and with a dog-leash, too. Do you suppose, Mr. Blend, that the murderer read or heard of this case and got his idea from that? But it's so long ago, and it's not likely to have been reported except in the local papers. Merely a claim for the value of the dog, and the cruelty charge seems to have fallen through. I should say it can only be an odd coincidence."

"The annals of murder are riddled with coincidence," remarked Mr. Blend in his most magisterial manner. "This little piece interests me because I am now classifying my crimes under 'method', and I am glad to have it to place beside Miss Pongleton. It was a chance remark by Mrs. Bliss that set me on the track. When I first read about how the old lady was strangled it struck me I'd heard of something of the same sort before, but I couldn't quite place it some-how. It bothered me. I connected it with a dog-leash, but not with a dog. Now you see what the magistrate said: 'True humanity shows itself first in kindness to dumb animals'; because they urged in this young chap's defence, you see, that he was a well-conducted, humane fellow, and wouldn't have done this save in self-defence. It was for that little saying that I kept the cutting in the first place. I used to quote that little bit at one time and Mrs. Bliss bore it in mind, and she came out with it on the evening of the very day the old lady was found throttled. That gave me the 'animal' clue, and I've been hunting for the thing ever since. I'm right glad I've turned it up."

Mrs. Daymer was not paying much attention to his meanderings. Her eyes travelled vaguely over the bad print and suddenly became riveted on one line.

"Did you notice the name?" she asked in a strained voice.

"Name of the young fellow? Oh yes, rum name, isn't it? But these reporters on local papers aren't any too accurate. Why, do you know, Mrs. Daymer, I could show you an account of a case in which the prisoner's name is spelt three different ways in half a column, and not one of them the right one, I'll wager. Now, let me see, where was it…?"

He began to gather up the scrap-book, but Mrs. Daymer laid a detaining hand on the page.

"No, don't take it away, Mr. Blend. It's a queer name and doesn't ring true. And extraordinarily like…Do you know, I begin to think that this is something more than a curious coincidence. What are you going to do about it?"

"Do about it? Why, I'm going to have that old cutting out and put it in my new book alongside of Miss Pongleton; a pretty pair they'll make!" Mr. Blend chuckled ghoulishly.

Mrs. Daymer was very disturbed. "I really don't know. It seems impossible, utterly impossible. Not the type, I should have thought. And yet—I must confess I have not been able to work out any convincing theory to account for the crime. Mr. Blend," she finished very firmly, "I really think that some-one ought to follow this up."

"Follow it up! You can't follow up a dog that was dead thirty years ago!"

"One might follow up the career of that nauseating young man."

"Follow up—I don't quite *follow you*. Oh, you mean to say that it might be the same chap? The name—like—mm! —someone we all know? Hm! Even if it is, what of it, Mrs. Daymer?"

"The man who did that might have done—this!" said Mrs. Daymer sepulchrally.

"We-e-ll, I wouldn't go as far as that. And to be sure, if there's anything in what you say, that's the policeman's job, Mrs. Daymer. The police can look this up, if they've a mind to."

"But it wasn't a crime, merely a civil action for damages. And the name—it's different, you see. He may have given a different name, or he may have been only too glad when they made a mistake about it, and refrained from correcting them. Anyway, I don't suppose the police have given two thoughts to the career of—that gentleman."

The implication which she saw in this discoloured record of an unimportant case of thirty years ago was so horrible and so fantastic that she could not bring herself to name the man whom it seemed to point to.

Mr. Blend nodded at her wisely: "You can follow it up for all I care, but I'm not doing any following up myself."

"Will you allow me to copy this report? I can do it on my typewriter upstairs in a minute."

"You're welcome to copy as much as you like, so long as you take care of my old book—a bit weak in the joints that scrap-book is, just like me."

Mrs. Daymer swept the notes for her novel unceremoniously into a flat case of soft leather embossed with a coloured pattern of plump apples. "My manuscript holder", it was grandly called, and the apples were referred to, when she was in humorous vein, as the fruit of the tree of knowledge. She bore the scrap-book reverently upstairs.

Before long she was down again and returned the book to the old man.

"Mr. Blend," she warned him, "I think it would be best if you said nothing of this to anyone here, for the present. You had better not leave *this* scrap-book lying about. And if you hear that I am paying a visit to the Midlands for the purpose of collecting local colour for my next book, please don't appear to attach any special significance to my expedition. And perhaps you had better not mention Coventry. Fortunately the name and address of the young man's landlady, the owner of that poor animal, is given in that cutting and may provide a starting point for my investigations. I suppose you wouldn't care to come with me?"

Mr. Blend was quite staggered by the graciousness of this offer, which was based, not so much on any desire of Mrs. Daymer's for the old man's companionship as on her feeling that it might be more conducive to the success of her plan to get him away from the Frampton.

"Well, really, ma'am," he said, relapsing, in his surprise, into his old manner of addressing his customers—"I feel that's a job for younger legs. I'm a bit wobbly on my pins and can't get about as I used to. But don't you fix your hopes on finding that landlady at that address. Thirty years is a goodish bit of time, and landladies aren't as a rule chickens." He chuckled to himself.

"I don't quite know whom to take," Mrs. Daymer mused. "There may be danger; I think it would be better to have a companion—and as a witness too." She sank into her arm-chair and ran through her friends. It was not easy to find anyone who would be willing to accompany her to Coventry at a moment's notice on mysterious business and who could, moreover, be relied on to remain satisfied with a subordinate part.

"Mr. Plasher!" she exclaimed at last. "I always thought him a very pleasant young man and one with a good deal of sense."

Mrs. Daymer meditated on how best to approach Mr. Plasher; she was experienced in the establishment of friendly relations with people, particularly men, whom she wished to study as "types". She planned her campaign and sallied forth, in a shaggy handwoven coat with cap to match, to the nearest telephone kiosk.

She learnt that Mr. Plasher was out but he would be back for lunch. Mrs. Daymer took a stroll by the ponds and returned to the station.

"Mr. Plasher—Mrs. Daymer speaking. You remember me, of course, at the Frampton? Now I want your help in a del-icate matter in connection with this murder. I must have a confidential talk with you. It affects Miss Sanders, of course, and therefore I felt that you were the person to approach.... Out to tea? Then before tea perhaps? But the Frampton is impossible! Oh, that would be very kind, but I think you had better not call at the Frampton. I will walk down Rosslyn Hill and you might stop in passing. Yes, on the opposite side of the road to the underground station. Thank you so much, Mr. Plasher; I knew I could rely on you."

Mrs. Daymer strode up the hill enjoying a sparkling sensation of pleasure and excitement.

After lunch she again donned the shaggy outdoor garments, with the addition of an immense woolly scarf, and strolled down the hill. Before long the grey two-seater came shooting up and drew in to the pavement near her.

"Mrs. Daymer!" exclaimed Gerry, with well-simulated surprise. "How about a little run over the Heath?"

"That is just what I was hoping for," Mrs. Daymer declared as she wedged herself awkwardly into the seat beside him. They snorted up the hill, and when they were sailing gently along the Spaniards Road Mrs. Daymer told Gerry of Mr. Blend's discovery and its possible significance.

Gerry was impressed. "By Jove, Mrs. Daymer! It's a rum go! But what are you going to do about it? What do the others think?"

"The others haven't had any opportunity to exercise their thinking powers upon it," Mrs. Daymer told him in a tone that implied that those powers were, in any case, of little value. "Mr. Blend has shown the cutting only to me, and I warned him to say nothing about it to anyone else for the present. He himself is not the practical type; he is only interested in this cutting as a specimen to be arranged in his scrap-book. He would not dream of taking any action. What I feel about it is this: it is too uncertain a clue to put in the hands of the police at present. It needs some subtlety of mind to grasp its significance. And then, of course, one cannot be sure, and one hesitates to make such an accusation against anyone without further grounds."

"Yes, naturally. It's not a pleasant implication. And even if the identity is established, I can't see where we are. It wouldn't be evidence of guilt in this crime—what? There seems nothing whatever to connect him with it."

"We cannot tell as yet. I have always suspected that there might be secrets in Miss Pongleton's past, and this may have some obscure connection with something of the kind. The very absence of obvious motive would give the murderer an assurance of safety in his horrible designs."

"But what sort of motive?" enquired Gerry.

"Who knows? Blackmail, perhaps. But we shall see."

"Her money goes to Basil—but of course there may be a later will which hasn't been found yet. By Jove! there probably is. Nellie says she and her young man witnessed one last Wednesday."

"Ah! You see!" triumphed Mrs. Daymer. "That as yet undiscovered will may reveal the motive."

"Beryl—Miss Sanders—didn't seem to think it really existed. But she's not keen on it being found. She thinks—we all think—that the money should go to Basil, but she was afraid her aunt might leave it to her—Beryl—if Basil annoyed the old lady."

At any other time Gerry Plasher would hardly have spoken his thoughts on the private affairs of the Pongleton and Sanders families in this unreticent way to a slight acquaintance. But the extraordinary circumstances which had deposited the gaunt Mrs. Daymer in the snug little seat of the Alvis which was generally occupied by Beryl made him forget all caution and babble on as if it were really Beryl at his side.

"This encourages me enormously," declared Mrs. Daymer. "Now this is what I propose to do. The clue must be followed up and I mean to follow it up myself."

"Mayn't that get you into difficulties with the police—if you go following up clues instead of handing them over for the police to deal with?"

"We'll not call it a clue—merely a curious coincidence which interests me as a student of human nature. If it becomes definite enough to provide a clue, then of course I shall inform the police at once. I propose to go to Coventry to-morrow, telling the people at the Frampton that I have to visit the Midlands for local colour in connection with my next book. You know, perhaps, Mr. Plasher, that I write?"

"Oh, rather! Jolly good story, that last one...."

Mr. Plasher was saved from what might have been an embarrassing lack of detailed knowledge of Mrs. Daymer's last book by her eagerness to explain her plan.

"Now, I don't quite like to go alone. The murderer must be a dangerous man. Doubtless he feels secure at the moment, but if he should happen to become suspicious he would stick at nothing. That is his type—ruthless and unhesitating."

"I don't quite see why his suspicions should be aroused, but certainly it might be nasty if they were—if he *is* the murderer. Perhaps you'd better drop it, Mrs. Daymer—at least, not drop it entirely, but put it in the hands of the police."

"No, Mr. Plasher; I cannot do that at this stage. But I must have a companion on my visit to Coventry. Someone reliable and with plenty of sense. That is why I have confided in you."

Mr. Plasher was so astonished when the significance of this remark dawned on him that he made the car swerve alarmingly.

"You mean t'say—me?" he enquired.

"I do," Mrs. Daymer told him decisively. "Will you come?"

"But, y'know, I don't belong to what they call the 'leisured classes'. Come to think of it, I don't know who does. I'm junior partner in a firm of stockbrokers—Oundle, Gumble, and Oundle"—Mr. Plasher had not been long in this dignified position and was still proud of it. "And then there's Beryl— Miss Sanders. Couldn't very well pop off to Coventry——"

"The Midlands, please," Mrs. Daymer corrected him.

"The Midlands, without telling her what I was up to— what?"

"No. I thought of that, and naturally I can't suggest how you will explain matters to her, but I should think that would not be difficult. Mutual trust between two young people in your position…" Mrs. Daymer waved a wool-gloved hand airily.

"Of course Beryl would trust me, even if I had to say that I was off on important business and couldn't explain it at the moment."

The idea of the expedition was obviously taking root in Mr. Plasher's mind.

"But what about the inquest to-morrow?" he asked. "I have to give evidence, y'know, about seeing the old lady on the stairs. They might arrest me after that, too! That's torn it!"

"Nonsense!" said Mrs. Daymer firmly. "The inquest will only take a few minutes; probably they'll adjourn it for further enquiries—including yours and mine in Coventry."

"The Midlands!" Mr. Plasher reminded her. "But then there's the firm. Well, I s'pose I could take a spot more time; have to be away in the morning for the inquest anyway. Dealing with some business affairs for Miss Sanders, perhaps. The boss has met her and Basil and he knows that Basil's pretty—er—well, not exactly a business man, and that she has no father or brother. It might be managed. I say, Mrs. Daymer, it's awfully decent of you to let me in on this. I mean, it's a regular wow, doing a bit of detecting on our own—what?"

Gerry had really decided that he would go on this wild expedition, but he was a little startled to find himself arranging a rendezvous with Mrs. Daymer. A glance at the clock on the dashboard showed him that he would be due in ten minutes at the Sanders' for tea. They were on the North Circular Road, and he drew in to the kerb and halted the car whilst they settled the final details and both noted them in their engagement diaries. Mrs. Daymer had looked up the trains to Coventry before she came out.

"Good idea!" he agreed, perhaps with too much enthusiasm, to her suggestion that they should travel by different trains—she by the nine o'clock, he at eleven-thirty. She delighted in making the affair as mysterious as possible.

"And we may be able to return the same evening," she told him.

"May be!" exclaimed Gerry in alarm. "You don't mean to say that I may have to spend a night—er…" He just stopped himself from saying "with you", and finished instead with "away from Town".

"I don't think you need worry about that possibility," Mrs. Daymer assured him. "Though I shall probably take some things, just in case——"

"Surely we can do it all in a day," Gerry insisted. "I really don't think I can stay longer. Might upset the police! Must think of their tender feelings, y'know!"

"If the police are watching you it might be risky," Mrs. Daymer agreed, but with reluctance. "We don't want them tracking us. You might observe some caution in going to the station."

"It'll be all right as long as I get back soon enough," Gerry declared.

It was arranged, and Gerry dropped Mrs. Daymer at the top of FitzJohn's Avenue and went on to Beverley House wondering just what he was to tell Beryl.

CHAPTER TWELVE

HUNT THE PEARLS!

On Sunday morning Basil delayed his start for Hampstead as long as he dared, hoping for a telephone call from Betty. True, he had told her that he would be setting off early, but, he thought to himself, Betty knows what my "early" is. At last a telephone call from his mother, to ask if he were "all right" and wasn't he coming soon, made him decide that he could wait no longer.

He arrived at Beverley House, where Beryl Sanders lived with her mother, in an irritable and dissatisfied state, and the sight of Tuppy nosing restlessly round the sitting-room did nothing to soothe him. Quite unreasonably he felt as though the stout terrier were responsible for his own unsatisfactory position.

There was a good deal of talk about "poor Phemia's things", and decisions were made as to the disposal of them.

"I'm only thankful Phemia didn't keep a cat; though it would have been just like her!" declared Mrs. Pongleton ambiguously. "The dog is quite enough; and why in the name of goodness did Phemia give him such a ridiculous name— Tuppy!"

Tuppy pricked his ears hopefully, but neither caresses nor biscuits followed.

"Didn't you ever hear the reason, Aunt Susan?" cried Beryl. "Aunt Phemia believed that Tuppy was very valuable. I think she had him from someone in settlement of a small debt—and they bamboozled her, I expect. Anyway, she was afraid dog-thieves might be after him, so she called him

Tuppence—Tuppy for short—to indicate that he wasn't worth much and so deceive them. Poor Aunt Phemia!"

"Childish!" snorted Uncle James. "Poor Phemia never was any judge of dogs; she could always have had a good puppy from me for the asking."

"I am so glad that Euphemia has left her pearls to you, Beryl dear," Mrs. Pongleton remarked. "They will suit your fair skin. It's not everyone who can wear pearls successfully—and *I* never had any to wear."

"Quite ridiculous of my mother to leave those pearls to Phemia," proclaimed Mr. Pongleton. "Of course she wouldn't wear them, and they wouldn't have suited her if she had done. They'd have looked better on you, my dear," he suggested to his wife—"though doubtless you'd have been spilling them all over the place."

"But then Beryl wouldn't have had them now," Mrs. Pongleton pointed out, ignoring the last part of her husband's remarks, as she often found it better to do. "I daresay it's all for the best—about the pearls, I mean."

"And do you know," enquired Mrs. Sanders—"they don't know where those pearls are, so Mr. Stoggins says!"

Basil eyed his relatives anxiously. If only Betty had hurried up and telephoned to him before this!

"What exactly did Stoggins imply?" asked Mr. Pongleton dryly.

"I don't suppose he meant that they are missing, did he, Mother?" said Beryl soothingly. She knew that Mrs. Sanders was fond of dramatizing a situation.

"They're not found, so they must be missing!" Mrs. Sanders declared. "The police turned all her things upside down, you know, looking for wills. They had been told how she hid things all over the place."

"Wouldn't it be most natural not to find the pearls in any of the obvious places?" suggested Beryl. "Aunt Phemia's things seldom were where you would expect them to be, and, after all, they haven't really looked for the pearls, have they?" She looked enquiringly at Basil, but he avoided her eyes.

"Why yes, of course," said his mother. "That will—in a drawer beneath her underclothes... well, really! And the *police* finding it there too!"

"That reminds me," said Beryl. "When we fetched Tuppy and his basket just now we heard about the possibility of another will. The maid at the Frampton said that she and her young man, Bob Thurlow, witnessed one for Aunt Phemia on Wednesday."

"*That* young man!" Mrs. Pongleton was shocked, as if the fact that Bob Thurlow had performed this service for Miss Pongleton increased the heinousness of the crime of which the good lady felt sure he was guilty. "But isn't that the one they found?"

"Mr. Stoggins told me that the will found so strangely in Phemia's drawer was made last April," Mrs. Sanders exclaimed. "And besides, it was witnessed by two people who were then staying at the Frampton and have since left—quite a nice couple called Briggs."

"What I think is that Aunt Phemia made one on Wednesday and tore it up the next day, having thought better of it," said Beryl firmly.

"That's very likely," Basil suggested eagerly. "She did that once in the summer. I saw her tear it up."

"But why should Phemia keep making wills in that undisciplined way?" enquired Mr. Pongleton severely.

"I s'pose she'd have a bright idea about some little detail," said Basil vaguely. "But next day it wouldn't seem so bright. Haven't you found that ideas are like that, Aunt Adela?"

Mrs. Sanders seemed uncertain that her ideas were so apt to lose brilliance in a night.

"The two wills which Mr. Stoggins has now are practically the same, aren't they?" asked Mrs. Pongleton.

"Oh yes, except for details," agreed Mrs. Sanders. She would not have been so indelicate as to point out that the main difference was the provision made for Tuppy in the later will, which provision, she suspected shrewdly, was not without its bearing on Mr. Pongleton's decision to take charge of the dog.

"I don't think we need worry about the possibility of a later will," said Beryl. "I'm not sure whether Nellie—the maid—has said anything about it to the police, but she sounded as if she hadn't thought of it until the moment when she mentioned it to Mrs. Bliss and me at the Frampton just now. If it doesn't turn up there's no need to search for it, because it probably doesn't exist now."

The gong sounded for lunch, and to Basil's relief the conversation turned to such matters as the price of chickens in London and the excellence of Yorkshire home-baked bread.

It was not until the arrival of Gerry Plasher for tea that Betty's note was discovered in the letter-box, where it had been resting all this time unnoticed.

Basil snatched it a little too eagerly from the maid—though this was not noticed by anyone except his mother,

Beryl having for a moment relaxed the careful watch she was keeping on her cousin, in order to greet Gerry. Basil read the letter quickly and frowned over it. He read it again, more slowly, and it began to acquire significance. Inevitably he looked round the room for Tuppy's basket, and his mother caught his eye.

"I hope it's no bad news, Basil?" This, she thought, was a tactful way of asking what was in the letter and who wrote it. Her remark attracted the attention of the others, who had been engaged in conversation with Gerry.

"No, no," muttered Basil with some annoyance. "Only about"—he turned to the opening paragraphs; there had been some quite innocuous remark there—"about a meeting with a friend. All my arrangements have been upset, of course, and I can't plan anything properly."

"You never were very good at plans, Basil dear," his mother pointed out. "But now it seems to me quite simple. Of course all your engagements must be cancelled for the next week or two. All your friends will understand."

"But business engagements can't be cancelled like that, Mother. You don't realize——"

"I always have thought that these artistic people that you go about with so much are a little lacking in understanding of what is suitable," his mother complained. "That man you brought up to Steyton once—his shirts so open at the neck...I couldn't get used to it at all."

Basil put the letter away...What puzzled him was why Betty should, as it were, send the pearls back to him. Was she playing a mean trick on him? Surely not! But what did she mean him to do? It might look queer if he showed now that he knew the pearls were there. Why couldn't she have let him know sooner?

Tea provided a diversion. Mrs. Sanders had felt that elaborate cakes were somehow not quite suitable for a family reunion in such tragic circumstances; a good fruit cake and some savoury sandwiches had been provided as more fitting. Gerry Plasher turned the conversation to the portrait which Peter Kutuzov was to paint.

"Beryl will wear her aunt's pearls," Mrs. Pongleton suggested. "And white, I think, Beryl? You look well in white. I hope this Russian artist is really competent. One never can tell with the Russians. Now, if Sir John Lavery could have done it… You mustn't have Beryl made to look a fright, Basil dear."

"Not even Peter could manage that," Gerry assured them cheerfully. "But seriously, Mrs. Pongleton, Peter's very good—not one of those chaps who puts your eyes in one corner of the picture and your ears in the opposite one. He's got a good idea for Beryl's picture—all in pale tones with a very pale blue sky behind, not so blue as her eyes."

"I should have thought a nice rich blue velvet curtain…" put in Mrs. Pongleton.

"I know you'll like it when it's done," Gerry assured her.

"And do you know, Gerry, the pearls are missing?" said Mrs. Sanders dramatically.

"Oh, Mother, don't exaggerate," Beryl protested. "They're not really missing. It's only that Mr. Stoggins doesn't know where they are. They are sure to turn up to-morrow when you go through Aunt Phemia's things—don't you think so, Basil?" Beryl's blue eyes gazed straight into Basil's grey ones, and there seemed to be some special significance in her words.

"Rather!" Basil agreed. "Now I wonder where she would have put them? Under the carpet was a favourite hiding-place for her things, but that would hardly do for pearls." He looked round the room, and his eyes lighted on Tuppy, now snugly settled in his basket at one side of the fireplace.

"Didn't she sometimes hang things up behind the pictures?" Beryl asked.

Basil shot an anxious glance at her and intercepted a look which seemed to imply: I know something, and I'm puzzled, but of course I won't give you away. To hide his embarrassment he whistled to Tuppy, who stirred sluggishly and then picked up the little blue cushion in his mouth, carried it to Basil's feet, and deposited it there.

"I say!" exclaimed Basil. "D'you think the pearls might be in this cushion? Tuppy may have more sense than we've given him credit for. Aunt Phemia kept his basket in her room generally, and she might have sewn the pearls up in the cushion."

"Phemia may have been foolish about her hiding-places, but hardly so scatterbrained as that!" Mr. Pongleton declared.

"But, really," urged Basil, "she did put her things in the queerest places. She thought they were safer if they were somewhere utterly unexpected."

"I think it's possible," Beryl agreed. "And, after all, her idea of hiding things wasn't so foolish, Uncle James. In a boarding-house, with strangers about, one naturally doesn't feel that one's things are so safe as in one's own home. Let's feel the cushion."

"There are such things as banks!" sniffed Phemia's brother.

Basil tossed the cushion across to Beryl, who poked and prodded it. But it was well padded and the pearls had been carefully laid in the middle, so Beryl could feel nothing.

"I could easily unrip it," she suggested.

"I won't have this foolery!" exclaimed Mr. Pongleton in annoyance. "Time enough to look for the pearls in such out-landish places when we have satisfied ourselves to-morrow that they are not in Phemia's own room. And pray why *this* cush-ion? Look at the animal's basket! It's lined with cushions."

"I don't think it's quite nice for us to be ripping Phemia's cushions to bits to look for her pearls when she's not yet laid to rest," said Mrs. Pongleton gently. "I mean, it looks so *impatient*. Perhaps you had better take the basket up to my room, Basil dear. I understand that the little dog is used to sleeping in a bedroom, and, although I don't approve of it, it may be best for to-night. When we get home he will have to be trained in better ways."

"Besides," put in Gerry suddenly, "the police have searched the cushions already!"

"Searched them already!" gasped Basil. "When?"

"Mrs. Bliss told us, when we fetched it this morning, that they had poked and prodded them before they let her take them out of Miss Pongleton's room. Don't you remember, Beryl?"

"Ye—es," agreed Beryl uncertainly. "She did say some-thing like that."

"That settles it!" declared Mr. Pongleton.

Basil picked up the basket and cushions, and made for the door.

"You don't know the room," Beryl pointed out. "I'll come and show you." She followed him out.

As they went upstairs, she whispered, "Are they there?"

"I—er—think so," stammered Basil. He looked at her suspiciously. "How do you know?"

"When I went behind your curtain yesterday to put on my hat, I had to tip the mirror to get at the light. Oh, Basil, what had we better do? I'll help you if I can. Why didn't you trust me?"

"Sorry, Beryl. Tell you the truth, I didn't want to bother you. It's all right, really. I can explain it all—later."

"But what do we do now?" Beryl whispered urgently. "Quick!"

They were in the room which had been assigned to Mrs. Pongleton.

"Don't rush me so," Basil grumbled. "We'd better not find them now—Father would be so mad. And besides, you heard what Gerry said, about the police having searched the basket. You see, the pearls weren't—I mean, they may have been put in after that, and if we find them there it may look fishy. No, I've a better idea. Can you get them out for me, Beryl, like lightning?"

"Come along to my room—it's not very safe here." Beryl, snatching the little blue cushion, hurried along the corridor to her own room, where she seized a pair of scissors and unripped Betty's stitches rapidly.

"Are you sure you've got a safe plan, Basil?"

"Yes, safe as houses; you see——"

"Don't tell me. It may be better for me not to know; but if you want me to help, give me the word."

"You're a brick. Is it undone?—are they there?"

Beryl's fingers searched the kapok. Suddenly Basil laid a hand on her arm. "Fingerprints! Put on gloves!"

Beryl gazed at him aghast. This really gave her the feeling of being involved in some criminal undertaking.

"But no one will look for fingerprints on them if—if—you arrange it properly!"

"You never know what they'll look for," said Basil gloomily. "Best to make sure."

Beryl searched for gloves, and, having put them on, again probed the cushion.

"Yes—here!" Carefully she drew them out.

"Paper, quick!" said Basil anxiously.

Beryl found tissue paper in which she wrapped the pearls, and Basil put the little packet into his breast pocket.

"Please be careful, Basil. I shall be awfully worried till I hear it's all right."

Her blue eyes looked at him appealingly. He almost wished he had confided in her to begin with—some of it, at any rate. It had seemed such a shame to bother her, and now he was bothering her after all. She looked frail and pathetic, he thought, in the black frock which accentuated her delicate fairness and her slender figure and the smooth, pale gold of her hair.

Basil roused himself. "All right, Beryl. I can't tell you how grateful I am. Don't worry. We must go downstairs. I say, what about the damn cushion?"

"I'll sew it up and put it back later. Aunt Susan won't notice that it's not in the basket."

They returned to the sitting-room. Basil was now racking his brains for an excuse for getting away from the family circle, and before long the excuse shrilled through the house with the voice of the telephone bell.

"Mrs. Bodylove to speak to Mr. Basil Pongleton," the maid informed them.

"Mrs. Body...?" Basil's mother could not quite bring herself to pronounce this exotic name.

"It'll be Waddletoes—my landlady, y'know," Basil reassured her, as he hurried rather too joyfully towards the door.

Mrs. Waddilove's fruity voice, thinned and metallicized by the apparatus, jangled in Basil's ear: "There's a young person called to see you, Mr. Pongleton, and won't give her name, and I was all for telling her to call again, but she was that persistent I really didn't know how to get rid of her, so there she is up in your room; settled herself quite at-home-like, and said she didn't mind waiting, so I thought best to let you know, sir."

"Quite right, Mrs. Waddy; thanks very much. Will you tell her that I'll be home soon? Yes, business. Er—what name did you say?"

"I've told you, sir, she won't give 'er name; and if it's business it's a funny sort of business, if you ask me."

"Quite so. I'll be along soon. You did quite right, Mrs. Waddy."

Basil re-entered the sitting-room, dragging on his overcoat with an air of urgency.

"Awf'ly sorry—someone waiting at my rooms to see me on business. Must fly. I'll be here to-morrow morning early to fetch you—about nine-thirty. Good-bye, Mother. 'Bye, Father."

Beryl came to the door with him.

"It's all right," he told her. "There really is someone waiting to see me. Yes—business, I think. But I'll dash up to the Frampton first and see about—you know—putting things right. Good-bye, Beryl. You're a brick!"

Beryl reflected that Basil was not usually so beset with pressing business affairs, especially on Sunday evening.

There was actually a taxi cruising up Haverstock Hill, and Basil, anxiously feeling the loose coins in his pocket with one hand, hailed it with the other. It set him down a few minutes later at the corner of Church Lane—he didn't want all the frumps peering out of the windows to see who was driving up to the boarding-house in a taxi!

Yes, Betty was in. What a blessing! He said he would wait in the lounge hall, and she came to him there after a few moments. He had the little tissue-paper packet in his hand ready; he drew her towards the corner by the front door, and pressed it into her hand.

"Betty, *dear*—you must do it again! Look here, put 'em in her chair—the armchair in the drawing-room; stuff them down the side—get the idea? Can't explain now, but please do just this one thing more for me. Yes, the other was splendid; it wasn't your fault that it got messed up. Can't explain, but I'll tell you all about it later. Thanks most awf'ly; you're a gem; don't know what I should do without you. Someone's waiting to see me at my rooms—business. Must fly!"

Betty kept her head, and only protested gently, "I do wish you weren't always in such a tearing hurry—there are heaps of things I want to ask you. But I'll see to it; to-night will do, I suppose?"

"Yes; good-bye. Family goes home Tuesday morning, and I may have more time then, if I'm still at large. Good-bye! I'll have to go in that beastly underground."

CHAPTER THIRTEEN

MAMIE TURNS UP

MRS. WADDILOVE was evidently on the look-out for Basil, for she heaved herself up out of the basement just as he let himself into the hall of her house in Tavistock Square.

"Well, Mr. Pongleton, I'm sure I'm glad you're back, for I don't like the idea of that young person left alone in your rooms, and that's a fact. And really, the trouble I've had these last few days, what with callers and newspaper men and those nasty perlice nosing around.... Up and down the stairs all the time! It's more than I can stand, and it's not what I'm used to. A friend to lunch or to tea now and again, that's within reason, I've always said; but these last few days I've had no peace at all."

Basil sighed. He knew that it was something more than the mere trouble of answering the door that had chilled Mrs. Waddilove's usual geniality and brought a note of bitter suspicion into her voice.

"I'm most awf'ly sorry, Mrs. Waddy, but I don't want them to call. Confounded bad management, I should say, to keep bothering us again and again like this instead of remembering what they want to know the first time. But have the police been again?"

"That they have, Mr. Pongleton; asking me this and asking me that till really I don't know what I've told them!"

"I hope you've told them the truth, Mrs. Waddy," said Basil, assuming a confidence he did not feel.

"The truth is what I've tried to tell them, as I always tell anyone. And there's no reason that *I* know of why I should tell them anything else." She looked up at him meaningly out of her little peering eyes, deep-set in her plump, flushed face. "What time did you go out on Friday morning, they want to know. I told them before and I've told them again that you went out at ten minutes short of the half hour by my kitchen clock, which isn't more than a few minutes fast, just to be on the safe side. And if you ask me, it's a great pity you didn't stay in bed a bit longer that morning, which wouldn't have been anything out of the ordinary. And did you have a hat on and what sort of a hat? Well, I told them, you're not one to go rushing round a respectable square—and respectable it always has been—without your hat; and if you came back without it—well, what can you expect when anyone's had a nasty shock like you had?"

"Quite so, Mrs. Waddy," Basil agreed. "It was a proper knockout blow. I think I left that bowler at Mrs. Kutuzov's at Golder's Green. D'you say the police asked if I came back without it?"

"Happen it were one o' them journalists asked that. Nosey, they are! And did you pay your rent reg'lar, they asked—that was the perlice. Well, I couldn't say reg'lar, meaning no offence, but you know well, Mr. Pongleton, that many's the time you've owed for a week or more, but I've made no fuss, knowing that your allowance came like clockwork——"

"Good heavens, Mrs. Waddy, do I owe you now? Saturday—of course. My aunt's death seems to have upset everything, you know, and I'd forgotten all about the date." He plunged his hand into his pocket, as the gesture appropriate to the occasion rather than with any hope of finding stray notes there.

"It's not *that* I'm bothering about, Mr. Pongleton," Mrs. Waddilove assured him—"though it's more than one week that's owing, as you may remember. It's all this prying and poking that I don't like, and never have done—not that I've ever been mixed up in things of this kind before. And strange men who look as if they're up to no good everlastingly hanging on the railings opposite. But that's not all. About that letter, they wanted to know...."

Basil made an effort to check the quick look of alarm that he realized he had shot at the garrulous old woman. "What letter, Mrs. Waddy?"

"That letter that came on Friday morning, and got you out of bed in such a hurry. I'm not one of the prying sort, and my gentlemen's letters are no concern of mine, but I couldn't help knowing that I brought a letter up to you that morning with the Hampstead postmark and a hand I've seen often enough before, and how you tore it open before I was out of the room, and shouted down the stairs after me to get your breakfast at once, which I did—and that accounts for you going off so early."

"But, look here, that letter—d'you mean a letter from my aunt?" Ideas whirled through Basil's head like a snowstorm. Was Waddletoes sure that the letter was from Miss Pongleton? Could he put her off the scent, muddle her somehow? What had old Slowgo advised him to say?

"It's not my business to know who your letters are from, and I never was one to be inquisitive," Mrs. Waddilove insisted. "It's not my way to go looking for trouble. But often's the time I've brought you a letter in that hand and you've mentioned, casual-like, that it was from your aunt—poor lady! And I little thinking what was in store for her! But what was in that letter, of course, I know no more than the man in the moon, and so I told those perlice."

"But, Mrs. Waddilove, this is the first I've heard about a letter from my aunt on Friday morning. I did hear from her not long before her death—let's see...I had tea with her on Wednesday, didn't I? She wrote asking me to go, of course, and I think she wrote again after that. Why, I may have the letter upstairs. But surely it came on Thursday? I didn't go to Hampstead on Friday, you know—I went to Golder's Green to see a man about a portrait of my cousin."

"So you told me, Mr. Pongleton; and where you go or don't go is no business of mine. But when the perlice ask questions they have to be answered, and that letter came on Friday, as I know well enough, though what was in it I can't tell."

"I should think it would be better if the police asked me about my own letters," Basil suggested. He feared they would do so only too soon. "But what about my visitor? I'd better go up and see her. Did you say a *young* lady?"

"Not so young, perhaps, as she'd like us to believe, and listening with the door open as like as not to what we've had to say, though I shut it myself, and made sure of it."

Mrs. Waddilove retreated towards her basement whilst Basil leapt up the two flights of stairs, cursing silently.

In his "rooms" he found, as he had expected, Mamie Hadden, lolling at ease in the biggest armchair with a cigarette between her lips—one of his own, he noticed, from the open box beside her—and her rather too fat legs, cased in shiny pink artificial silk, stretched out to the fire. He did not know why he had expected to find Mamie, except that she seemed to represent the only point in his complicated and besetting affairs that had not jabbed him within the last forty-eight hours, so he felt that she was due to turn up soon.

She turned her head towards him, and nodded without taking the cigarette out of her mouth.

"Good evening, Mr. Pongleton-Brown! Thought I'd better see how you were getting along and make sure you weren't forgetting me. Your old lady here was in a fair to-do about letting me in, but I wasn't putting up with any of her airs, so I just said to her: 'I'm an old friend of his and I'm here to see him on important business, and you'll hear about it if you don't let me in!' So here I am!" Mamie's pinched and prim enunciation reminded Basil of his first meeting with her, when he had "picked her up" in a cinema for the sake of having someone to talk to. She had relapsed into broader, more natural accents when they became more friendly.

"I wish you hadn't come!" Basil informed her frankly. It was a relief to tell the truth, if only for a moment. As he noticed Mamie stiffening herself in indignation and even putting her hand up to her mouth to remove the cigarette, he added hastily, "For your own sake chiefly. I didn't want to bring you into this."

"If you didn't want to bring me into it, you should have thought of that sooner, Mr. Clever, and not come asking me to help you pawn those pearls, and then come beggin' me to help you get 'em out agin! When am I likely to get my fifteen poun's back, I'd like to know? I'm a poor girl, an' I can't afford to go throwing my savings down the drain. I might've done the dirty on you over that deal. Those pearls were worth a lot more'n fifteen poun's; we might've got 'em copied so's you'd never've known. Didn't think of that, did you, Mr. Pongleton-Brown?"

"Good Lord!" exclaimed Basil aghast. "D'you mean to say I haven't got the real ones? Oh, Mamie, you wouldn't——"

"Don't you worry yerself," Mamie advised him—"I'm not that sort; but you're that innercent. Not fit to go gettin' yerself mixed up in a dirty business like this."

"But, Mamie——" Basil protested.

"No need to go Mamie-ing me like that. Now just you listen an' I'll explain a few things. You're wondering, p'rhaps, how I foun' my way here and foun' out your right name. Oh, you thought you were sharp, didn't you, Mr. Brown?—but you didn't think your picture'd be in all the papers, an' your name in full—nephew of the victim of the underground murder! No mistaking you, either, with your comic hat an' all."

Basil had chucked the "comic hat"—a black felt, of "Chelsea" character, with wide brim—across the room, and thrown his overcoat over a chair. He stood on the hearthrug looking down at Mamie and wondering how best to deal with her. Mamie, who had always been kind and consoling, had now, like Mrs. Waddilove, "turned nasty". Of course they both suspected him of being concerned in the murder of his aunt, and, instead of trying to shelter him, they could only think of their own petty difficulties.

"Look here, Mamie—I told you I was in a hole when I saw you on Friday night, and you turned up trumps then and helped me. I hadn't forgotten you—after all, that's only the day before yesterday. I haven't had time to get the money yet. Besides, as I told you, I didn't want to bring you into the mess. The police are keeping an eye on me; you see, they haven't caught the murderer yet, whoever he is, and they have to keep their eyes open and watch everyone who might be mixed up in the affair, in the hope of getting a clue. That's why I didn't want to go and see you or you to come here. There's a man on the watch outside this house, and he'll probably follow you when you go away and ask you awkward questions."

Mamie tossed her head. "And you don't want me to tell them all I know about you, Mr. Pongleton-Brown! Of course not!"

Basil seized a humpty, drew it up beside Mamie's chair, and sat there. Her small, plump hand, with stubby fingers and red lacquered nails, lay on the arm of the chair, and he put his own hand over it.

"You've been so kind to me, Mamie, and I've trusted you— surely you won't let me down now?"

"Trusted me!" snorted Mamie. "Couldn't even tell me your right name!"

"What did my name matter, anyway? I went to you when I was in a hole on Friday night, and you helped me, as I knew you would."

Mamie turned her long-lashed, greenish eyes upon him coldly.

"But you knew when you came to me on Friday that the old lady had been murdered, and yet the news wasn't in the papers then!"

"What makes you think I knew?"

"Weren't you in a nice state of mind? I knew something'd upset you, but I didn't know what till later. Then I began to put two an' two together, after I read the news an' saw your picture. The paper said you lived in Tavistock Square. Well,

I've got frien's here, an' it didn't take me long to find out from them where you lived. With that hat, y'see, anyone'd notice you. Nice hat for a murderer, I mus' say!"

"Mamie, you don't really think I could do that horrible thing? Besides, I didn't wear——" He stopped himself abruptly. "Mamie, I swear to you that I had nothing to do with it. If I had, why should I want to get the pearls back? If Aunt Phemia had been alive I should have been able to pay you back before now. Her death hasn't done me any good."

"Don't you get her money?" enquired Mamie.

"What makes you think she had any money? And if she had I don't know whether I get it or whether it goes to my cousin. Anyway, I haven't got any of it yet. Surely you can wait a bit longer, Mamie? My aunt isn't buried yet—that's to-morrow, and they'll read the will after the funeral. But even if she left her money to me, they won't hand me a bag of gold right away."

"I'm not quite so soft as you think," Mamie informed him. "I know all that, but I want some security. I'd like an IOU in your own name, Mr. Basil Pongleton, and that's what I came here for."

"Of course I'll give you that—but you won't hand it over to the police? It wouldn't help you, and it might make things difficult for me. Be a sport, Mamie!"

"Looks as if bein' a sport was goin' to cost me a lot!" Mamie complained, but her voice sounded kinder.

Basil went to his desk and took out some paper. He unscrewed his fountain-pen slowly, meditating. It was risky, but it seemed only fair. Could he trust her? In any case, if she were going to be vindictive and should choose to show his original IOU—in the name of Geoffrey Brown but in his own handwriting—to the police, that might look even more fishy than one in his own name.

Mamie sat polishing her fingernails on the padded arm of the chair. She was, as Mrs. Waddilove had said, not so young as she would like people to think. Basil had never thought of her as young, but she did not suspect that. Her make-up was carefully put on, but exaggerated. There was a metallic glint in the red curls on to one side of which a tiny knitted blue cap was apparently glued. Her skimpy blue coat, with immense "coney" collar, was thrown open and showed a dress of paler blue artificial silk. The three blues just failed to match.

Basil handed her the IOU which he had written out. She glanced at it, folded it, and opened her scarlet handbag, from which she took a soiled paper. Flipping it open under his eyes she scrunched it up and hurled it into the fire.

"Just to show you I'm not cattish—Geoff!" She smiled at him from her tired eyes. "The p'lice would like to get hold of that! Might look fishy!"

"I knew you were a good sort!" Basil exclaimed with relief. He patted her hand, and she turned up her face towards him. He bent down and gave her, without enthusiasm, the kiss she expected.

"But you're a bit of a mug," she added. "You should have asked me for the other one before you gave me this!" She tucked the clean paper into her bag and snapped it shut.

"That'll show you I'm not a hardened criminal but merely a bit of an ass who has got himself into a mess through being short of cash!"

"I dessay. But how am I ter know?"

"You've simply got to go on trusting me, and you shall have the money back with interest—I swear you shall." Basil sat down again beside her. "I didn't fool you over 'Geoffrey'. That really is my name—my second name."

"You didn't fool me at all. I never thought you were Mr. Brown—that's too easy. Now, if it'd bin de Vere, say, I might've believed you. I always had a fancy for a boy friend called de Vere."

"Mamie, you're a dear! We'll go to the pictures again when I'm clear of this mess."

"P'raps you'll be gettin' married when you come into the money?" suggested Mamie, a little sadly.

"Well—yes, I hope so; I don't know if she—if anyone will want to marry me after this. Doesn't make me look much of a hero, does it?"

"Women are all fools," Mamie assured him. "Soft!—that's what we are. Else why'd I do all this for you?"

"Because you're a good sort," Basil told her. "I knew you were, from the moment when I first met you at the pictures, and you've been a brick all through."

"That was *Hearts Aflame*, wasn't it? Soppy sort of picture. A good comic is what I reelly like. Tell you what, you can take me to the new Jack Hulbert; I'd like to see that while it's still at one of those big places where you can't get in under three an' six—makes the other girls a bit jealous to tell them I've been there. It'll just do for our good-bye razzle—and a bit of supper, with some fizzy wine?"

"Rather! But not good-bye?"

"If you're goin' to be married it'd better be good-bye," said Mamie sagely. "Oh, I know there's no harm in it, but who'll believe that? Not your girl! And anyway, you'll want to be takin' *her* out."

"You don't understand what she's like, Mamie. She'll believe me, and she'd like you for having been so kind to me."

"Don't you believe it, and don't you go messin' things up agin by telling 'er anything about me. You men are all alike—think everyone believes you. She'll believe you all right so long as you don't give her anything too difficult, but don't take no risks!"

"I'll have to take some risks when I start explaining things to her. But it'll be all right. You've cheered me up a lot, Mamie. I've had an awful time these last few days—simply hell!"

"I'd better be off." Mamie rose from the chair and began to pull her coat around her and fasten it. The blue cloth hugged her plump figure tightly, and Mamie smoothed it self-consciously.

"I'll just take a look in your glass to do me face," she said, whisking behind the curtain. From the other side her voice continued. "Oh yes, I had a look round while I was waiting. Nice little place you've got here but your old lady downstairs—she's a tartar! I'll get some black looks when I go out; and she'll be prying round and looking at the bed, if she can find an excuse to come up here, I'll be bound!"

"She's all right," Basil said. "But the police have been worrying her, and she's scared of harbouring a criminal."

"The old cat!" Mamie declared.

"That reminds me, the fellow outside may follow you when you go away and ask you who you are and what you know about me and the rest of it. What are you going to tell him?"

"I don't want those busies around my place. Tell you what, have you got a taxi fare on you?"

"Depends how far you want to go," said Basil cautiously. "But you can't throw them off the scent by taking a taxi. They'll get his number, and ask him where he took you."

"You don't think I'd be such a soft as to drive up to me door? I'll just take a bob's worth down the Tot'nam Court Road and hop on a bus, and if they catch me I can tell the tale—came to see you on a matter o' business; your mother's wantin' a companion, isn't she?"

Mamie came out from behind the curtain, giggling with joy, and took a few mincing steps with prim, downcast looks. "Quite the lady, aren't I? Now you go and ring up a taxi, that's a good boy, Geoff!"

Basil hurried downstairs to obey, and Mamie followed more slowly. At the bottom of the staircase she waited, swinging one leg and pointing the toe thoughtfully.

"You'd better not come again, Mamie," he exhorted her after he had rung up the taxi rank and ordered a cab. "Though I'm glad, after all, that you did come this evening. You know, I wanted to see you and tell you it'd be all right, but I didn't know how to do it."

"Don't you worry. I'll sit tight and wait till you come along. I say—they haven't reelly got anything against you, have they? I mean, it's the inquest to-morrow, and these busies—if they can't get the right man they'll get the wrong one, just to show they're doin' something."

"It'll be all right. But I wish they could find the man. The puzzling thing is to find who'd benefit by my aunt's death. That's why they're on to me, you see, because I'm supposed to come into her money."

"M-m." Mamie polished her fingernails against the palm of her hand. "It's funny, the things that'll make people do murder. You'd never believe——Is that the taxi?"

Basil saw her off and hurried upstairs, affecting not to see Mrs. Waddilove, who hovered behind a half-open door.

CHAPTER FOURTEEN

BETTY DECIDES TO COOK THE EVIDENCE

The Sunday after the murder was a harassing day for Betty. It began with the troublesome plans for sending news to Basil of her deed overnight. Then followed a walk over the Heath with Cissie, who enjoyed a thorough review of all the details of the crime known to her and many others imagined by her, and tried to fix the guilt conclusively on a variety of persons, from Mrs. Bliss to Nellie, not excepting Basil. On their return they heard how Beryl and Gerry had called for Tuppy and carried him away with his basket and cushions. That threw Betty into a state of agitation, but after some flurried thinking she came to the conclusion that perhaps it was a good chance. Basil would get her note directly he arrived at Beverley House, and would probably manage to "find" the pearls.

Betty was of a placid temperament, and the minor difficulties which life had so far put in her way she had been able to cope with by practical measures. She was, therefore, disposed to think that every ill could be cured by "doing something". She thought happily that she had successfully done her part towards clearing up Basil's latest schemozzle, and now Basil would doubtless do his and all would be well.

After lunch she settled in a corner of the smoking-room to write her weekly letter home. It was impossible not to mention the murder, and as soon as that subject was let loose, the idea of Basil came to the fore again. Since her walk with him on Saturday evening her mind had been so occupied with practical plans that she had not indulged in much consecutive thought on the whole situation. Now she began to go over what he had told her and try to sort it all out.

Basil went to Golder's Green on Friday morning to see the man who was to paint Beryl's picture. He went home—when was it?—in the afternoon—or the evening, did he say?—and he had some business to see to and then he had supper in Soho because it was too late to go to his rooms for dinner. What did he say about the business? Something he didn't want to tell anyone about at present, which sounded as if it were something to do with his aunt, for Basil was not much occupied with business as a rule, except for interviews with editors, and there was no reason why they should be wrapped in mystery. But how could it be to do with Pongle? Ah, the pearls! It must have been something to do with those pearls. But he didn't know then that his aunt was murdered; he had said that he read it in the paper while he was having supper. He had told Beryl that he had supper with a friend; he had told the police that he also went to see *The Constant Nymph* at the New Vic. But Betty realized that she herself had not been told whether the "friend", the supper-companion, existed or not. The whole affair was very bothering, and why should Basil be driven to all these subterfuges?

He was under suspicion of some kind, or thought he was. There must be some cause. Could it be that he knew who murdered his aunt? That he was trying to shelter them in some way? Betty was really fond of Basil; sufficiently fond of him to be able to look squarely at his weaknesses and accept them as part of him. Also she trusted him, though it may seem strange that anyone who had much to do with Basil should trust him.

She believed that in spite of all his prevarications and evasions and reluctance to tell anyone, even her, the whole truth about anything, he would not deceive her about any truly important matter. She felt sure, too, that he was incapable of crime or brutality, but generosity, perhaps misplaced—that was exactly in Basil's line. The more she thought about it the plainer it seemed to her that the whole puzzle could be explained by the theory that Basil had in some way found out—probably before the news was in the papers—about his aunt's murder and who the murderer was, and that he was determined to shield that person at all costs.

Betty was pleased at having found a key to the mystery, but it did not abolish her worry. She was vague about criminal law, but surely the shielding of such a criminal must be punishable in some way, she thought. And whom could he be so anxious to protect? He must feel that there was some strong extenuation, some cause which had driven the murderer to desperation beyond control. Betty could only think of Bob Thurlow. She believed that Pongle had probably threatened him with exposure and frightened him badly; perhaps Nellie had been threatened also with dismissal and disgrace. Betty had never been able to see Bob as a murderer—but who else could it be? Bob, rather a noodle, scared and helpless, without influential friends to help him, would be just the person whose plight would appeal to Basil's mistaken chivalry. For although Betty felt a glow of sympathy for what she had decided was Basil's readiness to bring suspicion on himself and get himself into a thorough mess in the hope of saving Bob, yet at the same time her commonsense told her that it was a foolhardy thing to do.

It was difficult to see just where the pearls came in, but Bob had stolen—or helped to steal—a brooch, and perhaps he had stolen the pearls too, and Basil was trying to help him to conceal that theft by restoring them.

Was it possible, in a purely material way, for Bob to have committed the crime? was Betty's next question to herself. The general idea was that the police did not believe Bob to be guilty. They seemed to be looking for someone else, but perhaps that was only because there was some hiatus in their evidence against him—a hiatus which Basil's knowledge could fill. Betty marshalled the facts relative to Bob: his motive; his presence in the underground passage near the foot of the staircase just before the crime; his possible knowledge, through Nellie, of Pongle's plans that morning; the dog-leash—ah! it was still uncertain, so far as Betty knew, when the dog-leash had been taken.

Nellie was sure the leash had been in the hall on Thursday night but not on Friday morning. Nellie, of course, might be protecting Bob, who was known to have waited in the lounge hall at the Frampton on Thursday evening, soon after dinner, to see Pongle.

Betty suddenly scrunched up the sheet of paper on which she had been drawing patterns to help out her thoughts, and hurled it with good aim into the fire. Hurriedly she scribbled a few sentences to conclude her letter to her mother, which she then sealed and addressed. She had left her stamps upstairs, she remembered.

As Betty came out of her bedroom a few minutes later with the stamped letter in her hand, Nellie passed along the corridor ahead of her, in hat and coat. It was her Sunday evening out.

"Please, Nellie," Betty called after her, "would you post this letter for me?"

Nellie turned and came back to Betty's door to take the letter.

"Seems dismal-like," she confided to Betty, "havin' no one to go out with. But I'm goin' to see Bob's fam'ly—maybe they can tell me 'ow 'e's gettin' on. Mr. Plasher's bin very kind—I 'spect you've 'eard, miss—gettin' 'im a lawyer an' all."

"I'm very glad, Nellie, and I hope it'll turn out all right. Have the police been asking you any more questions? You told them, I suppose, that you remembered seeing the leash in the hall on Thursday night and not on Friday morning?"

"I tol' 'em that, miss, the very first, an' they did ast a lot about it then. About Wednesday, too; you know Bob an' me come in an' put our names to a paper for Miss Pongleton—'er will it was, Bob said, but Mr. Plasher says no. Mr. Basil 'ad bin 'ere to tea with 'er, but 'e'd gone before we came in and brought the leash back. Seems no one took Tuppy out on Thursday, it bein' so wet, so no one noticed perticler whether it was there or no, but I saw it for certin sure that night when I put Mr. Grange's umbereller in the stand. The p'lice've bin astin' a lot o' questions about that Thursday night, an' I 'ear they're comin' agin to-night to ast some more. I'm sure I wish it was all over, an' I expec' you do too."

"What do they want to know about Thursday night?"

Nellie seemed embarrassed. "Well, miss, it wasn't me as told 'em." The girl cast anxious glances up and down the corridor, and Betty, thinking uneasily that she ought not to stand gossiping with Nellie, but curious to know what more she had to say, retreated into her room with Nellie following. Betty sat on the edge of her bed, and Nellie, fumbling with her hand-bag, opening it and snapping it shut again, continued:

"A-course, miss, you know you was the las' one in on Thursday night. None of the others wasn't out—not late; an' the door was left unbolted for you. Well, miss, a-course no one knows but you what happened when you come in that night!"

"Nellie!" The exclamation was so sharply interrogative that Nellie raised her eyes for a moment to meet Betty's brown ones that gazed at her, puzzled, perhaps a little angry. "What do you mean? Nothing *happened*. What do you think happened?"

"Well, miss, I didn't mean no 'arm, but I thought p'r'aps as you ast me about it you'd better know that the p'lice are comin' to-night to ast about it. Mrs. Bliss was astin' everyone about who locked up that night—yesterday evenin' it must've bin, when you were out with Mr. Basil. Miss Fain, I think it was, told 'er you went to the pikchers on Thursday night with Mr. Basil an' 'e saw you 'ome. Oh, miss, that's all. I don' know anything—an' I think I'd better go now."

"Wait a minute," Betty commanded severely. "I don't understand why you think this is important. The police came and questioned us all on Friday night, as you know, and they asked everyone about Thursday night, and seeing the leash, so of course they know I was out late. That's all there is to it. I didn't notice the leash, one way or another. I wish I had noticed. Yes, you'd better go now; you're late." As Nellie edged away, Betty added more gently, "Don't worry—it will all come straight."

Nellie hung on the door-handle with her head inside the room for a moment, to declare earnestly, "I'm sure I 'ope so, too, miss. An' I 'aven't said a word, not to a soul, an' not a word will I say!" With this mysterious declaration she slipped away, leaving Betty to ponder with a puzzled frown over what might be in the girl's mind.

As a matter of fact, something *had* happened in the lounge hall of the Frampton on Thursday night when Basil brought Betty home. It was an event of some importance to Betty, but she could not see that it had any possible bearing on the crime, nor could she believe that Nellie, or anyone else beyond Basil and herself, knew of it. Basil had stepped inside the door and had kissed her—spasmodically and with slightly inaccurate aim, for he was nervous, and a little doubtful as to how she would take it. His only previous experience of kissing was of the casual sort which Mamie understood and took as a matter of course, giving him every assistance. Now this experience became useless as he realized that Betty's reaction to the kiss was going to matter terribly. Betty had done rather more than receive the kiss passively, but, almost immediately, after a quick hug, she had bundled him outside the door, blown him another kiss, and then locked and bolted the door upon him and tiptoed up to bed in a pleasant flutter of excitement.

In her first interview with Inspector Caird on Friday evening Betty had told him that she came in alone on Thursday night, locked and bolted the door, and went straight up to bed, not noticing whether the dog-leash was on the umbrella stand or not. It had not occurred to her that the presence of Basil in the hall for a moment was of any importance, one way or another, and so far as the world in general was concerned, she had come in alone. Now the inspector was apparently going to question her further about that evening. He knew, evidently, that Basil had come up to Hampstead with her that night; Basil himself may have mentioned it, or Mrs. Bliss may have heard of it from the expansive Cissie and passed it on.

The idea in the inspector's mind, thought Betty, was that Basil took the leash from the hall on that night before the murder. Apart from Betty's inability to believe that Basil could have connived at the murder beforehand—much less committed it—she was positive that he could not have taken anything from the hall on that romantic occasion. He had only just stepped inside the door. She knew well that his arms were fully occupied. She had pushed him out and locked the door immediately afterwards. But how explain all that to an inspector, even a comparatively human one? Wouldn't it be safer to stick to her original story—told, not with intent to deceive but because it was the truth, Betty said to herself, so far as inspectors and such outsiders were concerned? If Basil were questioned he was sure to say that he didn't go inside the door. He would realize that to admit that he did go inside would incriminate him and perhaps bring suspicion upon Betty too.

"Confound it!" Betty muttered. "If only I had had more time to talk to Basil I might be sure about that!" But it must be all right. She would have heard before now if there had been any discrepancy between her story and Basil's. Had she better telephone to him to make sure? No, that was too risky; he would be at Beverley House and couldn't answer freely. And if the police found that she had been telephoning to him, that might arouse their suspicions. No, she was sure it was safe to say that he didn't come in; and really true in spirit, too, if not in fact.

Betty went downstairs to tea, taking with her a new detective story which she had obtained from Mudie's before the Pongleton affair had linked detective stories with life as Betty knew it. She tried to settle down to read it after tea, but it didn't sound right. There was a lot of telephoning in the book—that seemed true to life—but all these people were provided with telephones through which they could have confidential conversations with others at any moment without fear of being overheard. What a blissful state of affairs, thought Betty with some annoyance.

She was interrupted by Basil's hasty call to hand over the pearls to her once more. His interview with her was so startling, and so rapid, that it was only when he was sprinting away again down Church Lane that she realized that she might have asked him what he had said to the police about Thursday night. Too late! She could never catch him up now, and someone was sure to notice her if she dashed out after him. She returned to the sitting-room, where Mr. Slocomb—comfortably settled in the chair to which his right now seemed firmly established—Mrs. Daymer in her draughty seat opposite, and Cissie on the sofa, were engaged in desultory conversation.

"I wonder whether the police will find that other will to-morrow," mused Mrs. Daymer. She looked across severely at Mr. Slocomb, who was working out a crossword puzzle. "*You* should be able to think where it might have been put," she informed him—"your mind being attuned to the solution of problems. But I have often noticed that the working out of abstract formulae is not necessarily conducive to an understanding of human nature."

Everyone in the Frampton had heard by now of Beryl's and Gerry's visit that morning to fetch Tuppy, and of Nellie's chance remark about witnessing what appeared to be Miss Pongleton's latest will.

Mr. Slocomb looked up from the dictionary. "I believe that it is not so much a question of understanding human nature as a matter of accident. Miss Pongleton had no system in her habit of concealing things in odd places; it was purely capricious. It is quite probable that someone will light upon the hiding-place of this will—if it exists—by the merest chance."

"That is likely," agreed Mrs. Daymer coldly. "Chance may, of course, intervene when human perspicuity fails. But if we could simplify our lives and get more closely in touch with nature, we might understand *people* better, and depend less upon the vagaries of chance. All my best work has been done in a simple cottage in the Cotswolds; the place *breathes* craftsmanship; a constant reminder of man's true function— creation, honest workmanship. It is good for the style, keeps it simple." Mrs. Daymer drew her peacock-hued scarf of hand-woven silk higher up on her shoulders and shivered delicately. "But we are degenerate; we are ill-fitted to bear the rigours of life which our forefathers barely noticed. Though I am bound to say that as regards the exclusion of draughts, with all the ingenuity of modern invention, we have not yet reached perfect accomplishment." She shot a glance of envy at the opposite chair.

Cissie was sprawling on the sofa, waggling her feet. Her theory that this exercise improved the shape of her ankles gave her an excuse for indulging in it conspicuously when she was bored.

"I wish we could hunt for the will," she suggested. "I suppose Pongle's room is still locked up? It would give us something to do and it would be too thrilling if we found it and it turned out that Pongle had left her money to someone quite different."

"There's no reason to suppose that she ever thought of leaving it to anyone except Basil or Beryl," Betty reminded her. "And then she often made wills and tore them up, I've heard, so this one that Nellie witnessed on Wednesday may not be in existence now."

"As between Basil Pongleton and his cousin, Miss Sanders, I believe it will make no difference as to which of them ultimately inherits the money," announced Mrs. Daymer incautiously. She wanted the others to listen to her, and had been disappointed when craftsmanship and draughts had failed to draw any response.

"What do you mean?" asked Cissie, bringing her feet down on to the floor, and thereby levering herself into a more upright position. "You can't mean—Basil and Beryl—but she's engaged to Gerry—whatever?"

"I mean," said Mrs. Daymer deliberately, "that Miss Sanders is quite well off, whereas Mr. Basil Pongleton is not exactly affluent, and has not so far met with much success—financially—in his authorship; perhaps he has not yet found his own line. Miss Sanders is of a generous disposition—I have observed that—and I do not think she would allow her cousin to be deprived, through some caprice of their aunt's, of money which everyone believes to have been intended for him."

"I don't see that all that amounts to much," said Cissie ungraciously. "Beryl may be generous, but who would give up money once they'd got it? Even if you're well off you can't have too much."

"And perhaps Basil wouldn't take it," said Betty, underestimating Basil's conviction of his genuine right to the money.

"But the Wednesday will, if discovered, may have some quite different content," remarked Mrs. Daymer with great significance.

"D'you think she really left it all to someone quite different and they've murdered her?" enquired Cissie.

"There's no knowing," declared Mrs. Daymer. "But you may feel assured that if the Wednesday will"—she liked that phrase—"merely names Miss Sanders, instead of Mr. Basil Pongleton, as legatee, it will make no real difference in the ultimate destination of the money."

Mrs. Bliss looked in. "Miss Watson, you won't be going out any more to-day, I suppose? And you too, Miss Fain?"

Betty shook her head.

"We'll stay put," Cissie assured Mrs. Bliss. "What's up?"

"The police inspector wishes to see you both; he'll be here any time now; he thought you might be able to clear up some little points. Dear, dear! They don't seem able to fit things together. It's all very confusing, I'm sure. About some letter Miss Pongleton wrote; I thought you might have posted it, Miss Fain. She'd sit up writing letters at night—the electricity she must have used! But we mustn't grudge it her now, poor lady! I know she often gave them to you to post in the morning."

Cissie's mouth fell open and her tongue shot out a little way. It was a grimace which she often made when suddenly reminded of something about which her conscience was not easy. It had led to her abrupt dismissal from her first job, for insolence, but even after that she had not cured herself of it. Mrs. Bliss did not notice this sign of confusion because she had come into the room and was shaking up a cushion here, pulling a curtain straight there, and generally "putting things to rights".

"I declare I miss that little animal," she murmured. "He may have been a nuisance, but the house doesn't seem the same without him. Poor little fellow! I hope he has a kind home. The Yorkshire climate is very severe, and they say dogs feel a change the same as humans. They know a lot, and we ought to be careful how we treat them."

"Do you feel a draught, Mrs. Daymer?" asked Mr. Slocomb suddenly. "A window?"

"No, no!" declared Mrs. Daymer, blandly wagging her head from side to side. "I am a great believer in the beneficial effects of fresh air."

Mrs. Bliss had put all the furnishing accessories in order and sailed away.

"What's up, Cissie?" Betty enquired. "Did you forget to post a letter?"

"Well, I did," Cissie admitted. "But I posted it later. Pongle gave me a letter to Basil to post on Thursday morning. I expect she wrote it late on Wednesday night, as Blissie said. She wouldn't give it to you to post, you know, because, although you were more certain to do it, Pongle seemed to think you might put a spell on it so that it would say samething different by the time it got to Basil. Anyhow, I forgot it and I found it in my bag when I got home that evening, and I actually went out again and posted it, before I'd seen Pongle, so that I could tell her without blushing that it had been done."

"Cheer up!" Betty admonished her. "They won't arrest you for having forgotten to post a letter. Was that the only one? It doesn't sound as if it had anything to do with the case."

"I don't think I posted another one. I hadn't thought any more about that one till just now."

"It's not such an unusual event, after all," said Betty rather unkindly. "You've forgotten to post lots of letters before this. Sure there's not another one still in your bag?"

Betty was trying to stifle her own anxiety by building up suggestions about other letters and the unimportance of this one. A letter from his aunt which would reach Basil on Friday morning! She couldn't see the exact significance of it, but it certainly seemed likely that it had something to do with his strange behaviour on that dreadful day.

"Of course!" exclaimed Cissie, loudly and triumphantly.

The others all stared at her.

"Pongle was annoyed with Basil on Wednesday for some reason—he came to tea with her and upset her somehow. She made another will on the spot—the one Nellie witnessed—and wrote to tell Basil. That's just what she would do: 'Naughty boy, you shan't have my money!' sort of thing. I thought there was a spiteful look in her eye when she gave me that letter. So there is another will—and perhaps Basil knows where it is! Too romantic!"

"In whose favour, I wonder?" enquired Mrs. Daymer solemnly.

"I'm sick of all this talk about wills," Betty declared. "Can't we think of something else? How is your new book progressing, Mrs. Daymer?"

"The atmosphere during the last few days has not been conducive to work, but it goes pretty well. By the way, I have to take a journey to the Midlands to-morrow; a matter of local colour. I am rather particular about local colour. People's surroundings influence their thoughts more than you would believe, and I want to get a fresh impression of a Midlands manufacturing town. That is the sort of place in which a tendency to crime is born."

"Oh, do you think Mr. Blend did the murder? He used to have a shop in Rugby—or was it Birmingham?" said Cissie.

"In that district, I believe," agreed Mrs. Daymer. "But not all the inhabitants of a manufacturing town are susceptible to its debasing influence. Yet how much better we should all be if we breathed unpolluted air and saw branches against the blue sky every morning."

"That would be rather a question of weather, I should think," said Betty with extreme politeness of manner which concealed weariness and exasperation.

At that moment Mrs. Bliss came back to announce that the inspector was here to see Miss Fain. Cissie heaved herself off the sofa with a sigh.

"I suppose I must confess?"

"Oh yes," said Betty, wishing she could give some other advice. "Get the crime off your chest and it will soon be over."

"From my own experience of being questioned by the police in this case," announced Mr. Slocomb cautiously, "I should say that they are better pleased if you answer their questions briefly and to the point, without volunteering any conjectures which may seem to you to be of value but to which they do not attach any special significance."

"Don't tell them more than I must, you mean?" Cissie, who had stood on one leg by the door to listen to Mr. Slocomb's advice, swung out.

Betty was glad Mr. Slocomb had given that advice, with his usual fondness for offering wise counsel. Certainly there was no need to put unnecessarily incriminating ideas about the subject of that letter into the inspector's head. Her own turn would come next, she supposed. She clasped her handbag firmly. Rather a joke to go and answer the inspector's questions demurely, with those pearls in her bag under his very nose!

Cissie's interview was short. She sank on to the sofa again with a sigh. "Not so bad! Now he wants you." Betty walked out resolutely, saying to herself over and over again: "Basil did not come inside the door."

Whilst she was talking to the inspector in the smoking-room she heard the supper bell ring, so she was not surprised to find the drawing-room empty on her return. She paused for a moment, until she had heard the front door bang and felt sure that Inspector Caird was out of the way. Then she stuffed the tissue-paper packet down the side of what had been Miss Pongleton's chair and went to join Cissie at supper.

CHAPTER FIFTEEN

BASIL REPORTS PROGRESS

As Mr. Slocomb reached the corner of Church Lane at half a minute after nine on Monday morning, he saw Basil hurrying across Rosslyn Hill from the direction of Hampstead underground station.

"Hullo!" Basil panted as he came within earshot. "Things have been getting a bit hot, but it's not so bad. Your advice did help."

"Considering the mesh of deception in which you have entangled yourself, that is fortunate—very fortunate!" said Mr. Slocomb severely as they strode together towards Holly Hill. Basil noticed that his companion, without any apparent effort, kept pace, by an easy gliding movement, with his own long strides.

"I've got six—no, seven—special points to tell you about. Been going over them in the train. The police came last night——"

"Ah!" said Mr. Slocomb. "To Tavistock Square?"

"You say 'Ah!' as if you'd sent them!" complained Basil. "Yes; to my rooms; two of 'em, and asked me politely to accompany them to the police-station as they thought I could give them further information which might throw some light on the crime. Hypocrites! Well, I went quietly, as the saying is—as quietly as their car would take me, but it was one of those noisy popping brutes. There they had what they call an identification parade, I think—I'm getting awfully good at all the crime lingo. I was lined up with a lot of others—and, by Jove! it gives you a pretty poor opinion of yourself to see the specimens that the police pick out as being roughly of the same type as yourself! There were two fellows came and looked at us. One of them I didn't know from Adam, and he didn't seem to know me either, which was a bit of a relief. But I'm sure he was there to identify me, though the police didn't say so. He kept dodging about and squinting at us from all angles, and I think the police were pretty fed up with him for making himself so conspicuous."

"You are sure you have no knowledge of him? Hm! Possibly he saw you at Belsize Park station?"

"Yes; I thought of that. Anyway, he didn't recognize me again. Then the other chap gave us the once-over and picked me out pretty soon. He turned out to be the ticket collector at Golder's Green. Pity I didn't get my hair cut yesterday—he asked us to take our hats off and swore that I hadn't a hat on when I left Golder's Green platform on Friday morning. That's why he noticed me specially, I think—that and having a ticket only to Hampstead."

"Your bowler hat," said Mr. Slocomb, his enunciation icily distinct, "which you profess to have left at Mrs. Cut-us-off's house, was—er—discarded at some earlier point. The stairs?"

"No, no! I can't have taken it off there. I've thought about it and I'm sure. Must have left it in the train. But I can't see that it matters much. No one could identify my bowler for certain; there must be hundreds like it."

"It is hardly possible that hundreds of bowler hats were recklessly abandoned in an underground train on the Hampstead line on Friday morning," Mr. Slocomb pointed out meticulously.

"I dunno. It's a thing anyone might do—take it off and forget it."

"I fear you under-estimate the abnormality of your behaviour," Mr. Slocomb insisted.

"The police didn't, you'll be pleased to know," Basil told him. "They were very inquisitive about that bowler. As if I hadn't a right to get rid of an old hat and go without one when I want to! I told them I thought I'd left the beastly thing at Kutuzov's, and anyway I never wanted to see it again, and the inspector said, 'I can well believe that!' in a nasty kind of way."

"Perhaps the best we can hope for is that someone—er—annexed your hat and will never produce it. Hm! Any enquiries about the time of your arrival at Golder's Green?"

"Nothing special. Seems pretty clear the ticket collector doesn't know just when I passed him. Someone else who hasn't always got an eye on the clock, y'see! But I thought of what I'd told Delia about getting to her house at ten, so I remarked, quite by the way, to the inspector that I got to Golder's Green station at ten to ten. Good, that!"

"And what else occurred?" asked Mr. Slocomb.

"The inspector asked me about the ticket. What ticket had I taken at Warren Street? Must say you helped me there. I remembered your bright idea, and I gasped out, as surprised as could be, 'By Jove! Was that the morning I booked to Hampstead by mistake?' The inspector said, as dry as dust, 'Possibly, Mr. Pongleton, it was!' So I told him the tale, as you suggested. Used to booking to Hampstead, go there often to see my aunt, did it out of habit. It seemed to go down pretty well, though he was a bit sarcastic about why I hadn't mentioned all this before. That's the second point I had to tell you about. That all right?"

"At least you do not seem to have made matters worse," conceded Mr. Slocomb. "The first man, who failed to identify you…Hm! Ah! Now, the next point?"

"The next is deuced queer. They measured my shoes! Didn't seem to give 'em much satisfaction. Suppose they've got a footprint somewhere, but how and where beats me! And that reminds me—Mrs. Waddletoes told me they asked to go into my room and took a look at my shoes there, when I was out."

Mr. Slocomb looked worried. "I do not understand this at all, but apparently this investigation led nowhere? That is the third point."

"Yes. The fourth one is more awkward. They asked a lot of questions about the dog-leash. First of all, on Wednesday: did I see it there when I had tea with my aunt? I know it wasn't there then, for the girl and her young man had taken the poodle out and they didn't get back till after I had gone. Then Thursday: the police knew already that I went out with Miss Watson. They asked me about going back with her to the Frampton: did I go inside the house? After a bit I saw what they were driving at—that might have been the moment when I got hold of the leash! I didn't think of that immediately because I had it in my head that everyone thought Bob Thurlow took it earlier that evening when he called to see my aunt about the brooch. Well, actually I did go inside the door that night, but only for a moment. However, everyone's been telling me these last two days that I only make things worse by not telling the truth, and I thought they'd have got at Betty for certain, and she's most frightfully truthful; bound to tell them right out that I did go into your beastly lounge hall. So I confessed to that, but swore it was only for a minute and said they could ask Miss Watson and she'd tell them the same. They looked a bit queer at that. Surprised, I suppose, that my story agreed with someone else's!"

"Hm!" Mr. Slocomb grunted. "Unfortunate, very! But that was probably the best thing to say. It is regrettable that you did not think of that incident before. Miss Watson—hm! I don't know!"

"Can't do any more about that, can I?"

Mr. Slocomb paced on in silence for a few minutes and then announced suddenly: "I am convinced, Mr. Pongleton, that I did notice the absence of the leash earlier that evening. I understand that no one else in the Frampton knows whether it was there or not after young Thurlow called. I have already mentioned to the inspector that to the best of my belief it was not there. The girl, Nellie, says that it was, but of course she is concerned to deflect suspicion from her young man. Yes, I think I can call to mind a little detail which would clinch my assurance and convince the police."

"But, I say—that will make the case blacker against Bob. I don't want to do that."

"I fear, Mr. Pongleton, that you yourself are in sufficient difficulty to make me feel that I—er—should not be justified in withholding any shred of evidence which might be of assistance in—er—exculpating you."

"I don't like it. You might wait and see how things turn out. But how's time going? I have to call for my people at half-past nine."

They were now walking down Heath Street, having circled the Leg of Mutton pond. "We must waste no time," Mr. Slocomb agreed.

"There's not much more. They asked about Aunt Phemia's letter on Friday morning; seemed to know all about it, so I owned up to having got it and said, as you suggested, that Aunt Phemia wrote it in a fit of annoyance and told me she had made a new will and cut me out of it. Also said that I tore it up, being fed up about it. That went down well, I think, though again they were a bit sniffy because I had, as they said, 'kept this important information to myself' for a time. And did I know that actually her latest will so far discovered was in my favour? I told them I had heard that and it gave me a pleasant surprise. Had I any idea where another will might be?— Not the faintest; stuffed up the chimney perhaps! They'll be searching like mad for another will now, I suppose—do me out of the cash if they can't hang me!"

"It may be just as well if they do find it," Mr. Slocomb suggested.

"Better of two evils! Maybe! It struck me, it's a queer thing that the first time I ever asked your advice was about money— d'you remember? You gave me a good tip about investing tuppence ha'penny, and you said you'd be glad to help me if I ever had any more to invest. I've thought of that during this weekend and, by Jove! if I do get Aunt Phemia's money I'll come to you with the lot and get you to stow it away safely for me."

"You might do worse," said Mr. Slocomb modestly. "Your aunt was—er—I might say, conservative in her ideas about investment, and was not willing to take my advice. Otherwise, I flatter myself, her fortune might have been considerably increased. I shall be only too pleased to help you at the appropriate time. Now I think you have mentioned five points, Mr. Pongleton. There are two more?"

"Yes. Let's see. They asked me a lot of questions at the end about Friday evening—just what I did. I was careful to tell them the same story, with a few more details about the New Vic.—what the film was and so on; they got rather bored with that. And, by the way, I've fixed that with Beryl—she won't say anything that doesn't agree with what I say. There were some of the old questions about Friday morning—when I left my rooms and so on. I think I did that part quite well and there's nothing special to report. All quiet on that front!"

"The inspector appeared to be—er—satisfied?"

"Of course he isn't really fond of me, but I don't think he caught me out on anything."

"That was the sixth point? Not exactly a point perhaps——"

"Just a sixth thing to tell you. Now the seventh point is one of my own. What about that notebook? You remember you wrote down a lot of things I told you in my rooms on Saturday, and you said you'd destroy those notes?"

Mr. Slocomb indulged in a dry chuckle. "So you are learning the need for caution! You need have no anxiety on that score, my young friend! You may realize, perhaps, that the whole affair is irregular, highly irregular, and I have no wish to be known to be concerned in any way in what might seem to be—er—an attempt to deceive the police authorities. Such an occurrence would be most distasteful to me! You have not, of course, mentioned to anyone that you have—er—confided in me?"

"Good heavens, no!"

"It might arouse—er—suspicion if we were thought to be—ah!—plotting together." Again that dry chuckle. "I may say that nothing but my regard for your aunt and my respect for your family, mingled with my concern for your own embarrassing situation and my—er—complete confidence in your innocence, would have persuaded me, perhaps against my better judgment, to connect myself with the affair at all."

"Of course I'm awf'ly grateful to you and all that, and I'll never forget it," Basil assured him.

"Well, well; I shall not neglect that notebook. I may need to refer to it again, but it shall certainly be destroyed in due course. And naturally the notes therein are quite—er—harmless. Merely a few jottings as to times of events. Here we are at the underground. I do not think there is any cause for undue anxiety. The situation seems to be developing—er—as satisfactorily as can be expected. Good morning, Mr. Pongleton!"

Basil strode on down Rosslyn Hill feeling that he was managing affairs rather well.

CHAPTER SIXTEEN

GERRY CAUSES ANXIETY

BERYL and Gerry slipped away from the inquest on Monday morning before the verdict was given. It was a dark grey day, soused with slanting rain, and the grey Alvis stood outside St. Pancras coroner's court with its hood up. Beryl, in a leather coat buttoned up to her chin, ran out of the court and through the old burial ground with her head down and bolted into the car like a rabbit, closely followed by Gerry. In a moment they were shooting along the crowded road towards Euston, Beryl at the wheel.

Two women, who had failed to find places in the court and stood waiting at the door in the hope of satisfying their ghoulish curiosity by staring at the principal characters in the Pongleton affair, saw the hurried departure of Beryl and Gerry.

"My dear! That's the car we saw behaving so oddly on the North Circular Road yesterday," one of them declared.

"Behaving oddly? I don't remember. What was it doing?"

"*You* know—it was just in front of us and it slowed down with practically no warning at all and drew into the side."

"Oh yes! And you nearly ran into it!"

"Indeed I did not! I avoided it very skilfully considering how it behaved. The driver ought to be very grateful to me. But I took a good look at it."

"Well, I couldn't be sure of the car myself, though it certainly was like that one. Did you see its number?"

"I can't say I could repeat the number from memory, though I'd know it if I saw it written down, but it was DV—I'm certain of that, because it seemed so suitable.

And—that—was—the—man!" The speaker evidently considered the identification to be of great significance.

"Can't say I looked at him particularly."

"But I did. When he stopped the car, he and the woman with him took out notebooks and began writing in them. Most extraordinary behaviour!"

"Was that the girl?"

"No—that's the strange thing. It wasn't a girl, but a middle-aged woman, all wrapped in woollies and rough sort of clothes. *You* know—sort of arty."

"Who d'you think she was?"

"I can't say, but there's more in this than meets the eye. That young man's the one who's engaged to the old lady's niece, and not only that, but he admits that he went down those stairs on Friday morning and passed the old lady, and no one saw her alive after that. I wonder he's still at liberty! And now look at him—dashing off like that before the inquest's over. I shall tell the police about this. It's my duty!"

The speaker, well satisfied that, although she had missed the inquest, she had created for herself a speaking part in the drama, went to seek a policeman.

Meanwhile the Alvis was nosing its way to Euston. Beryl was a clever but rather reckless driver, sliding the car through the cumbersome traffic with a nonchalant air. Gerry loyally professed perfect faith in her driving, though it often gave him bad moments.

Gerry had arranged with Beryl on Sunday that she should drive him to Euston and take the Alvis back to Beverley House. "Urgent business," he had said to her—"and confidential. I'll explain on the way to the station."

"Urgent business has become a sort of disease," Beryl had thought. "Gerry has caught it from Basil."

"It is business," Gerry told her, as they drove to Euston, "but not Oundle, Gumble, and Oundle's business. It's to do with the murder, and it's really nothing to do with me at all. It's awfully difficult to explain and I hate making a mystery of it to you, Beryl. After Basil's mysterious complications I expect you're about fed up with mysteries, but I can't tell you the whole story because it affects two other people."

"You needn't tell me a thing if you don't want to. I'll take it on trust," Beryl assured him. But she did sound a bit fed up, he thought.

"I'd rather give you an idea of it. It's like this: someone, whom we'll call X, has more or less accidentally discovered something about another person, Q, which may have some bearing on the crime. But the connection is so far-fetched that one really can't take the information to the police as it stands, especially as Q doesn't seem, so far, to be concerned in the affair at all." He thought he detected a faint sigh of relief from Beryl at that.

"X is going to make some enquiries which may clear it up a bit," Gerry continued, "and I'm just going to help. If we get anything more definite we'll pass it on to the police."

"If your enquiries are successful will it mean that you've found who the murderer was?"

"I can't say that. Honestly it all sounds a bit unlikely to me. I'm inclined to think that X is after a red herring."

"Is it worth going?"

"It may not be, in one sense; but I think it's better that X should not go alone. I mean to be back to-night. I've had to tell old Gumble that I wanted the day off to attend to business matters for you. I'm sorry about that; I suppose I might have asked for the rest of the day without giving any reason, leaving him to guess that I wanted to attend the funeral, but Gumble almost put the words into my mouth and made no bones about it."

"If you don't get back to-night, shall I know where you are?" asked Beryl. There was a hint of complaint in her voice and Gerry feared she was taking it badly, though he knew she wouldn't make any fuss.

"But I *shall* be back. I'm not taking any luggage. If I am delayed—but that's impossible—I'll telephone. You mustn't worry, Beryl darling. There's no danger or anything of that kind, and I'll tell you all about it when I come back. I do hope you won't have a too beastly day, and that it won't create a bad impression, my not being at the funeral. I say, you've got me here in ripping time."

The car skidded round on the swimming road to draw up against the pavement outside Euston station.

"Good-bye, darling; you're an angel!" Gerry extricated himself from the car with the neatness of long practice and sped into the booking-hall. Beryl drove away, reflecting that the chief qualification for angelic status seemed to be a readiness to do odd jobs for distraught young men without asking too many questions.

She returned to St. Pancras coroner's court in case the inquest was not yet over. Leaving the car outside the old graveyard, she found people gathered in a hesitating group at the entrance of the court, buttoning up coats and opening umbrellas. Pushing her way through this throng to the gloomy hall, she saw her mother, her Aunt Susan, and Uncle James standing uncertainly in a corner, looking around and making incomplete remarks. It was clear to Beryl that Aunt Susan was "in a fuss".

"Oh, Beryl dear!" Aunt Susan hailed her. "I am so glad you've come back. The police want to see Gerard again, and really they have been in quite a state over the way the two of you vanished suddenly like that."

Uncle James was "shushing" his wife fiercely; her high-pitched voice, with a slight gasp of anxiety in it, had caught the attention of the loiterers at the door, and some of them turned round to look inquisitively at Beryl and her relatives, whilst others pointed at the little muddy grey car drawn up against the pavement, and whispered eagerly.

"That's the niece."

"Drove off in that car with that young Plasher—the one that said he saw the old lady walking down the stairs."

"Sporty little car...."

"Sporty young feller, too, if you ask me...."

"Bit too sporty fer the police; where's he got to now?..."

The scattered remarks pricked Beryl's consciousness like little barbed darts. She hunched her slim shoulders against them.

"Let's get away, Mother. I've got Gerry's car here. I can take you home, and Uncle James and Aunt Susan can get a taxi."

"But where is Gerry?" asked Mrs. Sanders.

A tall man approached them unobtrusively. Beryl recognized him as Inspector Caird who was in charge of the case.

"Excuse me, Miss Sanders, but can you tell me where Mr. Plasher is? We want him to clear up a few little points."

"I'm afraid you won't be able to see him to-day; he has gone away on business, but will probably be back to-night."

What was the meaning of the expression that flickered for a moment in Inspector Caird's eyes? Beryl wondered. Was it merely surprise, or wasn't there a hint of dismay and anger? He unobtrusively signed to her to follow him into an empty room opening off the hall.

"Can you tell me where Mr. Plasher has gone? We want some important information, which I think he can give us, without delay."

"I'm sorry, but I can't tell you. I don't know." Beryl spoke slowly and deliberately. She looked at Inspector Caird and then beyond him at a yellow fly-spotted notice on the wall.

"I don't want to worry you, Miss Sanders, but I must impress upon you that if you will help us to get into touch with Mr. Plasher it will save much waste of valuable time. After all, you have just driven him away from here in his car."

"I'm sure Mr. Plasher had no idea you wanted to interview him again," said Beryl wearily. It was too bad of Gerry to leave her to deal with this situation. She seated herself on the edge of the dusty table, as if realizing that there would have to be a good deal of explanation before she could escape.

"I blame myself for letting him go. One of our men was waiting to give him a message from me, but no one took much notice when he slipped out of the court; we all thought he was merely taking you outside the room, Miss Sanders, for a breath of air. You looked very pale, you know—a very painful ordeal for you and your family. Believe me, I sympathize with you. But we must know where Mr. Plasher is."

Beryl had gained a little time, as she hoped to do, and had decided that it was useless to refuse to say where she had taken Gerry; that could easily be traced. Why should she conceal anything? Only because she knew so little that her story might sound thin. But she couldn't help that; Gerry shouldn't have been such an ass. And, so far as she knew, he didn't specially want to keep his movements secret from the police. He had hurried her away from the court, but that was only so that he might catch the train and to avoid being seized by any of those tiresome reporters.

The inspector stood stiffly in front of her, waiting for her to speak.

"Really, Inspector Caird, I can't tell you much. We left in a hurry because Mr. Plasher had to catch a train. I drove him to Euston in his car and left him there. He will be back to-night, or to-morrow at latest."

"Can you tell me what train he was catching, Miss Sanders, and where he was going?"

"He left no address, so far as I know—he wouldn't be likely to as he meant to come back to-night. He took no luggage. I think he mentioned Chester, but I'm not really sure. It was some business matter."

"Ah!" Inspector Caird seemed relieved. "Then doubtless his firm can give me some more information."

"I don't think so. No, I'm sure it's no good asking them. It was not their business, but some private business for a friend. Beyond that I know nothing. We got to Euston between eleven-twenty and eleven-twenty-five."

Inspector Caird was recalling, in his mind, the times of the boat-trains, but Beryl did not know that. He thought she knew a little more than she had told him or intended to tell him, but he was sure that she genuinely believed that Gerard Plasher would return that evening or the next day. He himself was not so sure.

"Thank you, Miss Sanders. Now there's one thing I want to ask you about yourself. Did you go driving with Mr. Plasher in his car on Sunday afternoon?"

"Sunday afternoon? No; I was at home. I went with Mr. Plasher in his car in the *morning* to the Frampton, to fetch my aunt's dog. Is that what you mean?" Beryl's tone was cool.

"In the morning you merely drove from Beverley House to the Frampton and back? Not round the North Circular Road?"

"Merely from Beverley House to the Frampton and back," Beryl repeated indifferently.

Inspector Caird thanked her and held the door open for her.

As she came out she noticed two figures in a dark corner of the hall, away from the door. A man who stood rather slouchingly, and wore a black felt hat with wide brim, had his back to her, but she was quite sure that it was Basil. His hands were stuffed in his pockets and he had an air of uneasiness. And whoever was that girl? Beryl wrinkled her nose distastefully. A tightly-fitting blue coat hugged a rather dumpy little figure on plump, shiny pink-stockinged legs. One of Basil's little weaknesses, doubtless, but he might have more sense of fitness than to chat with her in a corner at such a time and in such a place as this!

Beryl hesitated. Would it be too frightfully tactless to make some excuse to speak to him and perhaps draw him away?

The woman noticed her and said something to Basil, who turned quickly and caught Beryl's impatient look. He blushed—Beryl knew how angry he would be to realize that he was doing so—and turned back to the woman with a negative shake of his head. Beryl joined her mother, who was waiting alone near the door.

"James and Susan have gone on in a taxi. Did you notice Basil talking to that woman? She waited there for him and pounced on him as he came out—simply pounced!—and they have been talking there for ages. Really I can't think what Basil has to do with her. His friends are too awful, but she doesn't look like one of his artistic set exactly. Do you think it is something to do with poor Phemia?"

"I haven't an idea, Mother. Perhaps someone from the Frampton," suggested Beryl wildly.

"Oh, I hardly think so, dear. Mrs. Bliss is very particular, and I believe they're all quite nice people. Not at all like that! I don't know how to put it, but really she hardly looks respectable! Her mouth! And her eyelashes!"

"But everyone makes up nowadays, Mother. I didn't see her close to. Shall we go home? Basil will follow, I expect. I know who that must be—some relative of Bob Thurlow's; a sister perhaps."

"I should hardly have thought…But you never can tell…" murmured Mrs. Sanders vaguely, as she followed Beryl to the car.

"Well, I don't like her," Mamie was saying to Basil. "I'm glad she's not your girl. But promise you'll get me the cash soon? I must have it—reelly—or I wouldn't have said a word now." She held on to the lapel of his coat. "Your father, now—can't you touch him for a bit?"

"I'll do my best; surely you realize that, Mamie? It's very difficult for me, and you only make it worse, catching hold of me here, with everyone looking."

"What's wrong with me?" Mamie demanded in indignation. "I thought it was *you* the p'lice had their eye on, not me. It's not very nice for a girl to be seen talking to anyone that's under suspicion like you are."

"What makes you think I'm under suspicion?"

"You told me so yourself, Geoff, when I came to see you Sunday, and you said there was a bobby watching outside the house. Nice thing for me, to have them watching me like that!"

"Well, I did my best for you and I told you not to come again. I can't stay here talking any longer. All the family will be wondering where I am."

"Oh no, they won't. They saw you standing here. Lor'! Anyone'd think you was a schoolboy, the way you can't stop and talk to a friend without everyone wanting to know what it's all about! But I won't keep you, Geoff. I don't want to get you into any trouble, but I wanted to make sure that you don't forget me."

She released him, and with a hasty good-bye he left her there and sped away from the court.

Mamie did not escape so easily. A thin, middle-aged man who walked alertly on his toes had been prowling about in the Victorian shadows of the coroner's court, and now he shot up from nowhere in front of Mamie as soon as Basil was outside the door.

"I'm the *Daily Chat*," he informed her confidently; "I wonder whether you can help me?"

Mamie jerked her chin in the air. "If you think I'm mixed up in this case, you're mistaken. I came along just to hear the case—nat'rally anyone'd be interested—but I know no more than you do. A good deal less, I reckon, consid'ring how you go prying around in corners!"

The *Daily Chat* was not discouraged. The principal figures in this case were singularly uncommunicative: James Pongleton was ferocious; his fluffy wife, who might have talked, was kept closely in tow by him; Gerry Plasher had been polite but apologetically "unable to say anything"; Basil sheered off like a timid colt and his only contribution had been: "The whole thing's a confounded muddle and I'm not going to help you make a worse mess of it"; Beryl Sanders had been haughty. But this young woman who had held Basil Pongleton talking in a corner for ten minutes or so seemed more promising.

"Miss—er—mm—you're a great friend of Mr. Pongleton's, I know; you will understand that I myself, a comparative stranger, can hardly trouble him at this time, though he has been very helpful—oh, very helpful. Of course he and all his family realize that the Press can give the police valuable assistance in unravelling the mystery. Now I believe you can tell us something——"

"I might tell you a lot," admitted Mamie saucily, "but it's not likely to interest you, and I can't tell you anything about this business, so you'd better not waste your time."

"You know Mr. Basil Pongleton well, of course? This is a dreadful thing for him."

Mamie nodded, slightly appeased. "I've met him now and then. Mind you, I'm not saying it's nice for anyone to have their aunt murdered like that, but he's got nothing to do with it. He's a real good sort, and you can put that in your paper! Wouldn't hurt a fly! Well, you see for yourself, he didn't have to go in the box this morning. You'd better get your eye on that young fellow Plasher—him that saw the old lady on the stairs, as he says."

"You know Mr. Plasher too, of course?"

"Never set eyes on him before to-day!"

"Ah! I had thought that perhaps you might be the lady whom he took for a drive yesterday afternoon."

"You did, did you?" Mamie was indignant. "What are you getting at? I'm not the sort to go in a car with any young fellow who's passing, even if he is quite the gentleman, which I will say for this Mr. Plasher."

"I quite understand," the *Daily Chat* assured her. "I thought that, being a friend of the family, you might know who went out with Mr. Plasher yesterday."

"You'd better ask him! I must be getting along." Mamie whisked away and left the *Daily Chat* disconsolate.

Meanwhile Inspector Caird was dispatching his minions in all directions to gather information which might help him to get on to Gerry's track, or at least to discover his destination and intentions. The inspector lost no time in sending a careful description of Gerry to all the west-coast ports, with commands that any would-be voyager of this appearance was to be detained. He considered the wisdom of asking the B.B.C. to broadcast the description and an appeal to Gerry to "communicate with the police", but decided to postpone this step until the afternoon.

Until Gerry's abrupt and unexpected disappearance from the coroner's court, Inspector Caird had not been paying very much attention to him. His story of his encounter with Miss Pongleton on Friday morning seemed to have no gaps in it and no inconsistencies, and although the inspector realized the possibility that Gerry might be the clever criminal playing a magnificent game of bluff, he did not give much thought to this theory, though he deputed a man to keep an eye on Gerry and to make some discreet enquiries. This man reported that there was nothing to indicate that Gerry had any opportunity to get hold of the leash; there was no evidence that he was short of money or that he had any means of knowing of Miss Pongleton's appointment with her dentist on Friday morning. Neither had he any grudge against the old lady. He was, of course, engaged to Beryl Sanders, who might possibly inherit Miss Pongleton's money; in fact, it now appeared likely that she would inherit it, unless the will made on Wednesday had been destroyed—by the old lady herself or by some other person. The inspector was beginning to believe that it might have been found and destroyed by Basil, and he feared that it might be impossible ever to obtain proof of this. The theory that Gerry murdered Miss Pongleton with the idea of obtaining her money indirectly through his marriage with Beryl seemed far-fetched, especially since there was nothing to show that he could have known of the will made on Wednesday, and its contents.

Gerry's sudden departure aroused alarm and suspicion in Inspector Caird's official mind. He relieved some of his anxiety by an outburst of anger against the man who should have kept an eye on Gerry and whose vigilance had been dulled by

Gerry's apparently normal behaviour throughout the last two days and his willingness to give any information asked for. The inspector told himself that if they had allowed the real criminal to elude them so neatly, his own career was ruined. But the frenzied activities of the police during that morning failed to disclose that Gerry had made any of the preparations which might have been expected of an escaping criminal. He did not seem to have provided himself with any large sum in cash, nor to have taken any luggage, nor to have obtained a passport. The only clue to his disappearance was the information given by that observant lady, Miss Miggs, that he had driven a middle-aged woman in rough, arty clothes in his car on Sunday afternoon along the North Circular Road, and that they had stopped to make notes in their pocket-books. Further investigation disclosed the absence from the Frampton of Mrs. Daymer. She had left early on Monday morning for an unknown destination, carrying a leather satchel in which she had packed what she might need for a stay of a few days. A description of Mrs. Daymer was sent forth into space to join the description of Gerry.

The inspector was baffled. Was this sudden flight the result of panic? And, if so, what had happened to alarm him? Or was it planned beforehand, with money carefully banked elsewhere in another name, and other supplies deposited, to be collected en route? In that case, what was the motive for the murder? The pearls! Miss Pongleton had owned a pearl necklace which had not so far been found among her belongings, though it had been thought that it would turn up in some obscure hiding-place. But, unless the Pongleton family had been deceived, or had deceived the inspector, about the value of the pearls, they were worth only from fifty to one hundred pounds, surely not enough to provide a motive for murder? It was remotely possible that the pearls were worth more than anyone supposed, and that Gerry was aware of this.

Assuming that the pearls might provide a motive, Inspector Caird began to test the case against Gerry. The footmark on the stairs seemed to belong to a small man who wore rather pointed shoes; it did not belong to Gerry, but it might possibly belong to a woman. Mrs. Daymer seemed to be definitely linked with Gerry's disappearance; the footmark might be hers, and she, living at the Frampton, would have been able to secure the leash for him. On Sunday afternoon a man named Jones had reported to the police that on Friday morning, at about 9.25, he had seen a slim man of middle height, wearing a dark overcoat and bowler hat, "slink away" from the passage leading past the foot of Belsize Park stairs. The inspector had immediately arranged an identification parade with the confident hope that Jones would be able to identify Basil, but he had been disappointed. Jones' description was vague and he had not seen the man's face, but he professed to be certainly able to identify him "in two twos" if only he could catch sight of his back once more. The inspector had not thought it possible that the "slinking" man was Gerry, who was six feet tall, broad-shouldered, wore a light overcoat and did not, so far as could be discovered, possess a dark one.

Basil corresponded to the description more nearly; he sometimes walked with a slouch, which Jones might call a "slink", and he had certainly set forth from Tavistock Square on Friday morning in a bowler hat. The inspector had decided that Jones was a mutt; now he began to wonder whether, after all, Jones might have seen Gerry. If that were so, Gerry must have spent some ten minutes on the stairs—and how had he occupied that time? Inspector Caird feared that the answer to that question was the solution to the puzzle. The time at which Gerry had reached his office on Friday morning had not been very surely vouched for, the inspector recollected; and Bob Thurlow was in such a state of terror and seemed so afraid that the truth would incriminate him further, that anything he said about the time when he had spoken to Gerry was quite unreliable.

The inspector looked up Mrs. Daymer's alibi for Friday morning; she had been engaged on "literary work" alone in the smoking-room at the Frampton; no one had enquired very closely into that. The inspector believed that if only Jones could identify Gerry, a plausible case might be pieced together against him. But now where was Gerry to be found?

CHAPTER SEVENTEEN

DISCOVERIES

THAT dark drenched Monday was the most wretched day of Beryl's life. The police gave her no peace. Clearly they were rattled by Gerry's unexplained disappearance. They visited his rooms and interrogated his landlord, as Beryl heard when she herself rang up his address in the forlorn hope that he might have left more precise information there. Beryl's feelings changed from annoyance to exasperation and finally to dismay. Was it possible that he had actually meant to give the police the slip and that he would not come back? She dismissed the idea indignantly but it returned again and again. She remembered what she and Gerry had heard at the Frampton on Sunday morning about another will. If it existed it was probably in Beryl's favour. The police of course were capable of believing anything; they might think that the possibility of Aunt Phemia's money going to Beryl would provide Gerry with a motive for ... Beryl refused to name it, even to herself.

Of course it was utterly ridiculous. Beryl herself was not badly off and Gerry was doing well on the Stock Exchange; at least, he always seemed to be doing well—he was never short of cash or worried about his rent, as Basil constantly was. But one did hear of people who seemed quite prosperous and suddenly crashed financially. That was absurd. Gerry wasn't a gambler. Besides, they had talked over their plans again and again; had even begun to look for a flat and mapped out the honeymoon tour. It was impossible to imagine that Gerry had been deceiving her all the time. That he could be in desperate need of money, need so desperate that ... Again she refused to put the possibility into words, even in her mind.

She wished that she had drawn the conversation with Inspector Caird to that possible will and made it clear that even if it disinherited Basil in her favour it would make no difference to him in the end. The money was always regarded in the family as due to him at his aunt's death, and certainly it would go to him.

So all through the day Beryl's thoughts tormented her, and to smother them she talked frantically to her family in a way quite unlike her usual calm manner—which had sometimes been described, spitefully, as blasé. Mrs. Sanders was annoyed to notice that Beryl was irritating her Uncle James by her random remarks.

James Pongleton disliked being away from home; his habits were almost as regular as Mr. Slocomb's, and he felt unhappy without his own familiar leather armchair and his own rooms in which he knew exactly where to lay his hand on anything he wanted. He was anxious to get things settled and return to Yorkshire at the earliest possible moment. It was all very distressing about poor Phemia, but they couldn't make things better by hanging around, and it was best to get the funeral over with the least possible fuss and go quietly home.

Mrs. Pongleton would have liked to stay in Hampstead a little longer. It was so difficult to get James to consent to any expedition from home nowadays, and the journey was tiring and expensive. Of course this was not really a fitting time for shopping and sight-seeing; nevertheless, it really was waste of a good journey to London to return home after only two days! Susan Pongleton would not have *spoken* so unfeelingly of the present melancholy occasion; she would be shocked if she could read her thoughts in cold print. But Euphemia Pongleton, her sister-in-law, had been almost a stranger, and in fact it had seemed providential that they had not met more often; Susan had always felt that it would be difficult to love Euphemia at close quarters, though it was possible to maintain a correct sisterly attitude towards her at a distance.

As for Basil, who had joined the rest of the family after the inquest, he had been in a state of wavering uncertainty all day, feeling that he ought to do something about the pearls, but unable to decide what he should or could do.

So in various states of discontent, irritation, and unhappiness, Susan and James Pongleton, Basil, Beryl and her mother, sat crowded together in the hired car in which they had followed Euphemia's body to the rainswept slopes of Highgate cemetery. They were all tired by the harassing events of the day, and Beryl, with her nagging anxiety about Gerry added to the strain of the inquest and the funeral, was in a state of wretched exhaustion. But when, in the evening, her Uncle James asked her to accompany him to the Frampton, where he was to go through Phemia's things, she thought that even that dreary occupation would be better than sitting, worrying about Gerry, in the restless atmosphere at home. So they drove up the hill in the Alvis and Basil was not able to make up his mind definitely before they left to give Beryl a tip about the pearls.

"Is your young man going to show up again before we leave?" Uncle James asked Beryl as they drove up the hill.

"I've told you, Uncle, I don't know," Beryl replied with weary exasperation.

"Seems to be a lot of mysterious business on hand," grunted Uncle James.

"Everyone's upset," replied Beryl shortly, and not very helpfully.

Inspector Caird and Mr. Stoggins, Miss Pongleton's solicitor, were waiting for them at the Frampton and they went at once to Miss Pongleton's room, which the detective unlocked.

Before they began to check Miss Pongleton's small collection of valuables by a list which Mr. Stoggins had brought, Mr. Pongleton handed to him a packet of letters neatly secured with rubber bands. Mr. Stoggins, a plump little man with a bald head and melancholy eyes, looked puzzled.

"These are a few of my sister's letters, covering a period of some years, which I have kept because they refer to her investments. They may be of help to you, but I believe her affairs in that direction are in order. Possibly Inspector Caird may wish to look at them, though I doubt whether he will find any clues. There is mention of some advice on investments which a friend gave my sister from time to time, but on which she did not act."

Inspector Caird took the packet from Mr. Stoggins. "The trouble about this case is that there are far too many clues, all pointing in different directions," he grumbled. "However, I don't want to imply, Mr. Pongleton, that we shall not track the criminal ultimately. I think I'll take a look at these letters."

Inspector Caird reflected that the discovery of the criminal might prove an unwelcome surprise for Beryl's uncle, and he was glad that the old man would be safely on his way home in little more than twelve hours' time. He sat down in a wicker chair near the fire and began to examine the letters. The others were investigating Miss Pongleton's jewel-cases and bureau-drawers systematically.

"Are you acquainted, Mr. Pongleton, with the gentleman mentioned in these letters who seems to have been so anxious to give Miss Pongleton advice on her investments? A Mr. Slocomb, who lives in this boarding-house?"

"I have never met him, and what my sister wrote about his confidential advice was so vague that one cannot judge of its wisdom. Her investments were perfectly secure and reasonably good, and therefore I counselled her not to disturb her money. She had no particular motive for wishing to gamble with her securities in the hope of large profits."

"Hm! I will return these to you, Mr. Stoggins." The solicitor stowed them away in his leather case.

Nearly all Miss Pongleton's valuables had been accounted for, but there was no sign of the pearls. Beryl was worried; she had hardly hoped to find them in this locked room, but yet had a wild idea that somehow Basil might have put them here. She opened a little case which seemed the kind of thing in which they might be found. It was empty except for a wad of cotton wool which clung to the lid. Beryl removed it and a folded slip of paper floated out, partly opening, so that Beryl saw something written on it in her aunt's hand. The word "Basil" started up at her from the spiky writing. She tried to suppress a little gasp and to occupy herself with another box, whilst peering surreptitiously at the inscription. Inspector Caird was behind her; she dared not look round; she dared not pick up the paper and put it back in the case or in her pocket. She took up another case and placed it upon the paper, which it did not quite conceal.

"May I come in?" called Basil's voice, and she turned to see him in the doorway. After a difficult half-hour with his mother, who was anxious to be assured that he was not making "undesirable friends", he had decided that the Frampton might be more restful than Beverley House.

Inspector Caird made an unobtrusive movement towards the chest-of-drawers near which Beryl stood, and helplessly she saw his hand reach out towards the leather case which she had just put down.

"Excuse me, Miss Sanders—haven't you overlooked something?"

He picked up the paper. Beryl held her breath and looked appealingly at Basil. Inspector Caird perused the note with interest and then he too looked towards Basil.

"You have arrived at the right moment, Mr. Pongleton. You can explain this, of course?" He handed the note to Basil, who took it with a puzzled look.

"Read it," commanded Inspector Caird, as Basil stood holding it and gaping rather aimlessly at the others. They all felt that this was a significant moment, though only the most ordinary remarks had been made.

"Oh! One of Aunt Phemia's notes. She often used to write little notes like this; memoranda, she called them, to make everything clear! But it doesn't help much in this case, does it?" He looked round anxiously at his relatives, avoiding the cold gaze of the inspector, who remarked sternly:

"The note states that the pearls were entrusted to you on a date some three weeks ago, to be restrung."

"That's so. I gave them back to Aunt Phemia last Wednesday, when I came here to tea with her. Can't think why she didn't put them back and destroy the note, but I expect she just tucked them away somewhere else for the moment."

"Of course," said Beryl quickly. "The sort of thing she was always doing!"

"Basil, what does this mean?" his father demanded sternly. "Why didn't you mention this before?"

"The note? I didn't know about it."

"Don't prevaricate, boy! You know we've all been speculating on what had become of the pearls. Why didn't you tell us that you had them until last Wednesday?"

"Didn't I? I mean, it didn't seem important," blundered Basil. "I thought you all knew that. I gave them back to her, and obviously, if they are lost, they have got lost since then, so it doesn't seem to make any difference."

There was an awkward silence. Uncle James abruptly remarked, "Wednesday? That was the day that young man Thurlow saw your aunt after you had left and, according to him and the young woman who was with him, witnessed a will for her."

"Tell you what," exclaimed Basil. "Those two came in and Aunt Phemia didn't want them to see the pearls lying about, so she tucked them away somewhere downstairs—in the drawing-room, where she was sitting. Let's go and look there!"

"And is it likely," his father enquired, "that she would leave them there all night and the next day and the next night?"

"It might be," put in Beryl hastily. "Aunt Phemia's memory was failing a little, and if she had really been making a will that may have put other things out of her head. We'd better look; don't you think so, Inspector Caird?"

"I think we had," the inspector agreed grimly.

Beryl led the way downstairs. Only Mr. Blend was in the drawing-room, and the inspector gently asked him to leave them alone. He shuffled out with some dishevelled newspapers under his arm. They all looked round the room vaguely.

"That's the chair she always sat in," said Basil, pointing out the one which Mr. Slocomb had annexed since Friday. "Try the crack down the side. It would be the natural place for anyone to stow things away."

"So it would!" Beryl agreed.

Inspector Caird aimed a quick look of suspicion towards her. He approached the chair cautiously, as if it were an animal of doubtful temper, and plunged his hand down one side—the side on the right hand of anyone seated in the chair—between the arm and the seat. He shook his head and tried the other side. His hand came up again holding an oblong buff envelope.

"That's not the pearls!" blurted out Basil in surprise and dismay.

"Correct!" said Inspector Caird, after feeling the envelope.

"The missing will, I think," suggested Mr. Stoggins gently, looking very melancholy.

James Pongleton stepped forward and put out a hand, but the inspector, disregarding him, placed the envelope gingerly on the mantelpiece and probed again in the side of the chair. They all watched him, open-mouthed in suspense. There was a slight rustling sound and he produced a small tissue-paper packet.

"Yes!" gasped Beryl and Basil in chorus.

"That looks more like them!" Basil added. "They were done up like that."

Inspector Caird sat on the sofa and opened the packet carefully. There lay the lustrous, delicate-looking necklace.

"Rather a slapdash parcel to come from a jeweller," he suggested.

"Oh, Aunt Euphemia opened the parcel to look at them," Basil explained hastily. He wondered anxiously whether one could tell by looking carefully—as Inspector Caird was looking now—whether pearls had lately been restrung.

"She was going to give them to Beryl as a wedding present," he added. "That was why she wanted them restrung now."

"Was your sister left-handed?" Inspector Caird asked Mr. Pongleton.

"No—no," replied the old man, too dazed by the startling events of the last few minutes to grasp the significance of the question.

The inspector had wrapped the pearls up again and slipped them into his pocket. Everyone noticed that, but no one liked to say anything. He took the long envelope from the mantelpiece, holding it by one corner. "Perhaps we had better look at this, Mr. Stoggins? If you have no objection, I will open it."

He examined it very carefully before ripping it open neatly with a pocket-knife, and drew out the document, holding it by the edges. He handed it to Mr. Stoggins, who took it with equal care.

"Yes, yes," muttered Mr. Stoggins mournfully. "Miss Pongleton's will, dated Wednesday, March fourteenth—last Wednesday—and witnessed by Robert Thurlow and Eleanor Foster. I think there is no doubt that this supersedes the one we read this afternoon. Perhaps it would be advisable for me to read it, Mr. Pongleton?"

"Yes, of course, read it!" snapped James Pongleton.

The will enumerated various small bequests and made provision for Tuppy, as the previous one had done. "A string of pearls, formerly the property of my mother and at the time of making this will in the possession of my nephew, Basil Pongleton, who is to return them to me as soon as they are restrung, I bequeath to my niece, Beryl Sanders. Five thousand pounds I bequeath to Mr. Joseph Slocomb as some return for his unfailing kindness and helpful advice. My nephew, Basil Pongleton, having incurred my grave displeasure, inherits nothing from me but his grandfather's gold watch. The residue of my estate I leave to my niece, Beryl Sanders."

"Irregular, most irregular," Mr. Stoggins murmured as he concluded the reading. "Should have been drawn up by a solicitor—but probably it can be upheld."

No one took any notice of him. They were all startled by the introduction of Mr. Slocomb's name; too startled to realize at once the significance of that phrase about the pearls, which Basil was supposed to have returned to his aunt *before* the will was made. But Basil himself was more interested in a voice and a step which he heard in the hall outside, than even in the confirmation of his fear that he had been disinherited.

"Just a minute," he muttered. "I want to speak to Betty."

He did not notice that the inspector followed him quietly to the door.

Betty, who had paused on her way through the hall to say something to Nellie, who was laying the tables for dinner, was pale, with dark shadows below her eyes. But she smiled at Basil.

"Had an awful day? Poor old boy! I've got a rotten headache and came home a bit early. What's up?"

"It's all right! They've found the pearls—in the chair!" he told her in a low voice. Betty showed no surprise. "And Aunt Phemia's will too," Basil went on. "It was in the same place—disinheriting me!"

"In the chair too!" gasped Betty. "But it can't have been—I mean it wasn't…"

"It was."

"Then it must have been put there later!"

She had come towards Basil and was on a line with the door of the drawing-room. Something drew her to look in that direction and she saw Inspector Caird standing in the doorway, gazing at her enquiringly. She grasped Basil's hand. Had she messed things up hopelessly after all?

Inspector Caird came forward. "Mr. Basil Pongleton, I think I must ask you to come to the station for a talk, to clear up one or two matters. And perhaps Miss Watson can give us some information?"

Beryl, followed by Uncle James and Mr. Stoggins, came out of the drawing-room. There were tears in her eyes and she blinked desperately, hoping to hide them.

"I think I had better take my uncle home," she said uncertainly, and with a question in her voice, to Inspector Caird. He nodded and they went out. James Pongleton looked dazed. The full significance of that sentence about the pearls in Phemia's will was dawning upon him, but he could not reason it out. He wanted to get away from this strange house. He felt old and helpless.

Inspector Caird signed to Basil and Betty to enter the drawing-room; he followed them and shut the door carefully. They sat side by side on the sofa and he faced them from the chair which had just disclosed its secrets. Betty sat upright and looked determined.

"As you know, Miss Watson, I overheard what you said outside this door just now. 'It must have been put there later.' I think you may like to explain that. You probably realize that we are hampered in our enquiries by lack of information which someone is withholding. Do you wish to tell me anything more?"

Betty had recovered her composure. She wrinkled her brows at him innocently. "I didn't mean anything in particular—only that Miss Pongleton must have put the pearls down the side of the chair after Basil gave them back to her at tea-time on Wednesday, and then she must have put the will there later, after Nellie and Bob had witnessed it. We've all heard about that. It's quite obvious, isn't it?"

"I see," said Inspector Caird, nodding slowly. "And you knew that Mr. Pongleton had them in his possession and—hm!—returned them to his aunt! I may have to ask you to make a statement later, so may I know if I shall find you here in, say, an hour or so?"

"Certainly. I'm not going out to-night. Is there anything more I can tell you now?"

"That is for you to say."

The door opened gently and Mr. Slocomb entered, for it was now half-past six, his usual time of arrival at the Frampton.

"Inspector Caird! This is very fortunate!" he exclaimed cordially. "I was considering the best means of communicating with you. A further scrap of information which may be of use, though I do not know if it has any bearing on the matter. Can you spare me a moment? Nothing confidential, you know," he added, with a glance at Betty and Basil.

Inspector Caird seemed to sigh, but he rose and walked over to Mr. Blend's table in the corner. Mr. Slocomb followed him.

"You may remember that during our conversation on Friday night I told you of my belief that the dog-leash with which Miss Pongleton was—er—strangled was not in its accustomed place in the lounge hall on Thursday night, after young Thurlow had been here?"

The inspector nodded.

"I am now *certain* that it was not there. A little incident has come to my mind which fixes the matter beyond doubt, and

I thought it right to inform you of this. On Thursday evening I had occasion to write a letter of some importance—on a business matter to a friend—and for this purpose I went into the smoking-room...."

The inspector nodded again, with a trace of impatience.

"On leaving that room at about ten o'clock, the question came into my mind whether Miss Pongleton's little dog had been taken for a run that evening. Miss Pongleton herself was reluctant to venture out in the night air in the winter and it was customary among us here—we are a friendly family party, Inspector—for one or other of us to take the dog for his constitutional, as is advisable before he settles for the night. I therefore looked on the umbrella stand, as I passed through the hall, for his leash. The absence or presence of the leash would normally give a clue to the animal's whereabouts."

Mr. Slocomb looked enquiringly at the inspector to make sure that he understood the situation.

"And you saw...?" the inspector asked, in a tone that indicated that his interest was aroused.

"The leash was *not* there."

"And did you make any enquiry, Mr. Slocomb, as to whether anyone else actually had taken the dog and the leash?"

"I made no enquiry. I assumed that the dog had been taken out on the leash, and I proceeded upstairs to bed."

Mr. Slocomb knew that the inspector had asked everyone in the Frampton about their movements on that evening and whether any of them had seen or touched the leash, and it was a matter of common knowledge that no one had taken the dog out that evening, because it was very wet. Tuppy had been forced to content himself with exercise in the back garden.

"You did not go out to post your letter?" asked Inspector Caird.

"No. Although important, it was not urgent and I reserved it for posting in the course of my constitutional next morning."

"You are doubtless aware, Mr. Slocomb, that the girl Nellie Foster states positively that the leash was on the umbrella stand when she herself went to bed that night, which would be soon after ten?"

"I have heard that, Inspector," Mr. Slocomb admitted pleasantly. "Her statement may, of course, be actuated by certain motives...."

"Yes, Mr. Slocomb, I think you can trust us to estimate the value of each witness," put in the inspector curtly.

"Quite, quite," Mr. Slocomb assured him.

"And on Friday you were not sure whether you had seen the leash?"

"I think we were all somewhat—er—distraught on that evening when you took our statements, Inspector," suggested Mr. Slocomb blandly. "Certainly this little incident entirely slipped my memory, which is generally—I may—er—flatter myself—a singularly retentive one. It was recalled to me when I received to-day a reply to my letter written on Thursday night—which reply, incidentally, confirms my memory, as my friend mentions the date of my letter. You will understand, accustomed as you are to following trains of thought, how it struck me that it was on the night preceding the murder that I had written to my friend. I recalled how undisturbed our life then was; I remembered how I left the smoking-room with my letter in my hand and, with what I may call—er—dramatic effect, I recollected how

I had thought of Miss Pongleton's little dog and had looked for his leash."

Whilst this conversation was going on, Betty and Basil sat side by side on the sofa, fearful of voicing the questions each was longing to ask the other lest they should say anything to rouse the inspector's attention. Betty realized that Basil was somehow in a worse mess than ever, and that her "explanation" of her remark to Basil in the hall had not gone down very well. She summoned courage to murmur in an almost inaudible whisper: "You must tell the truth—all of it." Basil did not commit himself, even by so much as a nod. They sat there in silence, holding one another's hands, until Inspector Caird was ready to go with Basil to the police-station.

CHAPTER EIGHTEEN

CLUES IN COVENTRY

MRS. DAYMER, awaiting Gerry on the platform at Coventry at 1.7 on that wet Monday, looked very long and unkempt in the shaggy brown coat which hung baggily to her ankles, and a shaggy brown cap rammed over her sandy hair. She peered through her pince-nez at the disembarking travellers and hailed Gerry excitedly by waving her leather satchel.

"I'm really very glad you've come," she declared, as they steered a wavering course out of the station. "I was almost afraid you might be kept at the inquest—imagination, you know.... But how *did* it go?"

"Much as we thought it would," panted Gerry. Mrs. Daymer pushed her way through the crowd with a stern disregard of the other passengers, who gave way to her timidly but with black looks. Gerry's progress was punctuated by dodges and apologetic hat-raising. "I say," he gasped, "what about a taxi and a spot of lunch? Must be a decent hotel here...."

"I noticed quite a reasonable-looking tea-shop," began Mrs. Daymer reprovingly.

Gerry rushed desperately at a waiting taxi, threw open the door, hustled Mrs. Daymer in and told the driver urgently, "A *good* hotel," before he followed her.

"But really, quite unnecessary expense," Mrs. Daymer was murmuring in protest. "A brisk walk through the rain would have refreshed your mind as well as your body."

"This is on me, please," said Gerry firmly.

"Certainly not!" declared Mrs. Daymer. "I most strongly deprecate the convention that a man must always treat a woman——"

"But you see I have a weak chest," Gerry improvised hastily. "And my digestion's not very good either; can't stand these cheap cafés. And you must be pretty wet already?"

"I don't mind it," Mrs. Daymer assured him airily. "My clothing is pure wool, handspun and handwoven—sheer craftsmanship without any damaging mechanical processes. The material retains the natural grease of the sheep, which is, of course, impervious to rain. As for my face, I use no cosmetics, as you see...."

Gerry sniffed surreptitiously. He had wondered why the air of Coventry was permeated with a farmyard smell; now he suspected that it was the natural grease of the sheep.

During lunch Gerry satisfied Mrs. Daymer's curiosity about the inquest. There had been the usual evidence of identity and concerning the discovery of the body. The medical evidence was to the effect that Miss Pongleton had been strangled, presumably by someone standing behind and above her on the stairs, who had whipped the leash with remarkable proficiency round the old lady's neck and pulled it tight, whilst she fell forward down the stairs so that the weight of her body helped the assassin. Basil had not been put in the witness-box and Gerry himself had only been asked to give brief particulars about how he passed the old lady on the stairs.

"They don't seem to be worrying about me at all," Gerry assured Mrs. Daymer, in blissful ignorance to the hue-and-cry that his disappearance had caused. "There was one old lady on the jury who gave me a nasty look, but the police didn't seem interested in me. Though, by the way, one queer thing has happened. The police called at my rooms on Saturday and asked to see my shoes, but after one look at them they showed no further interest. Surely there can't be any footprints?"

"Blood?" mused Mrs. Daymer ghoulishly. "Hardly. Mm! I regret having to miss the inquest."

"It was perfectly beastly! Beryl was pretty badly upset and I was quite glad of an excuse to whisk her away."

He thought sadly and anxiously of Beryl and felt no enthusiasm at all for this fantastic expedition with a strongminded woman in peculiar clothes. In fact, he neglected to ask Mrs. Daymer how her own enquiries had progressed, but when she had extracted from him all the details he could give about the inquest, she volunteered an account of her doings. She had found that the landlady, Mrs. Copping, was dead, but she had traced a former neighbour who had given the address of the landlady's daughter.

She flicked over the pages of a reporter's notebook. "Here it is: Mrs. Maud Birtle, Godiva Villas, Number eight, or it may be eighteen, but anyone in the street will know."

"Godiva Villas!" Gerry snorted with laughter. "Sure they weren't having you on, Mrs. Daymer?"

"After all, we are in Coventry," she told him severely. "I have great hopes of Mrs. Maud Birtle. The street where they used to live was much as I expected—monotonous, flat, mean; the kind of place in which the germs of crime sprout unchecked." Mrs. Daymer almost licked her lips in appreciation.

"Well, I suppose we trot off now to see Mrs. Maud?" Gerry suggested hastily.

They set forth through pelting rain, Mrs. Daymer having shot off ahead before Gerry had time to tell the porter to call a taxi.

"I almost think I ought to try my hand at a crime novel after this," Mrs. Daymer mused coyly. "Treating it in a psychological way, of course—not merely superficially, as most crime novelists do."

Gerry had felt more cheerful after lunch, but now the cold rain leaking down the back of his collar depressed him again. Mrs. Daymer strode on, serene under the protective natural grease of the sheep.

"About the third turning on the left," she said slowly, trying to remember some directions. "Johnson Street—or was it Thompson Street?" She stood precariously on one leg and the tip of one toe in the middle of the crowded pavement, where people came charging blindly along under umbrellas, and balanced her satchel on her knee whilst she extracted the notebook. "Yes, Johnson Street, and then Fairview Terrace on the right, and then Godiva Villas on the left."

"Let me take that!" Gerry held out a hand for the notebook, anxious to put an end to Mrs. Daymer's balancing tricks before she should upset the contents of the satchel all over the wet pavement so that he would have to scramble after papers, powder-boxes—no! she used no cosmetics, fortunately, or was it unfortunately?—her nightdress, perhaps, and goodness knows what else among the slimy mud and the legs of passers-by.

To his relief she handed over the notebook to his care.

"What do we say to Mrs. Maud when we get there? I mean, to explain ourselves?" Gerry asked.

"It depends upon her type; but I am used to dealing with people," Mrs. Daymer assured him complacently.

"She must have dealt pretty thoroughly with old Daymer," Gerry reflected.

Godiva Villas were on the outskirts of the town, a row of Victorian houses of liverish brick topped by cold blue slates.

The vagueness of the address—Number 8, or it might be 18; or perhaps 78 or 108, thought Gerry—increased his hatred of the interminable succession of silly little gables that ran down either side of the street, diminishing and huddling together more closely, away into a wet blur at the end. Once more he cursed the idiocy which had led him to come to Coventry with Mrs. Daymer. He had felt that it was going to be rather a lark; now he only felt a fool.

The bay-window of Number 8, Godiva Villas, displayed a large dirty card, propped up between the glass and the coarse lace curtains, which announced baldly: "Apartments".

"Probably the right number," Mrs. Daymer announced cheerfully. "I was told that Mrs. Birtle takes gentlemen in and does for them."

The door was opened by a small woman of about fifty, with little flickering eyes, a nose jutting out at a sharp angle and beneath it a long upper lip which was turned tightly in to her wide mouth. She had a lizard-like look. This was Mrs. Maud Birtle herself. Mrs. Daymer presented her card, which Mrs. Birtle read carefully and then turned over, as if she expected to find something really interesting on the back. Disappointed by its blankness, she handed it back and her eyes flicked from Mrs. Daymer to Gerry and back again enquiringly.

"I believe you can help me very much, Mrs. Birtle," Mrs. Daymer began, "if you will tell me something about an incident which happened in Coventry rather a long time ago, of which you possibly have knowledge. It was Miss Triggs sent me to you; I understand that she was a friend of your mother's when she was alive?"

"Friend!" snorted Mrs. Birtle. "That's as may be. Neighbour she was to us, and my poor mother always liked to be on good terms with her neighbours."

"I don't know Miss Triggs very well," Mrs. Daymer hastened to explain. "I only came across her in the course of my enquiries as to the whereabouts of any member of your family. I am a writer and at the moment I am studying curious examples of cruelty and perversion—the psychological aspect, of course. I have come across a remarkable instance: the case of a young man who strangled a dog. From the contemporary newspaper accounts I learn that he was lodging with your mother at the time, and I am in hope that you may be able to clear up some points connected with the case. Of course your name would not appear in anything I may write about the matter—unless you wish it."

Mrs. Birtle was obviously flummoxed by this flood of explanation, but the concluding words had been quite clear and she replied to them, ignoring the rest.

"That I don't indeed," she declared emphatically.

"Then you'll tell me something about the dog-strangling episode?" Mrs. Daymer asked.

Mrs. Birtle considered. "Yes," she said, after a tense silence. "I remember the affair, though it's many years ago, and a nasty affair it was too. Won't you come in and sit down?"

"This is very kind of you," Mrs. Daymer enthused. "I was sure you would help us."

Mrs. Birtle led them through her narrow hall into the front room. From the odour that hung about the hall Gerry surmised that she "did for" her gentlemen with kippers and onions. Mrs. Daymer seated herself on the end of a hard couch upholstered in green plush, and Gerry lowered himself gingerly into an armchair decorated with white lace bib and cuffs.

"I'm not quite sure what it was you wanted to know," Mrs. Birtle began. "Something to do with the Cruelty to Animals, are you, perhaps?"

"I won't deny that they may be interested in my enquiry," Mrs. Daymer prevaricated.

"They went into the case at the time, but they said if I remember rightly, that there wasn't not to say *cruelty*. What I mean is, if you had a right to dispose of a dog, that way wasn't so much worse than another."

"Quite so," Mrs. Daymer assented. "Your mother brought the case against him, I believe, for killing a valuable dog?"

"That was the way of it, and he had to pay for the dog, but of course nothing made up to Mother for poor Dido. Funny thing that you should come here to-day asking me about it, for I well remember the day when the case was on; the rain was torrential! Just such a day as this! How it all comes back! I was quite a young girl at the time," Mrs. Birtle added, flicking a coy glance at Gerry.

"Can you remember anything about the young man who strangled poor Dido?" asked Mrs. Daymer sympathetically.

"I remember him well enough," Mrs. Birtle declared, smoothing her black hair towards its knob at the back of her head. "You see, he was a smart enough young man, and I, being young and romantical, thought a lot of him—until that affair with Dido. That gave me a nasty shock, to think that such a pleasant-spoken, quiet young man could act so brutal."

"I suppose he didn't stay with you after that?"

"He did not! But he stayed in Coventry for a bit and he spread a story about that he strangulated that poor dog in self-defence. Made out that it was vicious! There was a lot who believed him, for he had such a smooth tongue with him and, as I told you, seemed so gentle and complacid that it was hard to believe ill of him. But my poor mother was a great sufferer to the day of her death, though never one to complain; the doctors could never diagonize her properly, and it's my belief that the shock of poor Dido's death was the root of her trouble."

"Most likely," Mrs. Daymer agreed. "The effect of shock upon the system is only just being studied with the attention it deserves. But did you ever hear more of the young man—what did you say his name was?"

"Joe Slocomb. That was his real name. And that was a funny thing. I don't suppose you've noticed it, not knowing the young man and not being interested in his name, if you take my meaning—but in the papers his name was given as Sokam—S-O-K-A-M—and that's how it was given in court, and that's the name he answered to there. Of course those who knew him knew that he was the one, but it was only when the papers came out that we noticed the mistake. My father made a to-do about it; it's what you might call mis-reputation, he said, and you could be had up for it. My mother said, 'It's all over and done with now,' she said; 'let it be.' So that's how it was—but it's my belief to this day that Joe knew what he was about when he gave that wrong name; or maybe he didn't give it, but they got it wrong and he didn't correct them."

"And his real name, you said, was...?"

"Slocomb. Sounds a bit like the other, you see, but spelt quite different. S-L-O-C-O-M-B. And there was something a bit mystrious about his first name too. Joe he was always called, and we took it to be short for Joseph, but he gave his name in court as Jonah! Did you ever hear of such a thing? When we came home from the court that day, I well remember—did I tell you what a day it was?"

"Yes; torrentential rain!" put in Gerry quickly, longing to try the word.

Mrs. Daymer frowned at him severely, but Mrs. Birtle seemed pleased.

"That's right, Mr. Daymer——"

"Just a friend of mine," interrupted Mrs. Daymer hurriedly.

"Well, as I was saying, it was just such a day as this and—where was I?—oh yes—as we were coming home my father—he was always one to have his joke and he was rather pleased, having won his case, and that was the only time he was ever mixed up in the law, for he was a clean-living man—well, my father remarked in his jocacious way, 'Jonah,' he said—'Jonah—well it's a good name for him. Looks as if he had swallowed a whale!' That was just my father's joke, of course, for he knew his Bible as well as any."

"And a jolly good joke too," declared Gerry emphatically.

Mrs. Birtle beamed upon him. "The gentlemen always enjoy a good joke," she remarked. "Now there was one of my young gentlemen——"

"Can you remember any more about how this young man—Sokam or Slocomb—strangled the dog?" Mrs. Daymer interrupted.

"Well, Dido was a great big dog, you know—one of these Sitters, if you know the kind of dog I mean. It's my belief to this day that Joe was jealous of that dog, though he never showed it till that last dastardily act. One day when my mother was out he entigled Dido up to his room. There was a sloping roof under his window—the roof of the scullery it was—of that congerated iron. He must have taken off Dido's collar and got that leash round her neck and pushed her out of the window, down the slope, and pulled it tight, all in a minute. There wasn't a sound anyone heard."

"And what did he do with the body?" Mrs. Daymer enquired eagerly, as if expecting to hear that he deposited it on the stairs of an underground railway.

"That was the cunning part! He was that artful! He hitched the leash round a hook on the window, so that it would look as if the poor dumb creature strangulated itself. And then he went out for a walk, just as if nothing had happened. There's callosity for you!"

"And how did you ever bring it home to him?" asked Mrs. Daymer.

"Ah! That was the invention of Providence, if you like! It just happened there was a boy scrambling on a fence, as boys will, and he happens to look up and sees the whole deed. He didn't say anything at the time, being afraid they'd ask him what he was doing on the fence, and not his own fence neither; but after a day or two he heard them talking about how poor Dido had strangulated herself out of the window and he says, 'That dog didn't ever strangulate itself—it was strangulated intently.' So of course that got round to our ears—though we couldn't hardly believe it, young Joe had seemed so cut up about Dido's death—and Father took it up."

"It must have been a dreadful shock to all of you," Mrs. Daymer declared. "And you never heard any more of the young man? He would be older than yourself, I suppose?"

"Not so much older. He was a young chap then, twenty perhaps; I reckon he'd be getting on for fifty now. It so happened we did hear of him again. You see, my sister Dollie was walking out with a young fellow by the name of Parsons; a decent chap he was, though it wasn't him she married in the end. Well, Dollie got a little money saved up; she was always a careful one, and she was a waitress at the Grand Hotel, and a nice little bit she used to get in tips sometimes, and living at home of course she hadn't much expense. Well, Dollie wanted to put this money safely away, and Parsons, he was in the same office with young Joe, and he told her that Joe knew of a good thing. Dollie didn't like the idea of that at first, but Tom Parsons got round her and in the end Joe took the money and got Dollie to sign some papers and that was the last she saw of it."

"Do you mean to say he embezzled it?" demanded Gerry.

"I wouldn't say that. He declared it was all a piece of bad luck and that his own savings were in the same concern, and he was in a concern too, or pretended to be. He did take on about it, Dollie told me. He said she'd get her money back in the end, and more too. But she never did, and it's my belief to this day that that's what wrecked Tom Parsons' chance with Dollie. She never forgave him, though I don't think the lad was to blame; it was said he lost his own money too."

"Did your sister sue Slocomb for the money?" Mrs. Daymer asked.

"She did see a lawyer about it, but it was all a bit awkward, seeing that Dollie didn't dare tell Father that she'd had dealings with Joe. She daren't make it public, and the lawyer said it would cost a lot and he wasn't sure they could get the law of him anyway, for there was nothing to show that it had gone into Joe's pocket, though it's my belief to this day that that's where it went. And would you believe it, that lawyer sent her in a bill for just telling her that. There's no accounting for some people!"

"His advice doesn't seem to have been worth much," Mrs. Daymer agreed. "This was a long time ago, I suppose?"

"It would be soon after Joe left us. I believe Dollie did hear more talk of how he'd got money out of others too, but soon afterwards he left that office and went up to London to reprove himself. Dollie married Fred Smithers, who was in the drapery. Father was in a nice way about that, our family not being in trade, though drapery is a gentleman's business, I always say! And Fred's got his own shop now, in Warwick Street, and doing well."

"We are extremely obliged to you, Mrs. Birtle, for telling us all about that unfortunate affair. I suppose this young man— Slocomb did you say his name was?—wasn't of a local family? Do you know where he came from?"

"That I can't remember. He thought a great deal of himself, but I daresay his family wasn't such great shakes as he made out."

"What was he like in appearance, this Joe Slocomb? I am not asking out of mere idle curiosity, you understand. Such matters are of great importance to me in my study of the types who are guilty of these excesses."

"Excessive you may well call it," declared Mrs. Birtle. "Even if poor Dido had got in his way—and of course she was a great big dog—did I tell you?—but house-trained—well, that wasn't any justifyment for such a deed. But you were asking what he looked like. A dapper little chap he was, not very big, with the smallest feet I ever saw on a man. Very fussy about his appearance he always was, forever brushing and polishing. A sort of betwixt and between in his colouring, so far as I remember, and quite a good-looking young fellow, though perhaps a bit sharp. Very good indoors he was too. A very fussy way of speaking he had and used long words—though that's nothing against him, for I always think that long words sound genteel."

"Now I really think we must be going," said Mrs. Daymer. "We have taken up a great deal of your time, and it is very good of you to have told us so much. It will be of great assistance to me."

"You'll have a cup of tea, won't you?" suggested Mrs. Birtle.

"I don't think we ought to trouble you further," Mrs. Daymer began, but Gerry was accepting the invitation with enthusiasm. He seemed to be fascinated by Mrs. Birtle's conversation.

"A pleasure!" Mrs. Birtle declared. "I like a nice cup of tea myself and a chat about old times."

Over tea Mrs. Birtle indulged in further reminiscences about her family, and Gerry listened with rapt attention and even drank two cups of the purplish mixture which she offered them. No further significant facts about Joe Slocomb were gleaned by the investigators, and the exact fate of Dollie's money remained a mystery, except for the recollection that Joe promised to "put it into a company".

As Mrs. Daymer and Gerry made their way to the station to catch the 5.20 train back to Town, Gerry expatiated on the charm of Mrs. Birtle.

"I never knew that such people existed. She's a gem—a dream! By Jove, I'm glad I came!"

His pleasure was to receive a douche of cold disillusionment on his arrival in London.

CHAPTER NINETEEN

CONSPIRACY!

BERYL and her uncle drove back to Beverley House from the Frampton in silence, and on their arrival they stood looking at each other in the hall, realizing that James' wife and Beryl's mother would be waiting for them, bristling with awkward questions. People's personalities seem to be changing, thought Beryl: Uncle James, who had always been rather ferocious and alarming, had become a pathetic old man who must be protected; whilst kind, fluffy Aunt Susan had become alarming and must be prevented from worrying Uncle James.

Beryl put her hand on her uncle's shoulder.

"Suppose you go into the study, Uncle. Don't worry—I'll see Basil later and find out what it's all about; I know it isn't as bad as it looks. Now I'll go and talk to Mother and Aunt Susan."

The old man moved uncertainly, with bowed head, towards the study door, and Beryl drew a deep breath. *Could* Basil give a satisfactory explanation of this pearls business?

Her mother looked up cheerfully as she entered the sitting-room.

"Well, dear? Is it all right? The pearls?"

Beryl rushed into a vague description of all that had happened at the Frampton and tried to fix their attention on what seemed to her the minor details.

"Well, really!" her aunt declared. "In the chair! I consider that the police are a great deal overrated. I'm afraid that inspector is quite incompetent. I hope James is writing to

The Times about it. You would think they might have discovered by this time who did that horrible crime, especially when they have got the man under lock and key, and without causing us all this inconvenience."

"But where is Basil?" asked Mrs. Sanders.

"At the police-station with Inspector Caird, trying to clear up some of this muddle."

"Well, if Basil can clear anything up I shall be surprised," his mother admitted. "Poor boy! He takes after me. Full of ideas but no head for business! And all the Pongletons are splendid business men. Such a pity!"

Beryl had a bad hour listening to a rambling discussion by her aunt of the situation and trying to lead them away from the more awkward points. When the telephone bell rang she leapt to her feet, thankful for an interruption as well as for the prospect of news.

"That you, Beryl?" came Gerry's welcome voice.

"Gerry! My dear! Thank goodness you're back! Where are you?"

"Euston. Sorry, darling, that I'm so late. Everything all right?"

"No!" declared Beryl desperately. "Everything's frightful. It's been a ghastly day, and wherever have you been? Inspector Caird wants you; he was in an awful state because you vanished so suddenly. I really think he believed you were running away." Beryl found that her voice was becoming trembly. The immense relief of knowing that Gerry, at least, was all right had brought her almost to tears.

"Suppose I'd better go and see him at once. I wonder where——"

"Hampstead police-station; he's there with Basil. We found Aunt Phemia's pearls and another will too, but there's some frightful mystery about the pearls and Basil's explaining—at least, I hope he is. Come round here afterwards. My dear, I shall be glad to see you!"

"So shall I," Gerry assured her ungrammatically. "Are you all right? Your voice sounds queer."

"The telephone," Beryl murmured.

"I was going to Hampstead police-station with Mrs. Daymer anyway, so that's all right," Gerry continued.

"*Mrs. Daymer?* Why on earth?"

"I'll explain later. All's well! G'bye, darling."

Meanwhile Basil had been escorted in a taxi from the Frampton to Hampstead police-station by Inspector Caird. In the gloomy silence of the journey the inspector mentally reviewed the situation. A foul case! he thought to himself. All these blasted clues, pointing in different directions: a brooch, pearls, wills, to say nothing of the extraordinary behaviour of Basil and of Gerry and the co-operation of such unlikely collaborators as Gerry and Mrs. Daymer. Basil and Mr. Slocomb too; his sleuths had reported three interviews between them, and now Slocomb appeared as a legatee under the new will. How did he come in?

The inspector ran through the evidence against Basil. He had to confess that Basil's own incriminating behaviour was the chief point against him. But there was one important point which Basil did not know about yet. He had left his fingerprints on the rail of Belsize Park spiral staircase, above the spot where the body was found. When the inspector interviewed Basil on Sunday night he had invited the young man to smoke, and indicated a silver box on the table. Basil, in helping himself, planted several fingers firmly on the polished surface without misgiving, and those prints had been identified, after a lot of trouble, with some of the multitude on the stairs. In the hope that Basil might give away something really useful, the inspector was keeping this evidence in reserve, but he had a suspicion that Basil might, with his engaging air of ingenuousness, be able to show conclusively that he had helped his aunt up those stairs on some previous occasion.

The footprint had seemed a piece of luck for the police, but it hadn't helped much as yet. Bob Thurlow, who had been pasting up notices on the platform, had slopped some paste out of his bucket in a dark corner near the foot of the stairs. Someone—presumably the murderer—had trodden in it and had left the mark of a rather pointed shoe, of small size for a man, on the lowest step, pointing upwards. It was not Bob's nor Gerry's; conceivably Basil might wear shoes which would fit it, but none could be traced among his possessions. Yet he had got rid of a bowler hat—could he have disposed of shoes also? He probably had time between leaving Tavistock Square and arriving at Golder's Green to commit the murder en route, though the times were a little difficult to vouch for accurately.

But how does the latest will fit in? thought the inspector. It disinherits Basil and therefore takes away his motive for the murder, which in any case seemed slight since the disposal of the money was always rather uncertain and there was evidence that his aunt, while she lived, frequently supplied him with cash.

His thoughts turned to Gerry. He was engaged to Beryl, who inherits under the new will. They were pretty certain that either Beryl or Basil would inherit. A ray of inspiration shot through the dark confusion of the inspector's thoughts. The whole thing's a damn conspiracy! he concluded. The pearls found in the chair, probably put there by Betty Watson, are fakes; these weren't ready in time for Basil to hand them to his aunt on Wednesday, and the letter—ah! the letter!—which Basil received from his aunt on Friday morning, telling him of her appointment with the dentist, provided him with the opportunity of meeting her on the stairs and made him decide to act at once. Young Plasher has gone off to sell the real pearls—but why so suddenly, at this juncture?

However, that may be cleared up; the thing is straightening itself out. The letter also told Basil of the will and gave a clue to its whereabouts. One of the gang abstracted it—is this where the Daymer woman comes in? They needed another accomplice in the boarding-house, since they dared not let Betty Watson into the whole plot. Betty—a really human feeling for Betty was breaking through the inspector's usual impersonal attitude towards every individual connected with a criminal case. He couldn't help liking that nice little girl, and he could hardly keep his hands off Basil, slouched in the opposite corner of the taxi, when he reflected that the brute had involved Betty in this nasty business. For she *was* involved—she had been detailed to put the fake pearls in the chair—and she'd be loyal to the last. Of course that was why she had lied about Basil having entered the Frampton on Thursday night; he *had* gone in and had snatched the leash, though Betty hadn't noticed at the time. Perhaps she now guesses this and is trying to defend him.

When Basil seemed to be under suspicion, the inspector decided, the gang planned to have the last will found, as it would tend to deflect that suspicion. The Daymer woman was to arrange that, but through lack of co-ordination, not knowing where Betty had put the pearls, she messed it up.

The inspector's thoughts turned back to Mr. Slocomb; probably he's in the gang; a wily bird, he may well be the brains of it. The footprint might be his—but why in heaven's name should they need to have three of them on the stairs, unless they thought there was safety in numbers and that the multiplicity of clues would confuse the police hopelessly. Gerry had since advertised his presence there, probably with the deliberate intention of leading the police astray; his rôle may have been to hold the old lady in conversation until the others arrived. He could help the others make an inconspicuous getaway and boldly show himself to Bob and act the innocent man. Slocomb had been very anxious to clear Basil by that volunteered evidence about the leash. The inspector glanced at his notebook. Had Slocomb time to get to Belsize Park? He had informed the police complacently, when questioned, that on Friday morning, as usual, he took a short constitutional before catching his train at Hampstead station at 9.40. The fact that he did travel from Hampstead at that time had been confirmed by acquaintances, but between 9.5 and 9.40 where was he? He walked, he said, down Downshire Hill and along the borders of the Heath, but there had been no definite confirmation of this. That had seemed only natural. He took his walk alone, and why should anyone notice him specially? But suppose he did not take a walk?

Beryl Sanders was slightly involved, too, but probably not seriously. She had certainly tried to conceal that damning note about the pearls, she refused to say where Gerry had gone, and she expected the pearls to be found. She might be fairly deeply implicated, the inspector decided.

As for poor Bob Thurlow, now waiting apprehensively in gaol, Inspector Caird believed that he was less guilty than any of the others who were still at large. The inspector realized that some of his subordinates engaged on the disentanglement of the Pongleton puzzle thought him barmy to ignore the clear evidence of Bob's guilt and waste time hunting for another criminal. He had a wide experience of guilty men telling lies— cunning lies, stupid lies, and bold lies. He also had a considerable, though less varied, experience of innocent men telling the truth—obvious truth, shameful truth, and almost incredible but nevertheless genuine truth. He had a personal conviction that Bob Thurlow's own story belonged to the last category, but there was little as yet to persuade a jury to agree with him.

When Basil and the inspector arrived at Hampstead police-station, Basil was set to wait in the outer office under the imperviable gaze of a constable. Another constable followed the inspector to an inner room.

"The Lost Property has rung up, sir, to say that they have a bowler hat answering to our description, which was found in an underground train at Edgware on Friday morning. The train would have stopped at Golder's Green at ten-fifteen, and it was a City train, sir—not from Warren Street. They're sending it along."

"The whole train? Hm! I think we've got him." Inspector Caird became grim. "He'll find it a bit difficult to explain how he set out from Warren Street at nine-thirty and arrived at Golder's Green in a train from the other line, and not until ten-fifteen. That gives him ample time. Any news of young Plasher and the Daymer woman?"

"Not yet, sir."

"Damn silly to let them give us the slip! Look here, take these"—he held out, very carefully, the pearls in their tissue-paper wrapping and the will in its envelope, encased in another piece of paper—"to Perrin to examine for finger-prints, especially on the will that's inside the envelope; then tell him to pass on the pearls to be tested to see if they're fakes. And—a moment—what about that other Johnny's time? He may have been there. Send a man to make this test: he starts from the Frampton, goes to Hampstead station and takes train to Belsize Park; there goes up the stairs to the point where the body was found; waits there—mm!—ten minutes; then returns to the down platform and takes a train back to Hampstead, where he crosses to the up platform and waits for a train. He is to move quickly but not so fast as to be conspicuous. He is to time himself carefully from the Frampton until the moment when he could board a Charing Cross train on his return to Hampstead station. He is to report here as soon as he has carried out the test. And now bring in Mr. Pongleton."

CHAPTER TWENTY

WHAT NELLIE HEARD

AFTER Beryl and her uncle, Basil and Inspector Caird, had left the Frampton, Betty retired to her room. She had spent an anxious day, wondering how Basil's affairs were progressing, and just when it seemed probable that she and Cissie would get away from the office early, Mr. Jamison, her boss, had come in with a long screed which must be typed immediately. Cissie, realizing that Betty was under the weather and also hoping for Mr. Jamison's favourable consideration of her plans for getting a specially long week-end at Easter, volunteered brightly to do the extra work. So Betty was able to return early and Cissie was not yet home when Nellie brought Betty's second course up to her room at about a quarter to eight.

Betty had asked for her dinner to be sent upstairs, for her appetite was usually impervious to worry and she had a theory that a headache may be cured by a meal. But she could hardly touch the food.

"Your favourite honeycomb mould, miss," said Nellie sympathetically, setting down a plate.

"Nellie, I've been thinking about you and your young man and that brooch." Nellie started and blushed.

"Nothing bad," Betty reassured her. "But there's something odd about that brooch that hasn't been explained. I can't think why Miss Pongleton had it with her on that morning!"

"Queer that you should ast me that," Nellie commented. "I allus thought it funny meself, seein' that Mr. Slocomb 'ad that brooch on Thursday night, an' I'd've thought 'e'd've kep' it."

"*Mr. Slocomb* had it? But why? I thought he didn't know anything about it till afterwards." Betty was so surprised that she forgot the caution she would ordinarily have exercised in remarking to Nellie on matters connected with the other boarders.

"Have you told anyone else about this?" Betty asked.

"Why, no, miss; the p'lice didn't ast that, an' Mr. Slocomb's bin very kind, I didn't 'ardly like to bring 'is name in; an' besides, I didn't ought to've known."

A bell rang downstairs. "Oh, miss, I mus' go——"

"Come back again to take away my plate, and bring me some coffee, very strong, please."

Betty prayed that Inspector Caird would not return at this moment to see her. Nellie was soon back.

"Tell me why you think Mr. Slocomb had that brooch," Betty demanded.

Nellie stood twisting her fingers and shuffling her feet.

"I think it's very important, and it can't make things worse for Bob," Betty urged her.

"Well, miss, I know I didn't ought ever to 'ave done it, but I was that put out about Miss Pongleton 'avin' got that brooch an' 'er threatenin' to tell the p'lice, so I thought maybe I could get 'old of it an' Bob would send it back to its rightful owner—which 'e would've done an' willin' by then, bein' in a proper state about it all. So Thursday night, when she was downstairs, I went up to 'er room an' 'ad a look. But she took it into 'er 'ead to go to bed early that night, 'cos of goin' to the dentist's nex' mornin'—she went on about that too, how Mr. Slocomb had made the appointment for ten, though she said eleven. Well, she comes up to 'er room jus' as I was lookin' in 'er work-basket, an' she says, quite pleased-like, 'It's no good you lookin' for that piece of stolen joolry, my girl, for I've given it to Mr. Slocomb an' 'e'll 'ave it locked up safe.' Oh, miss, you won't tell on me? Mrs. Bliss would be that wild!"

Betty hardly seemed to notice Nellie's distress. "Mr. Slocomb," she was thinking. "If he had it…?"

"But, Nellie, you don't know that he really had the brooch. Miss Pongleton may have said that to prevent you looking for it again."

"She knew it'd be safe with 'im," Nellie declared. "Besides, she ast 'is advice about it—she told me so—what she ought to do an' all. She thought a lot of 'im an' 'is advice, an' 'e do know what's what, now don't 'e?"

Betty was beginning to think that emphatically he did.

"Well, Nellie, I don't see exactly how this affects the case, but I'm sure you ought to tell the police about it. We must help them by telling them all we know." She said this without a blush, but hoped she would not have to follow her own advice. Or would it perhaps be a relief to tell her own story and not to have to make up any further "explanations"?

"I mus' go down, miss, or Mrs. Bliss'll be at me," said Nellie uneasily.

"Very well; but come back again to fetch my coffee-cup; and don't talk to anyone else about this."

Nellie was back before long and still the inspector hadn't reappeared—thank heavens! thought Betty.

"Nellie, I'm quite sure the way to help Bob is to tell the police everything. They won't take any notice of a little thing like your having looked in Miss Pongleton's work-basket."

"Are you sure, miss? I thought as 'ow they might get me for that."

"I'm perfectly certain they won't. But isn't there something more—it's best to get it all over at once, you know. About Thursday night; I thought…"

Nellie became very apologetic. "Oh, miss, I wouldn't tell about that, not for anyone. Don't you fear!"

"Nellie, whatever do you mean? I insist on you telling me!" Could Nellie have come down the stairs and seen Basil kissing her? Well, what of it? It wasn't criminal. But of course she had told the inspector that Basil had not come inside the door; however, Basil might be confessing even now that he had done so. She *must* get it cleared up. At least she must know what Nellie knew.

"Reelly, miss, I don' think no wrong, but men are—well, *silly*, aren't they? An' why should Mr. Basil be blamed for bein' in the 'ouse when that leash was took?"

"I suppose," Betty began slowly, trying to be dignified and not to feel like a schoolgirl caught in some misdemeanour—"I suppose you mean you saw me and Mr. Basil—come in—on Thursday night?"

"No, miss, I didn't *see* nothin'—I was in my room—but I 'eard."

A wave of relief swept away Betty's embarrassment. Nellie slept on the second floor in a little room at the top of the stairs, just along the corridor from Betty's room in which they were now talking.

"But *what* did you hear?"

"Well, miss, you see, I was layin' awake. I couldn't sleep for worry about Bob an' that brooch. I 'eard the front door when you come in an' I 'eard steps come along pas' my door up 'ere, an' I jus' thought to meself, 'That's Miss Betty goin' to bed.'"

"And so it was, I suppose. But what else?"

"After a time, I 'eard steps go down agin; it weren't so very long after. Then they come up agin, a second time. The steps goin' down I thought was only one person; it was jus' a step now and agin like, an' a creak of the boards; but when I 'eard a step comin' up agin an' wondered what it all was, I thought of the door—and sure enough it was bolted on the inside when I went down in the mornin'. So I thought to meself, 'It might've bin two comin' up and two goin' down, and one comes back alone.' I couldn't 'elp guessin' 'oo it would be, knowin' you was out with Mr. Basil."

Betty stared at the girl and deep colour flooded her face and neck as she grasped what Nellie was thinking. Basil's steps! That was the conclusion Nellie had jumped to.

"Nellie, it's dangerous to guess and you have guessed wrong. I see now why you didn't say anything about this before, but what you heard doesn't mean what you think it means. You say you heard the front door shut when we—I— came in. Didn't you hear the bolts? You know what a noise they make?"

"That's the funny thing, miss. I 'eard the door and the bolts shot to when you come in. They do make a noise, you're right. They ought to be seen to, but it's my belief Mrs. Bliss likes to be able to 'ear when people come in at night."

"And later, when you heard the steps go down again, did you hear the bolts again, or the door?"

"No, miss, not a soun', though I gen'rally 'ear the front door from my room, let alone the bolts, bein' jus' above it like, an' I was list'nin' too."

"Nellie, I don't know whose steps you heard, but the only time you heard me was when I came up to bed. No one came up with me and I didn't go down again. I shut the door when Mr. Basil left and bolted it."

"Lor'! Miss Betty! You mean-ter-say it wasn't you arter all?" Nellie gasped at her. "A-course, I couldn't reckernize the steps; it was jus' a sort of little noise like someone creepin' along, an' a creak or two."

"It was only because you imagined so much that you ever thought it was I," Betty pointed out severely. "Now those other steps—there's only one other room on this floor occupied now——"

"Mr. Slocomb's," said Nellie, almost in a whisper.

"It looks as if you had been making a great fuss about nothing," said Betty brightly. "Mr. Slocomb may have gone downstairs for something. But I think you ought to tell the police about this."

Slocomb, thought Betty—what could he want to fetch from downstairs at dead of night? What *had* been fetched from the hall mysteriously, no one knew when or how? The leash! Could it be possible?

Nellie stood expectantly before Betty, the empty coffee-cup in her hand, waiting for more definite instructions.

Steps—not faint, creeping steps in the night, but quick, thumping steps—came along the corridor. Cissie burst in, in her outdoor clothes clutching an evening paper.

Betty thought wildly, "Basil must have been arrested!"

"Betty!" Cissie exclaimed in great excitement taking no notice of Nellie. "The brooch was found in Pongle's *bag*, not in her pocket!"

"Good heavens! Have you gone off your chump? What difference does it make?"

"It all came out at the inquest." Cissie waved the mauled paper. "The judge—no, he wasn't a judge—well, never mind—he said he wanted to clear this up because wrong statements had been made in the papers——"

"But why shouldn't it be in her bag? As a matter of fact, I don't believe she had any pockets." Betty was exasperated.

"Don't you see, it wasn't in her bag when she started!"

"What do you mean? How do you know? It must have been!"

Cissie seated herself violently on the bed. "It wasn't. I can swear to it! I was going along Pongle's corridor that morning, on my way to put on my hat and coat, and as I passed her door there was a sort of scuffle and clatter inside and Pongle called out: 'Cissie, is that you? Please come and help me—so tiresome—I've upset my bag!' You know that mammoth reticule she always lugged about with her? She'd caught it on the door-handle and turned it all upside down, and there were pennies and hankies and notebooks and pencils and veils and goodness knows what, all over the floor. She sat down and emptied what was left into her lap and said—you know her fussy way—'Now we must pick everything up'—*we* was me, of course—'and put them back in their right order.' I had to pick the things up and hand them to her one by one, and she packed them all in, and I'm absolutely positive there was no brooch!"

"But it was in an envelope, I think," said Betty doubtfully.

"Yes; with Bob's name on it. There wasn't any envelope. It's about the only thing there wasn't. She repeated everything she wanted to take, to make sure there was nothing forgotten. I never thought about it before, when I read that the brooch was found in her pocket, but now I come to think of it, you're right—she hadn't any pockets—had she, Nellie?" Cissie realized the existence of the girl who stood behind her, gaping in a dazed way with the coffee-cup still in her hand.

"No," Nellie agreed, with a little shake of her head as if she were just waking up.

"And Pongle went off as soon as she'd repacked the reticule," Cissie continued. "I saw her go down the stairs."

"Yes," said Betty slowly. "Do you remember, I was waiting for you at the front door and Pongle passed me just before you came down? She certainly didn't turn back. Do you see what this means?" she continued, very impressively. "Someone must have put that brooch in Pongle's bag after she was killed. The one who killed her perhaps; *the one who had the brooch!*"

Nellie gasped and put up her hand to her mouth, as if to suppress her secret knowledge.

"But who——?"

"Have you told anyone else?" Betty enquired severely.

"Not a soul! I simply tore home because I was so hungry—too ravening!—and rushed up here to tell you."

"But didn't you tell the police in the beginning about the bag being upset?"

"No, I didn't. The inspector was so sniffy and kept snubbing me when I wanted to tell him lots of things about the Frumps and Pongle. And, anyway, I didn't think much about the bag being upset. There have been so many other things to think about—too distracting!"

Betty was on her feet and had seized her hat. She pulled it on decisively with quick, neat fingers.

"You'll have to come to Hampstead police-station this very minute—and Nellie too—and tell the inspector. Nellie, put on your things, quick!"

"But, I say," Cissie protested, "I haven't had any supper. It's after eight; that typing took me years and years, and I'm starving."

"This is desperately important. What you have to say and what Nellie has to say fit together in the most marvellous way, and we can't wait a moment. Take these biscuits—you can munch them on the way."

No one asked whether Nellie had had any supper. In a few minutes the three were hurrying down the hill towards the police-station, leaving Mrs. Bliss in a state of bewilderment, her self-assurance shattered by Betty's explanation, fired at her like a round of cartridges: "Nellie has to go immediately to the police-station with Cissie and me, to interview Inspector Caird. It's urgent. They had better have some supper when they get back. Don't say anything to the others!"

"Well, really now, who'd think I'm mistress here?" Mrs. Bliss lamented to herself. "And my poor nerves..."

CHAPTER TWENTY-ONE

"SOME VALUABLE INFORMATION"

MRS. DAYMER and Gerry stepped out of a taxi outside Hampstead police-station at a quarter to eight. They were startled by the warm welcome—with an undercurrent of surprise in it—which they received.

"I want to speak to Inspector Caird as soon as possible," Mrs. Daymer announced importantly to the constable. "I have some valuable information to give in connection with the Pongleton case."

"I never thought a policeman would be so glad to see me," Gerry remarked, when Constable Potts had gone to inform the inspector of their arrival. On his way the constable met a colleague to whom he remarked that Mr. Plasher and Mrs. Daymer were here, "cool as you like", and Mrs. Daymer was offering "some valuable information".

"If you ask me," Constable Waterton replied, "everyone comes telling us far too much in this case. We might get on a great deal better without all this vall-you-bull hinformation."

Basil was sitting in Inspector Caird's office, struggling to explain "the pearls business" without involving Beryl in any way, and exonerating Betty as far as possible, and leaving Mamie out of it altogether, and not admitting that he had been on the stairs on Friday morning. The truth oozed from him in reluctant driblets.

Constable Potts entered with the news that both Mrs. Daymer and Mr. Plasher had reported themselves. Basil did not hear exactly what was said, but he gathered that someone wanted to see the inspector.

"Look here, Inspector," he suggested. "Let me sit by myself and write this story down. I can spew it out better that way."

Inspector Caird considered the suggestion. It might not be a bad idea.

"But don't leave anything out," he admonished Basil sternly. "I know a good deal more than you think, and I'm less easily fooled than you imagine."

"I'm sure you are," Basil agreed. He was conducted to another room and there provided with paper and left in charge of Constable Waterton, who sat stolidly looking at nothing with an air of not having been introduced to Basil. The constable had an unfinished look without his helmet, and yet was somehow more alarming, and Basil did not find his presence conducive to literary facility.

The inspector had said he would see Gerry first, but when he turned at the sound of his door opening again he saw Mrs. Daymer. Constable Potts had been quite unable to cope with her without using force, and he had no authority to do that. He hoped, however, that the inspector might order her immediate arrest.

Inspector Caird, recovering from his annoyance, looked at her feet. His hopes wilted. Mrs. Daymer's unvarying devotion to *Trutoze* footwear—wide and rounded and peculiarly inelegant—for once stood her in good stead.

"Good evening, Inspector," she greeted him cordially. "I must plead guilty"—the inspector started and Constable Potts involuntarily prepared himself to whip out his handcuffs—"to kidnapping Mr. Plasher, but we have been carrying out a little enquiry of which we will now report the results."

She seated herself squarely in the chair just vacated by Basil, with her feet—those exasperatingly innocent feet—planted widely apart, and began her story.

"Thirty years ago," announced Mrs. Daymer brightly, "a young man of obscure origin, living in Coventry, strangled his landlady's dog with its own leash."

"Really, Mrs. Daymer," the inspector protested, "we are very busy at this moment, and unless your information is relevant to the Pongleton case I must ask you to tell your story later, or to someone else. I am dealing with very urgent matters."

"You will hardly be able to grasp the relevance of my story unless I begin at the beginning," Mrs. Daymer informed him scathingly. She looked for confirmation to Gerry, who had followed her in and was seated beside her.

"I admit it all sounds batty, Inspector," he said uneasily; "but there is a connection, I promise you."

Mrs. Daymer proceeded with her narrative and got through it with some difficulty, overwhelming the inspector's protests again and again and forcing him to admit that at least she had done her job thoroughly, and that he could obtain confirmation from the two women, Mrs. Maud Birtle and her sister, Dollie Smithers, whose addresses she supplied.

Inspector Caird regarded her quizzically. He could hardly doubt that she and Gerry had spent their time in Coventry as she described. He wished he could doubt it; he wished he could believe that she had been engaged in some nefarious occupation for which he might order her arrest. If he could really establish a connection between Joseph Slocomb, the late Miss Pongleton's valued friend, and Jonah Sokam who strangled a dog and embezzled young women's savings in

Coventry some thirty years ago, it might be useful, though it wasn't exactly evidence. But was Mrs. Daymer giving away an accomplice or had she really made a discovery?

He sent for a constable and instructed him to ring up Scotland Yard with a request for information about Joseph Slocomb, or Jonah Sokam, formerly of Coventry, especially with regard to shady financial dealings. He turned again to Mrs. Daymer.

"You realize that it is a serious matter to accuse anyone— even by implication—of murder, without a shred of real evidence?"

"I make no accusation," replied Mrs. Daymer with dignity. "I merely report facts which have come to my notice. The rest seems to me to be the business of the police, and I will leave you to deal with it. Good evening!"

Mrs. Daymer rose and stalked out of the room. Inspector Caird sniffed the air suspiciously and resettled himself in his chair.

"Hope you don't think I put the woman up to it, Inspector. I was as wax in her hands. Dunno what to make of the affair, but I can tell you I've been feeling like a blithering idiot, trailing after her round Coventry all day."

"I can sympathize with you, Mr. Plasher," said Inspector Caird gravely. He proceeded to question Gerry, who was engagingly confidential and did not seem to be concealing anything. The conspiracy theory was not working out very well.

Meanwhile Betty had arrived at the police-station with Cissie and Nellie, all out of breath. The constable who met the three of them at the door groaned almost audibly.

"We must see Inspector Caird immediately," Betty told him imperatively. "These two ladies have some entirely new and valuable information."

"We'll 'ave the 'ole of 'Ampstead 'ere with hinformation before the night is out," the constable muttered as he stumped along the passage.

In the room where Betty and her protégées were asked to wait sat Mrs. Daymer, exhaling a damp odour of the natural grease of the sheep.

"You!" exclaimed Betty, in not very polite surprise. She had hoped to see Basil.

Mrs. Daymer smiled at them grimly. "You have some valuable information, I heard you say. To avoid disappointment you had better accustom your mind at once to the idea that its value will not be clear to the police. I have been giving them some valuable information, but they have not received it in a very grateful spirit."

"What——" burst out Cissie.

"I expect we'd better not ask," said Betty sagely.

"I don't think I'll wait," said Mrs. Daymer, rising. "Mr. Plasher is in with the inspector now. You will perhaps tell him from me that I have gone home, with a hope, unfounded on former experience, that I may get something to eat."

"You may get my supper!" suggested Cissie gloomily, as Mrs. Daymer stalked away.

But Gerry was wondering hungrily in a room by himself why he was still not allowed to go home. The inspector couldn't quite make up his mind to lose sight of him again, and he was meditating on some information he had extracted from Gerry to confirm his own memory. Yes, Slocomb was rather under middle height and of slim build; his feet were small; he wore a dark suit and overcoat and a bowler hat.

The man who had been sent to test the time needed for what the inspector now believed were Mr. Slocomb's movements on Friday morning came to report: "Half an hour, and a fair wait for one train. They run more frequent in the mornings, if that's what you're thinking of."

"Half an hour! And our friend had thirty-five minutes."

Constable Potts followed on the man's heels to announce stolidly: "There's three ladies from the Frampton, sir, to see you, with vall-you-bull hinformation. One of 'em's Miss Watson."

"*Three* of 'em?" demanded the inspector incredulously. "How many ladies are left at the Frampton, Potts?"

An unofficial grin upset the constable's orderly countenance, but he deemed this to be a rhetorical question rather than a request for information.

"I do want to see Miss Watson," Inspector Caird admitted. "You can bring her in. Mr. Pongleton can remain with Constable Waterton until I send for him, but let me know if he asks to see me at any time. Mr. Plasher must also wait. Jones not here yet, I suppose?"

"No, sir, but the car ought to be here with him soon, unless he's not at home."

The telephone shrilly demanded the inspector's attention.

"Bring the ladies in as soon as I've finished with this call," Inspector Caird instructed Constable Potts before he picked up the ear-piece to learn that Scotland Yard was calling him.

"Jonah Sokam—yes; identical, I have reason to believe, with Joseph Slocomb of the Frampton Private Hotel and Slocomb's Business Agency. You know Sokam?"

Inspector Caird's eyebrows rose higher and higher as he pencilled rapid notes.

"No, I had nothing against Slocomb until half an hour ago; I have a good deal against him now. We're just getting a warrant for his arrest for the Pongleton murder. Motive and opportunity; a few gaps in the chain of evidence, but I think we're linking it up. You hadn't a suspicion of any connection between Sokam and Slocomb, you mean? Oh, not at all"—the inspector became very modest—"quite an accident put us on the track—and the usual carelessness, over a detail here and there, by an unusually careful criminal. You'll investigate that business agency immediately? But he's an artful customer. You'll probably find it all O.K. That's the respectable side of his life. You'll look into the Coventry business, of course? Got the addresses of those two women? Other connections in Coventry?—Ah! Large sums! I gather you're quite pleased that we've identified him for you? Yes, I've evidence that he was after Miss Pongleton's money while she was alive, got her to leave him a substantial legacy and probably hoped to get a good deal more out of her silly young nephew."

"Confound that Daymer woman!" he muttered as he replaced the receiver. "There'll be no holding her! She was on the right track, and I don't know how we should have hit upon the connection between Slocomb and his shady double if she hadn't blundered on that evidence in Coventry. Odd that he should have worked under a name so like his own, but he may have thought that its very similarity was a shield!"

Constable Potts entered with a report from the fingerprint expert. "Nothing on the pearls, sir; but the envelope had been opened, it seems, and sealed down again, very expert; but there *is* a print on the dokkyment inside—made, it seems, by whoever opened the envelope, with a damp finger. Not identified yet; doesn't belong to the nephew; they'll send a full report later."

"Good. I'm ready for the ladies now."

Inspector Caird reviewed the evidence in his mind. "I'd like a few more facts, but it seems to hang together pretty well," he concluded.

CHAPTER TWENTY-TWO

MR. SLOCOMB IS SURPRISED

"Well, Miss Watson, I can't tell you how relieved I am to have this elucidated; if only you could have persuaded this young man a little earlier in the proceedings that it would have been better for him to come out into the open, it would have saved us a lot of trouble. Probably you both feel happier now that you have got it off your chests! I have sent men up to the Frampton to keep watch, and at all costs to prevent the escape of a certain gentleman, but I don't think he has the wind up at all, so he's not likely to try to bolt. Keep quiet when you get there and keep those others quiet too, if you can, and I hope to goodness Mrs. Daymer hasn't been making a song about her little expedition! We shan't be long. And remember, don't tell any more tarradiddles!"

Inspector Caird smiled at Betty and Basil in a fatherly way. He had admitted handsomely that Betty had extracted from Nellie and from Cissie vital information which he himself had failed to elicit. But he felt such a glow of human satisfaction at being able to restore a chastened young man, completely vindicated of criminal misdeeds, to the "nice little girl", that he was not unduly downcast by these blows to his professional pride.

As Basil walked arm in arm with Betty up to the Frampton, he told her those parts of the story which he had at last been induced to reveal to Inspector Caird.

"You do understand, don't you, Betty? I'm an utter worm. But I was desperately hard up when Aunt Phemia handed over those pearls to me, and it seemed a good idea to raise a bit of cash on them. I made sure that I'd get all that and more for my story, *Pearls Before Swine*. I called it that to make it a good omen, but it seems to have been a bad one, for the story was an utter dud. Never tamper with the omens!"

"Nor with the heirlooms!" Betty added.

"When I realized that Aunt Phemia was dead and those pearls sitting in the pawnshop, my one idea was to get them out. Mamie had helped me put 'em in—took me to the shop and all that—and I thought she'd help me get 'em out again, as she did. She's a real good sort, Betty. You do understand, don't you?"

"What I can't understand is why you should have gone to *her*—to that sort of girl—when you might have come to me. You know I would have helped you, Basil."

"But can't you see, you wouldn't know about pawnshops and I couldn't ask *you* to lend me money? And I didn't want to mix you up in the business!"

Betty's sudden laugh startled Cissie and Nellie, who were walking a little way ahead. She felt so absurdly happy that she simply couldn't bother about Mamie just now. She was so thankful to have Basil safe that she could have swallowed half a dozen Mamies and still have laughed. A delirious kind of feeling, backed by a confidence, perhaps a rash one, that there would be no Mamies in the future.

"There's quite a lot I don't understand, Basil dear, but I don't think you'd better explain it now. I can't take in any more."

"I don't know when I've been in such an explaining mood," Basil told her. "And I don't know when I shall be again. Hadn't I better go on with it?"

"No, here's Church Lane and there's not time. I'll come to supper with you to-morrow. Oh dear, this is going to be rather horrible."

Basil squeezed her hand. Nellie was dithering at the door of the Frampton. She was in a confused state of mind, especially as Cissie had been elaborating the situation as they walked up the hill; but she gathered that Mr. Slocomb, Mrs. Bliss's most valued boarder, was deeply involved in some dirty work.

"Reelly I don't 'ardly like goin' into the 'ouse where 'e is," she complained. "Gives me the shudders like, an' 'oo'd've thought it?"

Betty took her firmly by the arm. "Go straight into the kitchen, Nellie," she commanded, "and get yourself some supper and don't talk to cook or Mrs. Bliss. You can say you had to give some more information about the leash and you can't tell them any more now. They'll know soon enough."

"And Miss Fain's supper?" Nellie enquired.

"Golly!" wailed Cissie. "My middle's caving in so that I can hardly stand upright."

"You must wait!" Betty declared. "And you too, Basil; if you missed *your* dinner it's your own fault."

He was installed in one of the wicker chairs of the lounge hall, and Betty and Cissie entered the drawing-room.

The scene struck them as curiously peaceful and normal. It was difficult to believe that something startling and horrible was about to happen.

Mr. Slocomb sat in the chair that had been Miss Pongleton's, with a crossword puzzle before him. Mrs. Daymer sat in the opposite chair with a strip of linen in her hands through which she jabbed a long embroidery needle ferociously, looking up now and then to shoot a suspicious glance at Mr. Slocomb. Mr. Blend was at his table in the far corner, happily pencilling the *Evening News*, and Mr. Grange sat meekly on the sofa near Mrs. Daymer, occasionally obeying her commands to reach the scissors or a skein of silk.

Betty and Cissie took their seats on the sofa, disregarding Mrs. Daymer's enquiring look.

"Is your headache better, Miss Watson?" asked Mr. Grange solicitously.

Betty jumped. Did she have a headache? Yes, of course, years ago at about six o'clock this evening. "Much better, thanks," she told him.

Mr. Blend got up and shuffled about the room, picking up a paper here and there and rattling the pages. In the course of his tiresome pottering and rustling he worked a devious way towards Mrs. Daymer.

"Restless old fellow, aren't I?" he mumbled aimiably. "Don't seem able to settle this evening! Did you get all the local colour you wanted, Mrs. Daymer? Not much colour there—grey old place!"

Mrs. Daymer scowled at him and he hurried back guiltily to his table. Mr. Slocomb's dictionary slid off his knee and thumped on the floor. The three women started violently.

"Tck! Tck! Tck!" he clucked in annoyance. "I believe I must have dropped off! At my age of course—and perhaps it is a little close in here?"

"You should beware of dropping off, Mr. Slocomb," Mrs. Daymer warned him. "It may become dangerous."

"Oh, surely not...." But now he seemed to be infected with the spirit of restlessness. He crossed, uncrossed, and recrossed his legs, drew his eyebrows together and pulled down the corners of his mouth, but made no progress with the crossword puzzle.

"Awkward problem?" Cissie enquired suddenly.

Before he could answer, the door opened and Basil entered. Betty, who had heard faint sounds from the hall and had been holding her breath in anxiety, gave a gasp. Cissie jumped up, shaking off Betty's restraining hand. She could not resist the opportunity to create a scene, although Inspector Caird, in laying his plans, had done his best to avoid one.

"Hullo, Basil!" she exclaimed. "Wasn't that a queer thing that came out at the inquest on your aunt this morning—that the brooch was in Pongle's bag, not in her pocket! I wanted to tell you about it because I *know* it wasn't in her bag when she started. She upset it and I helped her to pick everything up. Too mysterious, don't you think? Who could have put it there?"

She looked straight at Mr. Slocomb, and the others, who had been looking at her, followed the direction of that enquiring gaze from her innocent blue eyes.

They all noticed how queer Mr. Slocomb looked as he rose slowly from his chair.

"Must fetch—er—another dictionary," he mumbled as he moved towards the door.

"I was just going to tell you, Mr. Slocomb," said Basil, standing in the doorway, "there is someone in the hall to see you."

Mr. Slocomb stopped short and put his hand in his breast pocket; his movements, usually so precise, were feeble and uncertain. He drew out a small black notebook and threw it into the fire.

"Done with—no necessity to carry it with me," he muttered, and walked to the door which Basil was holding open.

Basil, seeing Mr. Slocomb's action, opened his mouth and raised his hand, but seemed unable to utter a word or make any further movement. Cissie, Mrs. Daymer, and Mr. Grange were all following Mr. Slocomb's progress with their eyes as if they were hypnotized, but Betty sprang into action. She was on her knees on the hearthrug in an instant and, without waiting to reach for the tongs, she had seized the notebook by a corner of its cover and flicked it on to the hearth, where she beat out the flames and sparks with the poker. Basil drew a breath of relief.

Mr. Slocomb looked at him quickly, suspiciously; then walked deliberately into the hall. Basil shut himself and the others into the drawing-room.

Inspector Caird and two constables in uniform faced Mr. Slocomb in the hall.

"Joseph Slocomb, alias Jonah Sokam, I arrest you for the wilful murder of Euphemia Pongleton, and I warn you that anything you say may be taken down and used in evidence."

Mr. Slocomb swayed slightly and gripped the door-handle behind him.

"There is some mistake. I can account for all my movements on the morning Miss Pongleton was murdered. Witnesses, who saw me enter the train at Hampstead..." His voice faded away.

The inspector looked from Mr. Slocomb's pallid face to his dapper feet and nodded thoughtfully. He made a sign to the policemen.

As the car in which Mr. Slocomb sat, closely guarded, drew up outside the police-station, another car slowed down and stopped behind it. Under the two big blue lamps which proclaimed "Police" in yellow letters on either side of the gateway, the flagged path to the door glimmered strangely; it seemed to be swimming with water, though the rain had stopped some time ago. Mr. Slocomb could not avoid getting his shoes very wet, and he left several good footprints on the clean doorstep. The inspector paused to give instructions to a man who was waiting in the passage.

"Photographs and measurements quickly, before they dry!" he commanded sharply.

Meanwhile the two men from the second car were coming towards the door.

"Hi! Look out!" the officer who had been left in charge of the footprints warned them. "Don't step here!"

The straight passage leading from the door was well lighted and Mr. Slocomb could be seen turning into a room at the far end of it. With its blue and white tiles it was suggestive of an underground railway station.

"That's him! That's him!" excitedly cried one of the two men—who was in fact the witness Jones, who had been snatched, after long delay, from his evening recreation at his darts club. "That's the chap I saw slinking away from the stairs in Belsize Park—just like that! I'd know him anywhere!"

Inspector Caird's case was complete.

CHAPTER TWENTY-THREE

COMMENTS BY THE FRUMPS

"The whole affair shows," Mrs. Daymer explained, "what a fetish we make of regular habits. Of course I suspected Slocomb from the start; but because he had apparently followed his usual routine on that fatal day, the police never gave a thought to him until I put them on the track."

Cissie would not take this lying down. "Betty and I had a good deal to do with it," she pointed out.

"Oh yes," conceded Mrs. Daymer; "you contributed useful pieces of information but——"

But the story of the Coventry expedition had been told too often in the Frampton; even the dutiful Mr. Grange was unwilling to listen to it again. So he hastily interrupted:

"Didn't Slocomb risk a good deal in taking the train from Hampstead so much earlier than usual that morning? He must have been pretty well known at that station."

"He was known by those who travelled with him at nine-forty; not by people he was likely to encounter about half an hour earlier. As for the ticket collector, Slocomb was clever enough to guess that he looks at the tickets rather than at the faces of those who enter the lift, and therefore wouldn't be likely to notice that Slocomb was so early. No, the great risk, as it happened, was that he might meet Mr. Plasher, who was probably talking to Bob Thurlow in one passage when Slocomb skulked up the other, towards the stairs."

"Afterwards, why didn't he just take the train on to Leicester Square from Belsize Park," enquired Mr. Grange.

"That was one of his cleverest moves," Mrs. Daymer explained. "He got back to Hampstead quickly enough to catch his train from there at his usual time, and probably made a point of exchanging remarks with several of his fellow travellers who knew him by sight, so that they would be sure to remember he was there—and it gave him what almost amounted to an alibi, in conjunction with that habit of taking a morning constitutional of which he was so proud."

"I suppose he may have had the affair planned out ages beforehand," Mr. Grange speculated. "When he found that at last she had made the will leaving him the legacy he'd been angling for, he was ready, and the appointment with the dentist gave him the opportunity——"

"And the affair of the brooch gave him a heaven-sent—well, not exactly that, perhaps—chance to plant suspicion on someone else. I believe he thought Bob probably would go up the stairs and find the body and actually steal the brooch and be caught with it on him!" Cissie elaborated.

"It was very clever of you to remember about the contents of her bag," said Mr. Grange admiringly. "But I don't understand about that will—did he find it?"

"That will probably never be known for certain," said Mrs. Daymer mysteriously. "But you may not have noticed—though it did not escape me—how cunningly he gained possession of this chair—Miss Pongleton's chair—on the very evening of the day she was murdered. My first thought was, of course, that he was no gentleman. But on considering it further I suspected that he had some motive."

"You mean he knew or guessed that the will was hidden there?" said Cissie. "Well, *I* think he had the will already.

Pongle is quite likely to have given him the will to take care of. Besides, he left a fingerprint on it; that probably means he opened it *before* he murdered her, to make sure it did really leave him the money. Probably he was fed up at finding that it left the rest to Beryl—he had hoped to worm it out of Basil, you see. He may have waited to see if any other will turned up which would also leave him something and the rest to Basil. When it didn't, he put the will in the chair to make sure of his own legacy. And of course he'd heard us say by then that the money would probably go to Basil in any case."

Mrs. Daymer was annoyed at being caught out. "Of course," she remarked with dignity, "my own little part in the affair will never be revealed to the public, and I am content that it should be so."

The others did not seem to be impressed with her magnanimity.

"Rather a joke, wasn't it," Cissie babbled on, "that the Porters were dragged in after all? After having put on those superior airs as if they couldn't possibly know anything about it! Of course Nellie heard Slowgo's footsteps when he crept downstairs on Thursday night to get the leash from the hall, but it was a good thing Mr. Porter saw him. Mrs. P.'s simply too terrified of burglars, and hearing someone creeping about she made Mr. P. open the door and look out. At the time he just thought Slocomb was fetching a book or something."

"Not a very perspicacious man!" commented Mrs. Daymer, implying that she would have been quite sure, had she happened to see Mr. Slocomb on that nocturnal expedition, that his intentions were sinister. "But even the most perspicacious may make a mistake, as Slocomb did in his notebook."

"Ah! That notebook! Betty was marvellous! But just why was it so important?" asked Mr. Grange, who was one of those people who always manage to know less than others, although constantly asking questions.

"My own theory," began Mrs. Daymer, "is that when young Mr. Pongleton rushed to Slocomb with his confession, Slocomb didn't quite believe it at first—thought he had been seen, perhaps, and that this was a trap. The notes were probably a test or even a counter-trap. Perhaps being rather startled, although at the same time believing himself quite free from any danger of arrest, he relaxed his usual caution. The notes in themselves, of course, proved nothing, though they did not quite tally with the supposition that they were made by an innocent man."

"They gave away a good deal," Cissie pointed out. "For one thing, the time of the murder was put down; then there were several notes about Slowgo's own movements which looked a bit fishy, and he made one awful floater. He put himself down as leaving *Belsize Park*, where he pretended he'd never been, and then crossed it out and wrote *Hampstead*. But you could still read it."

MR. SLOCOMB'S NOTES

Basil P. leaves Tavistock Sq.	..	9.20 a.m. approx.
Warren St. station	..	9.30
reaches Belsize Park	..	? 9.45
Euphemia Pongleton leaves		
Frampton	..	9 a.m.
J. S. leaves Frampton ..	..	9.5
E. P. on stairs, Belsize Park	..	9.15 onwards
G. Plasher on stairs, Belsize Park		9.16–?9.18
Murder	..	9.22–9.25

J. S. leaves ~~Belsize Park~~ Hampstead ..	9.40	
B. P. leaves Belsize Park	? 10	
reaches Golder's Green ..	? 10.10	Say 9.50
Kutuzov's	? 10.30	Say 10

LEASH.	THURSDAY.
Bob Thurlow in hall, Frampton ..	8.30 p.m.
Basil P. in hall, Frampton ..	11.20

Leash *not* in hall after 8.30.

"It is just the sort of futile carelessness that a clever criminal is apt to commit," remarked Mrs. Daymer with an air of great experience.

"And have you heard about Bob?" enquired Cissie. "Basil has persuaded his father to find work for Bob in the garden of their house in Yorkshire, and Nellie is to be housemaid there until Bob can marry her. Betty thought all that out; she's too marvellous!"

"I should not have thought Bob Thurlow's experience in the underground would give him much knowledge of gardening," Mrs. Daymer remarked coldly.

"Most gardeners know a sight too much," Cissie assured her. "They're always telling you you're wrong. It'd be a jolly good thing to have one who didn't know."

"And Basil Pongleton will inherit his aunt's fortune, after all, in spite of the last will?" Mr. Grange asked, perhaps because he feared that the subject of gardening would let Mrs. Daymer loose on her favourite theme of Nature.

"Yes, he's to have it as a wedding present," Cissie explained. "My hat! Betty is lucky—thirty thousand pounds! But she deserves it—don't you think so?"

"I'm inclined to think that Basil Pongleton is the lucky one," said Mr. Grange.

Basil would have agreed with him. He was convinced that his luck was greater than any good fortune that had ever befallen any human being. As for Betty, he was sure that she deserved any luck she might get.

They walked across the Heath one spring morning to see how Kutuzov was getting on with Beryl's portrait. Woolly clouds streamed across a pale blue sky above the bleached and limpid colours of the earth. Betty strode briskly along, swinging a daffodil-hued beret in her hand.

"D'you remember the last time we were on the Heath?" Basil enquired, with a sideways look towards her.

"Why, no. When was it?—Oh! Of *course*... We sat on a tree down there near Ken Wood. One of those times when you were being such an utter ass!"

"I wasn't such an ass as I might have been." He looked at her again, cautiously. What a dear she is, he thought. "Did you know that I was nearly hugging you that night, on the log? I wanted to. I was pretty wretched and just aching for a little comfort, but I thought just in time that it would have been rather caddish to make love to you then, when I was asking you to involve yourself in my trouble in order to help me. So I didn't. Did you know, Betty?"

"Yes, I knew." There was a twinkle of amusement in Betty's brown eyes, but she put out a hand to meet his.

"Would you have minded?"

"Well—of course I was feeling rather angry with you; I hated being kept in the dark."

"But that wasn't my fault; you know what a rush I was in; there wasn't a moment to explain. And besides, the less you knew, the less you were involved."

"You darling idiot!"

"Betty, you did always believe in me?"

"Ye-es. I'd have done anything to help you, Basil, and of course I never thought you had killed Aunt Phemia, but I rather wondered just what you had done and just how far it was—well, not criminal, but illegal."

"I believe Beryl thought I was capable of anything."

"Oh, she didn't! Beryl behaved like a brick! And so did Gerry. Poor old Gerry! Do you remember how he was kept waiting at the police-station for years and years on that Monday night when Slocomb was arrested, because everyone forgot about him? And he began to think that they must be going to arrest him after all! And poor Beryl had a ghastly time trying to keep the family calm and thinking the police-station had swallowed first you and then Gerry without a trace!"

"It was a pretty foul occasion altogether. Do you remember how we sat on the sofa at the Frampton while Slowgo talked to the inspector?"

"Don't I!" Betty squeezed Basil's hand. "D'you know, at that moment, when you seemed to be in the most awful mess, as we sat on the sofa I was suddenly absolutely definitely sure that I was—was very fond of you, enough for anything and for ever!"

"Just at that moment? Queer—I believe it was just then that it came over me that the whole beastly affair was bound to turn out all right because I really did care about you so much that it was simply impossible that it could all be wasted!"

Everyone knows that when two young people who are in love for the first time begin saying, "Do you remember?" and recalling their feelings on this and that marvellous occasion, their conversation becomes utterly idiotic to any third person. So we will leave Betty and Basil to their reminiscences as they swing across the Heath in the sunshine.

THE END

Also available from British Library Publishing

MR BAZALGETTE'S AGENT

Leonard Merrick

With an Introduction by Mike Ashley

When Miriam Lea falls on hard times, an advertisement for private agents catches her eye, and within weeks she finds herself in Mr Bazalgette's employ as a private detective in pursuit of an audacious fraudster. What follows is a journey through some of the great cities of Europe – and eventually to South Africa – as Miss Lea attempts to find her man. Miriam Lea is only the third ever professional female detective to appear in a work of crime fiction. Originally published in 1888, *Mr Bazalgette's Agent* presents a determined and resourceful heroine who grapples with some very modern dilemmas of female virtue and vice.

ISBN 978 0 7123 5702 9
144 pages
Also available as an ebook (978 0 7123 6307 5)

Also available from British Library Publishing

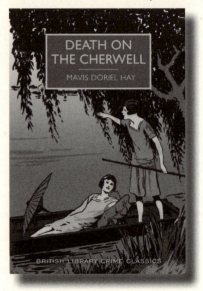

DEATH ON THE CHERWELL

Mavis Doriel Hay

For Miss Cordell, Principal of Persephone College, Oxford, there are two great evils to be feared: unladylike behaviour among her students, and bad publicity for the college. So her prim and cosy world is turned upside down when a secret society of undergraduates meets by the river on a gloomy January afternoon, only to find the drowned body of the college bursar floating in her canoe. The police assume that a student prank got out of hand, but the resourceful Persephone girls suspect foul play, and take the investigation into their own hands.

ISBN 978 0 7123 5726 5
288 pages